# BRANDED

**Also by A.C. Abbott**
*Wild Blood*

# BRANDED

A.C. ABBOTT

CUTTING EDGE

ISBN-13: 978-1-952138-90-4

Published by
Cutting Edge Books
PO Box 8212
Calabasas, CA 91372
www.cuttingedgebooks.com

# CHAPTER ONE

O<small>N THAT</small> Saturday afternoon when Rock Kendall rode into the sprawling town of Wellton, he looked as tough as his reputation claimed him to be. The dust of a long hard trail coated his worn garments and dulled the coat of the big solid-brown Morgan he rode. Even a three-day stubble of black beard could not hide the grim set of his jaw; and his eyes, piercing, steely gray under the low-pulled brim of his black hat, touched every man and every movement in sight.

He put his horse into the crowded rack in front of a barber shop and had just swung off when a rider coming out of a side street caught and held his attention. It was not her face that stopped him—the distance was too great for him to see her features clearly. It was the way she sat her horse, loose and easy in the saddle but with a square-shouldered grace that hinted of pride and confidence and an independent, vivacious spirit.

Rock stood immobile, one hand on his saddle horn and the other on his horse's mane, watching her approach. She was dressed in a man's clothes, Levis, half boots, a wide-brimmed hat riding well forward on her head. She handled her horse like a man, too, but she was all woman. The hat couldn't hide the glorious shine of her gold-bronze hair any more than the soft blue shirt could hide the contours of her well-rounded body.

She came on at an easy jog. Rock could see the smooth clear tan of her throat now, the rich warmth of her mouth. Her eyes were in shadow but he felt them touch him, briefly and with no particular interest, as she rode past.

Still he watched, his face stony but his blood stirring with a quick, unwonted drive. She swung down in front of the two-story Town House across the street, handing her reins to a cowboy who stepped out to take the horse. Rock caught the flash of her smile, the friendly lift of her voice. When she turned into the hotel, she moved with the same sure grace that characterized her riding.

Not until she had disappeared did Rock think to look at the horse she had ridden. It was a fine black, with a blazed face and four white stockings; and it bore the Triple X brand. This, then, was Katherine Sinclair, half owner with her brother of the herd of Texas longhorns Rock had used to cover his entry into the country.

Without glancing at the hotel again, he shoved away from his horse and tied the animal with a knot that could be jerked loose. As he ducked under the rail, he became suddenly aware of a man standing at the edge of the awninged board walk, one brawny shoulder tipped against a post. The fellow had his thumbs hooked lazily in his cartridge belt, a cigarette dangling idly from his lips, but his pale eyes were fixed on Rock with an icy, unswerving regard.

That look was a shock that jolted Rock out of his brief, unguarded moment. Instantly wary, he straightened, his right arm brushing the butt of the .45 holstered low at his hip. The second gun inside his gray flannel shirt pressed against the muscles of his stomach, giving him a deadly self-assurance.

"Well?" he said, with cold challenge. "Seen me before or figuring to know me next time?"

The man spat his cigarette into the dust without taking his eyes from Rock's face, a gesture that was maddening and vaguely insulting.

"What," he asked in a low metallic voice, "were you looking at so steady?"

"A woman," Rock said, "that isn't hard to look at."

"My boss happens to be mighty particular about that woman, stranger."

"Can't blame him for that," Rock said cynically. "Good-looking *and* rich."

"*And* taken," the man said, his voice a narrow threat. "You know her?"

"I know the brand on her horse. That's all."

"That's enough," the man said flatly. "That's as close as you need to get, cowboy."

A breath of warning touched Rock, a whisper somewhere in his mind that told him to pull his elbows in and play it safe; but he couldn't restrain the feeling of animosity this hard-faced man aroused in him. Stepping up onto the walk, he paused to look the fellow up and down with cool, deliberate insolence.

"You own all this country?" he drawled.

"I'm telling you, stranger. One look's enough."

"Thanks," Rock said with dry sarcasm. "Thanks for the tip."

He nodded with mock courtesy and strode on across the walk to enter the barber shop. The first thing he saw as he closed the door behind him was his own name, jumping at him from a reward poster tacked up between two gleaming, spotless mirrors. His glance touched it impersonally and went on without pause to the slight, gray-haired barber waiting expectantly behind the chair.

"Howdy," he said pleasantly.

"Afternoon, stranger," the barber responded, with a nod that was polite but not friendly. "Like to get out from behind those whiskers?"

"And out from under a load of dirt."

"Plenty hot water in the back room."

Rock eased his long body gratefully into the chair, then let his glance wander around the room with casual interest before bringing it back to the poster. It was like the others he had seen. No picture. Just a description. A Texan, Rock Kendall. An inch or two over six feet tall, something less than thirty years of age. Worth a thousand dollars dead or alive.

"Town seems to be booming," he commented.

"Business is good," the barber agreed. "Especially since the railroad came through. We draw from a wide territory."

"Awful big country," Rock said. "Those mountains to the south must be twenty, thirty miles away."

"All of that," the barber conceded. "And those Mescaleros are rough, I'll tell you."

Rock lay back in easy comfort, staring at the ceiling as the barber went to work. He had favored those mountains with a speculative survey as he rode into town, knowing they were too far away; but that danger couldn't stop him any more than the poster could. He had learned through careful inquiry in a bar a hundred miles to the southeast that a man answering Ash Carlton's description had been seen in this part of the country. If that man were still here, Rock Kendall was going to have a look at him.

"You just get in?" the barber asked.

"Yeah," Rock said casually. "Came up with that last Sinclair herd."

"Oh? From Texas?"

"From Texas."

Not recently from Texas, he thought sardonically. The cattle were from there, but Rock hadn't set foot on Lone Star soil for nearly three years.

"Well! So you're a Triple X man," the barber said, instantly hearty. "That's a good outfit. Fine people, John and Kathy Sinclair. They're Texans too, you know. Came in here several years ago and have built up a fine big ranch. I just hope they're not making a mistake now."

"How so?"

"Bringing in too many cattle. Why—" The barber paused to wave a finger emphatically at Rock. "They've brought in thousands of head in the last year or two and more still coming."

"Plenty of range," Rock said, visualizing the vastness of the gray, broken country sloping gradually up to the dark timbered mountains to the south.

"Too much range," the barber retorted with dark significance. "The country's too big and too rough. The Sinclairs won't keep all those cattle." He renewed his attack on Rock's beard, working almost grimly. "And John still down in Texas getting another herd together."

The barber shook his head in obvious concern, but Rock had no comment to make. He had joined the Sinclair outfit a week ago merely for the cover of respectability it would afford him. Now that he had used it to introduce himself, he was through with it.

He said, "Lot of people drifting in here?"

"Everyone," the barber retorted, "who ever had to get out of anywhere in a hurry is coming to Arizona these days. Sheriff Lackey isn't too cooperative, though, about letting some of them stay."

Rock grinned with a deep-lying appreciation. "Tough lawman, huh?"

"Plenty tough."

"Well, that sure scares me," Rock drawled, "but I reckon I'll have to stick around for awhile, anyway. I'm looking for an old pard, and I've got a hunch he might have drifted out this way."

"Who's that?"

"Bill Brown," Rock lied, glancing hopefully at the barber.

"Common name."

"Yes, but he isn't a common-looking man." Rock looked back at the ceiling, fighting to keep the hatred out of his eyes and voice as he described Ash Carlton. "Big fella, a little over six feet tall and built like a man's supposed to be built. Awful good-looking man, and he's got a mighty pleasant way about him. Blue eyes, but it's his hair that really sets him off." It was his hair that had given him the nickname of Ash. "It's a real light blond, almost gray. Ash blond, I think they call it."

"Cowboy," the barber said with a laugh, "you've just described Ed Claiborne right down to the ground. Best-looking man in the country and the nicest fellow you ever met."

"Ed Claiborne," Rock repeated softly, and he turned the name over in his mind. Ash Carlton. Ed Claiborne. Same ring to it.

"You bet," the barber said with enthusiasm. "Ed came in two or three years ago. Bought out the Bar Circle and since then has bought several other brands. He was well heeled when he came and has sure made money since."

Ash would have been well heeled. Even his own half of the K Bar C would have set him up. Both halves, his and Rock's, must have made him rich.

"Ed's a handsome cuss," the barber prattled on. "Devil with the ladies, I hear. But he's a fine man. Never packs a gun. He keeps going, he'll be governor some day."

"Wrong man," Rock drawled, his face like granite. "This pard of mine will never be a governor."

A growing hope was putting a pound in Rock's blood. It all fit—the time element, the fact that this Claiborne was never seen to carry a gun. Ash Carlton used a shoulder holster, always out of sight. He'd been a devil with women, too—and a worse devil when he thought he'd lost one.

"Bar Circle," Rock said softly. "Tough outfit?"

"They're all tough in this country. Have to be." The barber wiped his razor for the last time and reached for a towel. "Old Pat Garrett's been cleaning house over in New Mexico, and he swept a lot of his dirt under Sheriff Lackey's bed."

Rock laughed; but as he sat up, he glanced at himself in the mirror and felt a momentary shock. His eyes were as bleak as a winter sky. He said with grim humor, "Dirt like that Rock Kendall, huh?"

"Not him," the barber snapped. "He'd never risk his life coming into a railroad town like this."

"Can't ever tell," Rock said, looking down at his big rough hands. "Maybe his life isn't worth much to him under the circumstances."

"It wouldn't be worth anything if he came around here, the damn woman killer!" The barber was suddenly hot. "Me, I'm a peaceable man," he said forcefully. "I don't get my blood pressure up over rustlers or horse thieves or *man* killers, as long as they leave me alone. But you take a man like him—" he stabbed his finger viciously at the poster "—that'd shoot a woman down in cold blood like he did that Dorene Mayberry—Why, even I'd load up a .30-30 to notch a sight on him. Or," he finished with a growl, "dig out a dull, rusty butcher knife and cut his damn throat. You want a bath now?"

"Yeah," Rock said and got up to move into the back room with a slow, heavy stride.

Long afterward, as he stepped outside and paused at the edge of the walk to roll a cigarette, the barber's words still burned in his mind. It wasn't new to him, this rabid feeling toward a man branded as a woman killer. It would be the same here as it had been everywhere else. This town didn't know his face—yet. Just his hated name, but it was only a question of time until someone spotted him. Then he'd have to fight or die on the spot.

With that knowledge goading him, he lit his cigarette and turned up the street, ambling along as if he had nothing on his mind except a desire to see whatever sights the town might offer. Only his constantly moving eyes belied his manner. He wanted to see this Ed Claiborne, yes, but he wanted to be very sure to see him first.

He walked the length of the main street, crossed it and sauntered back without seeing anyone he knew or who seemed to know him. With the thought that the influential Mr. Claiborne would frequent only the better places, he turned into the Town House, made a sweeping survey of the crowded lobby without seeing the handsome blond head of Ash Carlton and turned toward the barroom. He had just stepped through the doorway when a voice back in the lobby arrested him.

"Mr. Claiborne coming in tonight?"

Rock spun sharply in time to see Kathy Sinclair, clad now in a light blue dress, pause to face back toward the man who had spoken.

She laughed lightly. "He'd better or I'll shoot him."

"Then I'll save his usual room."

"I'm sure he'll want it," Kathy replied and moved on toward the street.

For the space of perhaps three seconds Rock hesitated, wondering whether this could have any significance for him. Then, with a slow, unobtrusive stride, he recrossed the lobby and followed the girl up the street.

Midway up the second block she turned into a store; and Rock, after a last searching glance at the bustling street, turned in after her. It was a dry goods store which, to his satisfaction, had more customers than it had clerks. He stepped away from the door, moving part way down the left-hand aisle before stopping and helping himself to a seat on the edge of the counter.

Kathy stood waiting not over fifteen feet away, and Rock covertly studied her. Her face was turned away from him so that he still couldn't see her eyes, but he could see the line of her cheek, firm and showing a rich color from exposure to the sun. And he could see the full yet delicate curves of her body, discreetly enhanced by the dress she wore.

Again Rock felt a stir of feeling, instinctive and resented, threatening to interfere with his cool appraisal of this woman. Kathy Sinclair could mean nothing but danger to him unless, in some way, she could help him get his hands on Ash Carlton.

As a clerk approached, Kathy stepped up to the counter and began, "I ordered some things—"

"Yes, Miss Sinclair, they're all ready," the clerk interrupted. She reached under the counter to bring out half a dozen parcels already wrapped. "Will you need some help in carrying these to the hotel?"

"Oh, I think I can manage," Kathy replied, but she was eyeing the pile dubiously.

Instantly, Rock slid off the counter, reaching for his hat as he strode up to her. "Excuse me, Miss Sinclair. Can I help you?"

She looked up at him, and Rock felt something of a physical shock. Her eyes were the deepest blue he had ever seen, clear yet disturbingly impenetrable. For a long moment she studied him, and Rock had the uneasy feeling that he was being gauged as no man had ever gauged him.

"I don't believe we've met," she said finally.

"My name's Rocklin, ma'am." That was no lie. Full name, Rocklin James Kendall, although that was one piece of information the reward posters had overlooked. "I came up with that last herd of yours."

"Oh?" A smile af tentative friendliness touched her face. "John hired you?"

"No, ma'am," Rock said truthfully. "I joined the outfit on the trail, after your brother had gone on to get the next herd lined up." He grinned. "But I still make an awful good pack horse if you need help with those bundles."

He saw her studying his grin, and he saw the answering smile light in her eyes even before it reached her lips.

"Thank you, Mr. Rocklin," she said. "I would appreciate the help."

She picked up two of the bundles and Rock gathered up the others, shifting them to his left arm as he followed her out of the building. On the walk she waited for him, looking at him with a sudden, startled interest.

"You," she said, and lifted one hand to brush her chin. "With whiskers. You were standing in front of the barber shop when I rode in."

"Yes."

For a moment she stood breathlessly still, confusion bringing a tinge of deeper color into her cheeks. Rock knew then that his brooding stare had not been unobserved, but he offered no apology for it as Kathy turned somewhat hurriedly along the street. They had taken several steps before she spoke again, her voice a little strained.

"Like our new country?"

"Haven't seen much of it yet."

"And that mostly dust and sage, I'll bet." She laughed nervously, but it was still a soft, pleasant sound that warmed Rock. "You can't appreciate the scenery when you're looking at it through a bunch of cows."

"You sound as if you knew," he said, with a rider's instinctive admiration for a woman who knew cattle.

"I've been behind a cow or two, but I don't enjoy working them down here on the desert. The real country is down south of here, in the mountains. Oh, it's beautiful out there! Timber, all kinds of game. That's wild country." She laughed again, giving him a glance that showed him, for a brief moment, the humor and the eager, high spirit lying deep in her eyes. "I love it. Unladylike, isn't it, to love a home like that?"

Rock left suddenly tight inside. "It—isn't unladylike to love any home," he said constrainedly.

That ranch on the Pecos had been in wild country, too, a broken country of canyons and cedars. A beautiful country. He and Ash had been making two drives a year to Dodge, with the price of cattle rising steadily.

He said, "There's money in cattle these days—if you can hang onto them."

The unintentional bitterness in his voice caused her to glance at him sharply. He waited, braced against the questions most women would have asked; but Kathy Sinclair didn't ask them. Instead she looked away, her lips suddenly compressed.

"Yes," she said, "if you can keep them. Are you staying on with the outfit?"

"Hadn't figured on it."

She looked up at him again, studying him with a narrow, penetrating speculation. Once more Rock had the feeling that she was judging him as a man would have judged him, only with deeper insight, more careful discrimination.

"I wish you would stay, Mr. Rocklin," she said finally, her voice as level and direct as her gaze. "We need riders." She flicked a glance at the gunbelt slanting across his body, then looked again up into his eyes and showed him a frank smile. "We need good men. Rough times ahead, I'm afraid."

The way she said it was a compliment and Rock looked away, strangely upset and at a loss for words. It had been a long time since anyone looked past his gun to see what lay inside of him. But she had judged him as a man, divorced from his real name. He wondered—and figured he knew—what her reaction would be if he told her with all the harshness he felt that he was Rock Kendall. The man Ash Carlton had branded as a woman killer!

He took her elbow as they crossed the intersection, feeling the soft warmth of her arm, knowing that she must notice the icy coldness of his own hand. But if she wondered about it, she gave no sign. As they stepped up onto the far walk, he saw, leaning indolently against the front of a saloon, the hard-eyed man who had warned him to stay away from this woman. A moment later the man saw them, and he straightened at once.

Kathy greeted him with a reserved smile. "Hello, Jud."

"Afternoon, Miss Sinclair," he replied, touching his hat. Then his eyes went past her, settling on Rock with chilling effect.

As they moved on toward the hotel, Rock could feel the man's glance still on him. He felt, too, the hair rising on the back of his neck, but he didn't look around.

"Who is that?" he asked quietly.

"Jud Moore, foreman of Bar Circle."

"Bar Circle," Rock repeated concealing his sudden, sharp interest. "Ed Claiborne's outfit."

"Yes. You know Ed?"

"Heard of him."

"His ranch is out on Cedar Creek, only ten miles from ours."

Rock grinned down at her. "Is that," he asked mildly, "why you prefer the mountains?"

Kathy flashed him a reproving glance, but her eyes were sparkling roguishly and her cheeks were warming with fresh color. "I would like Clear Springs, anyway," she informed him, with just the right emphasis on the last word.

"Shucks," Rock drawled. "And here I was about to stake out a claim."

They turned into the hotel, where Rock deposited his bundles on the desk and once more removed his hat. Kathy still had a twinkling look about her, but Rock had lost his smile. He was watching her now the same way he had watched her ride into town, with an involuntary, futile hunger.

"Thank you, Mr. Rocklin," she said with a smile.

"I got my money's worth," Rock said evenly.

Her smile faded under the intensity of his gaze, and a wondering glint crept into her eyes. Rock saw her glance touch his hair, his mouth, then come back to his eyes, appraising him; and his jaw tightened.

"I hope you'll reconsider about staying on with the outfit," she said quietly. "If you do change your mind, come out to Clear Springs."

"When will you be going back?"

"Tomorrow. I just came in to receive the herd and attend the dance tonight."

"I'll think it over, Miss Sinclair."

He nodded to her, then stepped back and turned toward the door, aware that her thoughtful attention was still on him. Rock put his hat on and pulled it down hard over his eyes. He knew Jud Moore would be waiting for him, and he had no desire to risk the attention a fight would attract. Not until he'd had his look at Ed Claiborne.

The moment he reached the walk, he saw Jud coming, lounging forward with apparent aimlessness. Rock turned down the street, striding rapidly, hoping to lose himself in the crowd. He didn't make it.

Behind him, he heard the swift rap of boots, the jangle of spurs. Then a strident voice yelled out.

*"Hey, stranger!"*

Instantly, it seemed to Rock, every eye within range was focused on him, startled, wondering, quickly suspicious. He stopped in his tracks, standing dead still while a cold, bitter rage swept up in him. Then, deliberately, he swung to face the Bar Circle foreman.

"Were you yelling at me?" he demanded in a clear, icy challenge.

Jud came to a halt not three feet away, his big chest heaving, his fists clenched. "Who did you think I was yelling at?" he countered harshly. "What were you running from?"

"Not from you," Rock retorted. He was aware of the crowd ringing them, watching closely. If he were spotted now, he was a dead man; and that certainty filled him with a reckless defiance. "I thought we settled that awhile ago."

"It looks," said Jud, his eyes narrowing, "like we didn't settle anything awhile ago. Who in the hell are you, anyway, and where you from?"

"I'm just a poor cowboy," Rock said sarcastically, "and I came from Texas with that last Triple X herd. Anything else you'd like to know?"

"Plenty," Jud bit out. He flashed a look down over Rock, then seemed to square off, his face twisting. "The fact that you came in with the Triple X herd doesn't spell anything, cowboy. There are a lot of killers coming up that trail."

Rock took a slow step forward. "That could be," he said, spacing his words with ominous care. "But don't say anything against my outfit that you can't prove!"

It was a bold move, and it had its effect on the crowd. Rock heard the ripple of approving comment. Jud heard it, too, and his face darkened.

"You talk tough, stranger," he said derisively, "but I'd like to know whether you came all the way from Texas or whether you joined that herd in New Mexico."

"What do you mean by that?"

Rock knew what he meant, but he wanted Jud to say it, to give him the excuse he needed to end this thing.

Jud turned his head to spit, the same insulting gesture Rock had seen once before. Then he said deliberately, "That Lincoln County War ended awhile back, but not *all* those rustlers went down!"

Rock hit him, a swift, solid blow that jarred his head and knocked him off balance. Before he could recover, Rock followed up with two more blows that landed like twin bolts of lightning in the pit of Jud's paunchy stomach. As Rock had suspected, the man had been drinking and that attack on his beer keg had a drastic effect. He turned a sickly greenish-white and, staggering, made a vain attempt to grab Rock for support. Rock eluded his grasp, stepped back and laid one on his jaw that knocked him flat.

Jud rolled over, gagging and gasping for breath, obviously too sick to get up. Rock looked up to sweep the circle of faces for any sign of hostility, but he saw none. Then he noticed the girl, evidently standing on her toes to peer over someone's shoulder. She was pretty in a dark, wild sort of way; but it was not her beauty that caught his attention. It was the expression on her face. Her dark eyes, fixed on Jud Moore, were gloating; and her red lips were pulled back from her teeth in a smile of undisguised, savage pleasure.

The sight jolted Rock, but he had no time in which to wonder about it. A voice hissed sharply, "There's the Kid!" And the crowd split with a significant, scrambling haste that brought Rock pivoting around. A slight, flashily dressed cowboy stood not ten feet away, his feet wide-braced, his hands on his hips just over the two guns he wore. One look into the Kid's flat, milky-blue eyes told Rock that he was up against a killer; and pressure closed in on him, cold and gripping.

If he had to throw a gun, these people would damn well know he was not an ordinary drifting cowhand. Then it wouldn't take them long....

# CHAPTER TWO

T HE KID flicked one brief glance at Jud before fastening his gaze on Rock. "Are you the man who whipped my bunkie?" he asked, his voice as thin and expressionless as his face.

"Shucks," Rock answered coolly. "I wouldn't say Jud was whipped. Just temporarily under the weather."

"How did you do it?"

"Reckon it was the whisky that did it."

"You're a liar!"

Rock felt the leap of cold anger but he held himself in check, saying softly, "You're mighty free with your language, sonny."

"Sonny, hell!" The Kid's nostrils flared with a quick fury. "I don't like your looks, stranger."

"Then we're even," Rock retorted bluntly. He could hear Jud stagger erect behind him, swearing thickly. Again that sense of angry frustration washed through him, turning him reckless, and he said, "You hurt my eyes, sonny."

The Kid made a furious gesture, then demanded, "What's your name?"

"What's it to you?"

"I don't like to send a man into a nameless grave!"

Rock laughed outright. "That's mighty considerate of you," he drawled insolently. "And while we're on the subject, maybe you better tell these folks how you want your epitaph written. Captain Kidd or Billy the Kid?"

A light came into the Kid's eyes, a strange, smug light. Like a cat when you pet him, Rock thought remotely. He waited, coldly balanced, watching that flicker of satisfaction fade into a thin, deadly purpose. The Kid's hand was starting to quiver when a voice boomed through the crowd like the blast of a gun.

"Hold it!"

Rock's nerves jumped. Then he froze, unbreathing as he watched the Kid, doubting that the man could be stopped now. He was aware of movement in the crowd, of someone shouldering his way roughly through; but he kept his eyes glued to the Kid, waiting.

The Kid's nostrils were flaring again, his lips curling back in a snarl of disappointment; but he evidently had a high respect for the owner of that voice. Slowly he eased out of his strained position; and Rock, with the beginning of relief, swiveled his glance to see the last man in the world he wanted to see. The sheriff.

Sheriff Lackey was a big man, with a gray mustache, a deeply-lined, leathery face and keen gray eyes. Boldly he stepped out between Rock and the Kid.

"What's the trouble here?" he demanded, his firm voice carrying an authority that had a quieting effect.

He flashed one warning glance at the Kid before turning his attention to Rock; and it was a piercing, penetrating attention that turned Rock stone-quiet, every nerve keyed for explosive action.

"What's the trouble here?" Lackey repeated. "Speak up, stranger."

"No trouble—now," Rock said, striving to be natural under the icy tension that gripped him. He managed a grin. "But I got a hunch you just kept me from dyin' awful young and innocent."

A nervous laugh went up from the bystanders, but Lackey's eyes narrowed.

"You didn't look to me like you were backing up very fast," he said evenly, "and I don't reckon that's the first time you ever squared off to draw on a man. What's your name?"

"Rocklin," Rock said promptly and dug out another portion of his unused, unclaimable name. "Jim Rocklin."

"Where you from?"

"Texas."

"Just get in?"

"I came in with that Triple X herd."

"I see."

Lackey paused, studying Rock narrowly, glancing critically at the hang of his gun, the well-oiled holster. The ice was still in Rock's stomach, creeping through his vitals, but he stood steady, judging the sheriff in turn. And he could see exactly what the barber had meant when he said this officer was uncooperative toward outlaws.

"Well, Rocklin," the Sheriff said finally. "I'm not saying this was your fault, but Triple X and Bar Circle don't usually tangle. What was the trouble?"

"Ask Jud Moore," Rock suggested evenly.

Lackey hesitated, still eyeing Rock as if trying to find some definite basis for a vague suspicion. Then he turned toward Jud.

"Well?" he said sharply.

Jud had no chance to answer. Someone called Lackey's name; and, as the circle of men turned and then split, Rock saw a dusty cowboy sitting his horse just beyond the hitch rack. Behind him, on a lead rope, was another horse on which had been lashed the body of a man.

Lackey swore viciously, then stepped heavily off the walk and strode into the street, the crowd closing in behind him. Rock didn't move, letting the men jostle past him as he turned a wary eye on Jud and the Kid. The Bar Circle foreman had lost interest in him; but the Kid, before dropping into the street, gave him a baleful glance that was a naked threat.

A moment longer Rock stood immobile, waiting for all attention to leave him. He took the time to roll a cigarette, inhaling with relish, listening to the run of talk.

"I sent him out," Lackey was saying in a hushed voice, "to see if he could find out who's behind this rustling."

"Looks like he found out," the cowboy said laconically. "I found him 'bout two miles out, just like that. And Lackey, if you'll look close, you'll see powder burns on the back of that feller's vest. They lowered the boom on him without bein' polite a-tall."

A general growl arose from the crowd, and Rock turned away. He made his way unobtrusively through the men remaining on the walk, stepped into the clear and was starting away when he again noticed the girl. She stood at the edge of the walk, one brown hand clutching at a post as she stared at the dead man.

Rock paused involuntarily, wondering about this girl, narrowly scrutinizing her. She obviously was not a product of the town. Her dark curly hair hung loose over her shoulders, adding to the impression of wildness that had struck him before. Her plain, poorly-made brown dress served to accentuate a figure that was lithe, supple, vibrant; and he noted that she wore beaded moccasins.

*A girl from the backwoods,* he thought distantly, *and she's seen that dead man before.*

Before he could move on, the girl swung abruptly away from the post, caught his gaze and stopped short, staring at him. Her lips parted as if to question him, but she didn't say a word. She just moved slowly back against the post, her dark eyes sweeping down over his body, then lifting again, centering on his face with provocative speculation.

Rock got out of there, not hurrying but certainly not wasting any time. He got his horse and turned up thé street, not looking back, but not until he had turned into a side street did he draw a completely normal breath.

"God bless us!" he breathed then, sleeving sweat off his face. "Boy, if you like my company, you better keep your runnin' shoes on. That man Lackey's got a nose like a bloodhound and a sense of humor like a double-barreled shotgun."

Rock knew he was juggling dynamite by staying in town now, but he wouldn't leave until he got his look at this man Claiborne. He would, however, have to hole up until after dark. He hunted up an inconspicuous rooming house on a side street, stabled his horse and carried his rifle and pack into a dingy little room. There he sprawled on the bed and lay staring at the ceiling in deep, restless thought.

The hope that his long-futile search would end here in Wellton still throbbed in his blood like a dull, distant drum. If Claiborne was Ash, Rock would get to him someway, force him to tell the truth about the death of Dorene Mayberry. It wouldn't be easy. You couldn't just walk up to a man and ask him to admit to a murder someone else was slated to die for, particularly when that someone else had been framed out of murderous, raging hatred.

Rock thought of Ash as he had known him when they were partners, cunning, arrogant, selfish, but a man who could be broken because he was at heart a coward. Ash had been afraid of him in Texas—his selling out and leaving when the posse failed to down Rock was proof enough of that. Perhaps in that fear would lie the weapon Rock needed.

As he lay there thinking, it was inevitable that the events of that tragic day should come back into his mind. Rock grew rigid as he saw it all again and, as always, one thing rose out of that memory to torture him: the unforgettable light in the green eyes of Dorene's eighteen-year-old brother. Red Mayberry, bursting into the room, had taken only one look at Dorene, then had fixed Rock with a damning stare that haunted him. With that one look he had thrust Rock out of the realm of manhood and condemned him as the basest of animals.

That was what hurt and Rock came off the bed with a lunge, stalking to the window and staring blindly at the street. There had to be some way to make Ash tell the truth. If there wasn't, Rock might as well walk out into the flaming guns now and get it over with. Only the driving desire to clear his name of an unforgivable crime had kept him going this long.

He was still hopelessly tangled in his brooding thoughts when he heard a sound at the door behind him. He whirled away from the window with his gun coming into his hand, and he noticed then how dark it was getting. Only a gloomy, murky light remained in the room.

He stepped back against the wall, watching coldly as the door swung open and a girl stepped in with a swift, furtive movement. She turned for a flashing look at the hall before closing the door, and in that instant Rock recognized the brown dress and the dark curly hair. It was the girl he had noticed in the street.

Surprise as well as suspicion held him rooted, his gun still in his hand. As she stepped away from the door, her glance went first to the bed. Then she saw him and stopped short, taking note of the gun without change of expression. This girl, whoever she was, was used to guns and the men who threw them.

"I guess," she said calmly, "you weren't expecting me."

"I wasn't expecting anybody," Rock said, sheathing the gun and stepping out into the room. He hesitated, feeling strangely awkward. "Is this the room you were looking for?"

"Yes. I saw you come here awhile ago and I was—curious."

Without taking her eyes off him, she moved to the foot of the bed and folded both hands around the iron post. Her movements were slow, guarded, but there was a litheness about them that suggested she could be lightning quick if the need arose. The fact that her moccasins made no sound added the impression of stealth. Like an Indian, Rock thought with skepticism—or a wildcat.

"My name's Rocklin," he said, with an inflection that carried a strong hint for her to introduce herself.

"I'm Rita Ballard."

"Rita Ballard," he repeated. "Haven't heard that name before. You live around here?"

She gave him a slanted look. "You interested?"

"Not much," Rock said bluntly, nettled by her manner. "What's on your mind, Miss Ballard?"

A brittle light sprang into her eyes. Rita Ballard, he guessed, knew men and had yet to meet the one she was afraid of.

"You," she said, just as bluntly. "From the way you were looking me over awhile ago, I thought you'd be worth knowing." She swept a glance down over him, then tilted her chin, eyeing him with an open challenge. "Maybe I was wrong."

"I'd hate to think it," Rock murmured, watching her now with a strict, wary attention.

He saw the tantalizing smile that started playing around her lips, the pulse that quickened in her throat under his gaze. She was, he thought, as unreserved as any creature in the wild country that had bred her. His own pulse quickened, began to throb; and Rock got a swift, hard grip on himself. He couldn't afford the luxury of unguarded desire.

He reached for tobacco, keeping his eyes on the girl but forcing his thoughts to consider the lawman she had recognized and the rustlers who had murdered him. And he wondered whether it would be wise to evince any interest in that business. It could be dangerous, but it could be pertinent, too. He couldn't forget the venomous glance this girl had cast at Ed Claiborne's foreman.

He tapered his cigarette with care, reached for a match and asked casually, "Where had you seen that man before?"

"Which man?"

Rock eyed her with cool derision over the flame of his match. "The one," he said pointedly, "who was riding his horse belly down."

"I'd never seen him before," she protested hastily. "Why, I don't even know who he was. I was just looking—"

"Yeah," Rock interrupted. "You were just looking at his carcass and remembering who you'd last seen him with, *alive.*"

"You're crazy!" Rita didn't move, but something about her expression reminded Rock of a cat, back up, sliding cautiously away. "I tell you I don't know anything about that man."

"Your eyes," he said mildly, "do a better job of telling the truth than your tongue does. I saw the way you were looking at him. I figured then that you knew him, and now I'm sure of it. But it's nothing to me."

"Nothing to you?" She eyed him doubtfully. "Then why did you ask?"

"Just curious," Rock said easily. "Wondering how a pretty girl like you got mixed up with a dead man, that's all. I've got no interest in this business whatsoever. If you hadn't come here, I'd probably never even have thought of it again, but—" He dropped his cigarette on the bare floor and stepped on it, then looked up with a faint grin. "I'm still curious."

"So am I," she said queerly, and he saw then the calculating gleam that had crept into her eyes. "Come to think of it, you weren't too much interested in the sheriff, either, were you?"

Rock concealed the start that gave him. "I didn't see any point in getting into trouble over something Jud Moore had started. You don't like him much, do you?"

"I hate him!" she flashed, with sudden, flaming passion. "The conceited coyote!"

Her outburst startled Rock, and he became suddenly, vividly aware of the wildfire that was in her.

"Mama," he breathed. "I hope you never look like that when you're thinkin' about me."

"Him and the Kid," Rita said bitterly, her breast heaving, "I was hoping you'd kill the damn little skunk."

"They been bothering you?"

"Bothering me?" she echoed hotly. "Every time they come—" She broke off sharply, flashing him a startled, fearful glance. Then slowly she moved forward, looking up at him with a narrowed interest. "Who are you, anyway?"

Rock shrugged. "Drifter." Her nearness aroused him, and he glanced at her parted lips, wondering about Jud and the Kid—and Ed Claiborne. He said, "Some men sure make nuisances of themselves, but I reckon you're pretty fast on the getaway."

She smiled with sudden coquetry, giving him a significant, sidelong glance. "When I want to run."

Rock folded his hands over her shoulders and pulled her close. "Maybe," he said, "I do care where you live."

"Maybe I don't mind telling you. On a ranch near Skeleton Creek."

"Where's that?"

"Down in the brakes, under the rim."

"And that," he said, "is where you saw the dead man."

"Yes," she admitted. "He rode into the ranch one day."

"Can't blame him for that," Rock said. "Reckon I'll have to ride out there myself some day, only I hope I don't come back the way he did. You come in for the dance?"

"Yes," she said and giggled. "My brothers were gone, so I sneaked off."

"You know Ed Claiborne?"

He threw the question at her bluntly, and the startled light in her eyes gave her away. It was just a flicker, but Rock knew.

"Everybody knows Ed Claiborne," she said evenly.

"Yeah." He looked at her lips again, his loneliness driving him, but abruptly he stepped back. "You better get out of here," he said gruffly.

"You going to the dance tonight?"

"I may drop in."

She smiled with frank invitation. "I'll be watching for you."

After she had gone, Rock leaned rigidly into the door for a moment, his jaw set and his eyes narrowed with a hard speculation.

"So," he muttered grimly. "The righteous Mr. Claiborne is no stranger to Rita Ballard. I—just—wonder!"

Abruptly he turned to his pack, dug out a dark blue shirt that wouldn't show up in the night and changed. He paced the room restlessly, lingering until full dark had settled over the town. Then he went out, feeling as cold and inexorable as the gun barrel pressing against his stomach.

He had his supper at a small hash house nearby, inquired the way to the dance hall, then sauntered to the intersection and turned up the main street. Across the street from the Town House he found a darkened alcove and stopped, tipping one shoulder idly against the wall as he kept an alert watch on the hotel.

It netted him nothing. A number of people emerged, some of them climbing gaily into waiting rigs and taking off for the dance, but he saw nothing of Kathy Sinclair or Ash Carlton. The moon came up while he waited, bathing the street with a clear, brilliant light that made Rock reluctant to leave his shelter. At the end of an hour, however, he knew that he had missed them. If he wanted a look at Kathy's escort tonight, he would have to go to the dance. And he wanted that look.

As he stepped out of the alcove, he nearly collided with two cowboys weaving drunkenly along the walk. Rock stepped aside, giving them all of the considerable room that they needed, but one of them, a lanky, sharp-faced man, stopped to peer at Rock intently.

"Say," he demanded with thick belligerence, "ain't you the feller that whipped Jud Moore?"

"No," Rock said and started on up the street.

"Hey, wait—"

"Aw, let him go, Hank," his companion protested. "That ain't the feller."

"It is, too."

"Well, Jud'll get him. C'mon. I gotta have a drink."

Rock kept on walking, ignoring their wrangling, but the incident had put him on edge. He had already attracted too much attention in this town, and every moment that he remained in it increased his danger. He cut across the street, turned into a vacant lot and headed directly for the dance hall, anxious now to get his look and get out of here.

The hall was on a side street almost at the edge of town, a low adobe building with but few windows and all of them small, high. Rock hesitated, looking at those windows, noting, too, the high wall showing behind the building, evidently enclosing a garden. He could see only one entrance, leading into a narrow, shed-like structure that had been tacked onto the building for use as a cloak room.

The place could be a death trap. Rock knew it, but he gambled on this very fact insuring him against suspicion. It was the last place anyone would expect to find a man with a price on his head.

Pulling his hat down well over his eyes, he stepped out of the shadows and strode boldly toward the hall, the sound of the gay, lively music bringing a sardonic smile to his face. He slipped quietly through the crowd of men lounging outside the door, scanning the faces, seeing none that looked familiar. As he stepped into the narrow entrance hall he was momentarily checked by the sight of the ticketed guns ranged along the wall. But it was too late to turn back now.

He stepped out purposefully, starting past the table and the gray-haired man behind it. The fellow held up his hand with authority.

"Check your gun, cowboy."

Rock paused. "I'm not stayin'. Just got a message for the boss."

"Who?"

"Claiborne. He here yet?"

"Yeah, he's here."

Rock nodded. "Won't take but a minute," he said, and strode on into the hall.

It was reassuringly dim, the only light coming from Japanese lanterns strung across the ceiling, and it was crowded. There seemed to be almost as many people ringing the floor, watching, as there were dancers.

Rock eased into the spectators, making his way slowly down the side of the hall. As the dance ended and couples came trooping merrily off the floor, he stepped back against the wall and waited, watching eagle-eyed. But he saw nothing of Kathy or the man he sought. When the music resumed, he took advantage of the confusion to move out again, working quietly toward the archway leading to the garden.

If he knew Ash Carlton, the man would sooner or later have his lady friend out in the shadows.

As he gained the archway, he caught one glimpse of Kathy Sinclair's shining head but lost it immediately and couldn't see who she was dancing with. Rock stepped on into the moonlit garden, strolled a short way down the path, then turned over to the wall where thick shrubbery formed a concealing shadow. The tension was beginning to hit him, bringing a cold sweat to his hands; and he leaned back against the wall, rolling a cigarette and turning his mind to the music. It was a dreamy waltz, and it brought him a queer, hollow feeling that was almost like homesickness. He had liked to dance, once.

He smoked his cigarette down, feeling the strain ease off into a renewed restlessness. He had extinguished his smoke and had just started to step away from the wall when the sound of footsteps on the gravel path stopped him. The next moment Kathy Sinclair came into view, her face radiant in the moonlight. Rock saw that much. Then his glance lifted to her companion, and his blood leaped with a tigerish, almost uncontrollable impulse.

He would have recognized that superbly built body and that self-assured walk anywhere, even if he could not have seen the handsome head with its shock of fair hair gleaming silver. It was Ash Carlton, all right, an engaging smile on his face as he gazed down at the girl.

Rock felt a flash of hot, driving exultation. Then he seemed to freeze, his fists clenched, and his jaw set with an aching restraint.

Ash led the girl off the path not fifteen feet away, stopping behind some shrubbery that would hide them from the path but that left them in clear view of Rock. There Ash turned the girl to face him, his hands on her arms, his smile fading.

Hungrily Rock studied that face, searching for the weakness and the dissolution he felt sure would be there. But they weren't. He saw only strength, confident, capable strength.

So intent was Rock on drinking in every detail of the man's appearance that he missed the first part of the conversation. It was the familiar smoothness of Ash's voice that recalled him.

"You're beautiful, Kathy."

Kathy laughed softly. "It's just the moonlight, Ed. It makes anyone look better."

"Well, something is sure raising Cain with my blood pressure. Kathy—" He hesitated, pulling in a deep breath and evidently struggling for words. Then, abruptly, he laughed. "Thunder. I guess there's no point in me loping plumb around the section when you probably already know what's biting me. Will you marry me, Kathy?"

For some reason, the question hit Rock like a thunderbolt. He flashed a glance at the girl to see her looking up at Ash with a faint, uncertain smile.

"I'll have to think that over a little," she replied.

Ash's grip on her arms tightened noticeably. "You know I'm in love with you."

"Yes."

"And I think you're in love with me."

"I'm afraid of it."

She laughed, her eyes sparkling with a mischievous light. Ash laughed, too, then deliberately folded his arms around her shoulders, pulled her to him and kissed her.

Rock strained forward, watching while a savage rage swelled up and knotted in his breast, threatening to overwhelm him. It seemed a mocking symbol, that kiss, of all the desolation of the past three years; and the desire to kill Ash Carlton became an unbearable throb in his brain.

He saw Kathy step back, flushed and breathless. He saw the way Ash looked down at her and he thought, *Not this one, Ash. You've had your last woman!*

"When, Kathy?" Ash asked intensely. "When will you know?"

"Probably not until John gets back." Kathy laughed in confusion. "You take my mind off my work, Mr. Claiborne."

"And I'm going to keep it off," Ash said forcefully.

He started to reach for her again, but Kathy stepped back and held up one hand in a mock-serious gesture that stopped him.

"I have the next dance promised," she said soberly, "and I would like to have a little of my composure left."

Ash laughed exultantly, then offered his arm with exaggerated gallantry. Rock watched, strung taut, until they were out of sight and hearing. Then, slowly, he eased back against the wall, wiping his hands on his pants, trying to relax. He couldn't do it.

This, then, was the man from whom he had to force the truth if he were ever to clear his name. Not a man looking constantly back over his shoulder with guilty fear, but a man standing firm and straight in a new country. A man who might feel that he had nothing to fear from a despised outlaw who would be gunned down the moment he was recognized.

Rock shoved abruptly away from the wall and stepped out of the shrubbery, turning toward the archway with a growing sense of urgency. He had his information. Now he wanted to get away from here so that he could figure out what to do about it.

The music was just starting up when he stepped into the hall. He saw Ash across the room, his back to the dance floor, talking to someone. With this reassurance, Rock started for the entrance, staying as near to the wall as he could while he made his way through the crowd.

He was halfway up the side of the room when he came face to face with Rita Ballard, her dark eyes shining with the excitement of the occasion. Rock nodded to her, started to step past. At that moment a hand grabbed his arm, his right arm, and a shrill, electrifying yell broke in his ear.

*"Rock Kendall!"*

# CHAPTER THREE

With that cry knifing through him, Rock spun, caught just a glimpse of flaming red hair, of glittering, hate-filled green eyes. In that split second he recognized Red Mayberry, and he lashed out blindly with his left hand. The blow caught Red in the face, knocking him back and loosening his grip. Rock wrenched free and whirled toward the door, plunging through the crowd with reckless abandon, turned coldly desperate by Red's frenzied yells.

"That's Rock Kendall! Stop him! *Stop him!*"

The hall was instantly in an uproar, the screams of women piercing through the booming, questioning shouts of men. The stunning suddenness of it was in Rock's favor. He was almost to the door before the significance of his headlong rush dawned on the startled dancers.

Hands grabbed at him but he beat them off, slamming a fist into any face that appeared in front of him, smashing his way ruthlessly toward the entrance. His momentum carried him through. He leaped into the clear, and dodged through the door only to find the entrance jamming with men hurrying in to see what the excitement was. Sight of him checked them, but Rock didn't hesitate. Throwing both guns with the speed that had made him notorious, he lunged straight at them, yelling stridently.

"Open up!"

They did, without stopping to ask questions, some of them swerving to the side while others ducked back out the door. Rock could hear the crowd spilling into the cloak room behind him now, heading for the gun rack; but he was in the clear. For a moment. As he broke out the door, he saw Sheriff Lackey not over twenty-five feet away, coming at a run and tugging at his gun as he came.

For the briefest part of a second, Rock hesitated, his finger tightening on the trigger, knowing it was the only safe thing to do. But he didn't. Without firing, he turned and raced for the corner of the building.

"What's up?" Lackey shouted.

"That's Rock Kendall! Kill him, Lackey! *Kill him!*"

Rock recognized Red Mayberry's voice an instant before a shot boomed out behind him, followed closely by a second. A bullet glanced off the side of his cartridge belt with a force that staggered him, and a roar of elation went up from the crowd. Then he had rounded the corner and was making a mad dash down the side of the building.

He had reached the garden wall before the firing broke out behind him again, more than one gun now. He could hear the thud of lead into the adobe wall, the ominous zing of ricochetting bullets, but his pursuers evidently were shooting on the run, and he reached the corner of the garden without being touched.

A stable and corrals loomed ahead of him, with a number of saddled horses tied on the outside; and Rock turned on a last resolute burst of speed, putting his guns away as he ran. He heard the wild yell of rage and fear as the men burst around the corner, knew that they would pull up now for more accurate shooting, but he didn't look back.

As the guns opened up, one of the saddled horses screamed, threw himself against the corral with a rending crash, then went down heavily, kicking and thrashing. Instant panic swept the others. Several of them broke away and stampeded, but the bay Rock was heading for couldn't break his bridle. Rock dodged the lashing hoofs, jerked loose the reins and threw himself into the saddle as the terrified animal plunged away.

The shooting, he realized then, had ceased after that horse went down; but now it opened up again in a savage fusillade. Rock felt a tug at his shirt, another at his belt. Then a spasmodic leap from the bay told him the animal had been hit, but it served only as a spur. With a wild snort, the horse stretched into a killing run; and Rock lay far over his neck, his face whipped by the flying mane as they tore away from the dance hall.

A row of trees gave them temporary shelter, and Rock swerved the horse into a vacant lot, cut between two houses on the other side of the block and came into a street that led to the open desert and the mountains to the south. The horse was still running with a wild straining effort that couldn't last, but Rock made no attempt to pull him up until they had passed the last unpainted shack of the town. Then he eased him into a smoother run and looked back.

At least a dozen riders were pelting after him, clearly visible in the brilliant light of the moon, and he knew there would be more coming as soon as they could get horses. He could see the flash of their guns, but he had little fear of being hit. A fall was the greatest danger, and Rock turned his attention to the rough floor of the desert ahead of him and to the horse under him. The bay was still running hard but his stride was free, unpanicked, and he gave no indication of faltering. Apparently the bullet had merely stung him.

Rock covered a mile before looking back again, from a slight rise. He had gained on his pursuers but they were still coming, doggedly, and he knew they wouldn't give up as long as they thought he was wounded. Then he lost sight of them as the horse carried him on over the rise, and again he turned his attention to the country ahead of him, scanning the moonlit desert for some form of cover.

He came onto the canyon suddenly, a deep, brushy cut angling down from the mountains in a northeasterly direction. Rock tipped off into it at a slant that would indicate he was going to follow it on toward the mountains; but once out of sight under the rim, he turned down country and spurred the horse into a lunging, sliding rush to the bottom. There he pulled up in the shelter of thick brush and waited, wet with sweat and heaving almost as badly as his winded horse.

As he had suspected, the men didn't take the time to cut for tracks. Some of them stayed on the rim, spurring out viciously in the hope of sighting him, while the others piled off into the bottom of the canyon and turned up toward the mountain.

"Good hunting," Rock grunted after them, and lifted his hand to his hat brim in an impudent gesture of farewell.

The lid was off now. Not only would every man in the country be out to hunt him down and destroy him, but Ash Carlton would be on guard. The only advantage Rock might have had, that of surprise, had been eliminated, but the knowledge did not depress him. Rather, the challenge of it exhilarated him; and he grinned to himself as he visualized the consternation that must have struck Ash when that frenzied yell went up.

"Give him something to think about," he drawled to the bay, "besides Kathy Sinclair."

He took the time to roll a cigarette before turning down the canyon at an easy jog, following its winding course until he figured he was about due east of town. Then, shoving the extra gun back inside his shirt, he rimmed out and spurred the horse into a lope back toward Wellton.

Lights were still shining all over town, but the streets seemed strangely deserted. Rock avoided the main thoroughfare, turning into a side street and holding his horse to a walk as he made his way quietly back toward the rooming house where he'd left his pack and rifle. He needed those items and he wanted the brown Morgan, a horse that he knew from past experience could outrun and outlast almost anything that could be thrown against him.

As he turned in at the rooming house, he caught a brief glimpse of a hurrying figure down at the intersection, just turning into main street. Rock pulled up short. He couldn't be sure since her form had been only an indistinct shadow; but it wasn't the actual sight that told him who it was. It was an impression of lithe speed, of catlike stealth. And he remembered then that Rita Ballard had been with Red Mayberry when Red spotted him at the dance.

Rock looked back at the rooming house, studying it narrowly while a dull anger stirred in him. Then he rode directly up to the front door and swung off, leaving the bay with reins dragging right beside the step. He paused only long enough for one sweeping survey of the moonlit street before entering the building, gun in hand.

It was perhaps foolhardy, but Rock had a strong hunch Red would be alone. The young cowboy hadn't had a gun at the dance but that hadn't kept him from jumping Rock, instantly and without fear, which would indicate that, given a chance, the redheaded brother of Dorene Mayberry would exact his own vengeance.

There was no one at the desk. Slowly, without making a sound, Rock moved down the dimly-lit hall and stopped before the door to his room. He laid careful hold of the knob, turning it silently. Then he threw the door wide open and lunged through it, leaping instantly out of the shaft of light.

Neither a shot nor a challenge greeted him. Swiftly, he moved to the corner where he had left his things and found them undisturbed. For a moment he stood hesitant, staring down at his pack and wondering. Maybe he was wrong about Rita Ballard—or maybe Red was in the stable. And maybe he *wasn't* alone.

Rock sheathed his gun and threw the saddlebags over his shoulder. Carrying the pack under his left arm and the rifle in his left hand, he went back out to the bay, fighting an urge to get out of here while the getting was good. He was crowding his luck, crowding it dangerously; but he wanted the brown horse, and he wanted to talk to Red Mayberry if he could manage it.

Mounting the bay, he rode back up the street, partially circled the block and turned into the alley that ran behind the stable. He quit the bay, leaving the horse and his belongings in the shadow of a shed, then went on afoot, again moving slowly and with infinite care. The stable was a small one with only three stalls, but Rock remembered that it had a window on the far corner, a blank hole in the wall that opened onto the alley. And that window would now be in shadow.

Rock eased up beside it and stopped, his back to the wall, his head turned as he listened intently. For several moments he heard nothing but the sound of a horse munching hay, rubbing against the manger and blowing the chaff out of his nostrils at frequent intervals. Then, distinctly, he heard the sound of a human sigh.

It was near at hand, just on the other side of the wall, and Rock froze. Moments longer he waited, hardly breathing, but he heard nothing further. Just one man, then, lurking in the shadow of this end stall, waiting for Rock Kendall to silhouette himself in the broad doorway.

In absolute silence, Rock lowered himself to pass under the window, then stole around the end of the building to the front. As he had expected, the door stood wide open, the moonlight streaming into the stable with deadly brilliance. Rock eased up beside the aperture, flattening himself against the wall, hesitating. Red would fight if he had any chance at all, and Rock didn't want to give him that chance.

He drew his gun, then picked up a small rock and tossed it over the building. He heard it hit on the other side. A second later, he heard the faint rustling of straw and knew that Red was now facing the window. Soundlessly, Rock slid around the door casing, taking one long stride away from the light before stopping, his gun leveled. He could see Red clearly, crouched in the stall, his gun lifted toward the window.

"Don't move," Rock warned, his voice soft but icy.

Red jerked spasmodically, then grew rigidly still.

"Drop that gun," Rock ordered.

Red hesitated, his hand beginning to tremble; and Rock thumbed his hammer back to full cock, the click adding deadly emphasis to his words.

"Drop it, Red," he repeated softly.

It obviously cost Red almost more than he could bear, but he let go of the gun. As it fell into the straw, he came slowly erect, turning toward Rock with his fists doubled. Even in the uncertain light, Rock could see the glitter in his eyes, the defiant set of his jaw; and he knew that one moment of laxity could be fatal.

"Come out of there," he ordered. Then, as Red reached the mouth of the stall, "That's close enough. Now you stand hitched, young fella, while I tell you a thing or two."

He paused, knowing Red wouldn't believe a word he said but driven to tell him. Red was taller than he remembered, a little wider across the shoulders, but he was still slim and wiry, his legs slightly bowed. He would, Rock guessed, be a tophand cowboy.

"Where'd you leave my horse?" Red asked coldly.

"Was that your horse I borrowed?"

"If it hadn't been," Red retorted, "I'd have been out there after you."

"Ahuh. Well, he's up the alley here. You riding for Ash?"

"For Ed Claiborne," Red corrected.

"You can come out of the bushes, Red," Rock told him. "I've seen your Mr. Claiborne." He laughed at a sudden thought. "That's pretty good, me making my getaway on a Bar Circle horse. Be sure to tell Ash how much I appreciate that."

Red was suddenly snarling, straining forward. "You skunk. You rotten skunk!"

The words took all good humor out of Rock. He held the gun steady, waist high and still cocked, waiting until the cowboy eased slowly back.

"I've been wanting to talk to you for three years," he said then, "to tell you I didn't kill your sister."

"The hell you didn't!"

"Ash was the one who killed her."

Red flipped his hand in a furious gesture. "You expect me to believe that?"

"No, I don't," Rock said evenly, "but I'll tell you, anyway. I'd gone to her shop that day looking for Ash. He wasn't there and we were talking." He paused. He could see her vividly, red hair piled high on her head, green eyes stormy in the dimness of her little dressmaking shop. "She was sore, Red. She figured Ash had been fooling around with other women on that last cattle drive, and you know damn well he had, too!"

"I don't know any such a damn thing! He was in love with Dorene, planned to marry her."

"Yeah, just like—" Rock bit down on the words, but he could not restrain the fleeting thought of Kathy Sinclair and Rita Ballard. "Ash has always been a sucker for women, and Dorene was just finding it out. I don't know what the hell bit her, Red. I guess she wanted to get even with him, to show him they could both play that game. Anyhow, she must have seen him coming that day. All of a sudden, she threw her arms around my neck and started to kiss me. It knocked me for a loop. I—couldn't help myself, Red. I grabbed her."

The memory filled Rock with a sudden agitation and he stopped, fighting for self-control. He wanted to justify himself but couldn't do it, and the blazing, bitter contempt in Red's eyes drove him on.

"I was holding her, kissing her when Ash came in. You know how jealous he's always been. When he saw me—like that—he lost his head. It was me he wanted to kill, but I heard the click of the hammer and spun around just as he fired."

Again Rock broke off. He could still see Ash's face, livid, twisted into a horrible mask of insane rage, and he could still feel Dorene's fingers digging convulsively into his shoulders for one terrible second before she sagged limp in his arms. Horror had held him rooted, but not Ash.

"I was just starting to lay her down when he jumped in and hit me over the head with that gun."

"Ash wasn't even packing a gun."

"*I'm* the one that wasn't packin' a gun." Rock's voice turned bitter. "That's a mistake I've never made since, but I was a respectable rancher in those days. Ash had a shoulder rig—does he still use one?"

"I don't know."

"Well, make it a point to find out," Rock said harshly. "It might tell you something about the precious gentleman. He's always carried a hideout gun, and he had one under his coat that day. He tried to shoot me in the back. Then when the slug hit Dorene, he saw a chance to frame me for the murder and he sure didn't waste any time doing it!"

The rest of it was vague but hideous nightmare to Rock. The blow on the head that dropped him, stunned; the wild accusations and the bleary faces of lynch-mad townsmen; the terrible moment when he knew they'd never believe him. Then the thundering ride out of town, slammed down over the horn by a bullet in the back.

"I reckon he thought I was plumb out," Rock said grimly, "because he dropped that gun beside me before he started yelling for help. If he hadn't, I'd have been strung up right then."

"Like you should have been," Red bit out. "You're wasting your breath, Kendall."

Rock cut him off. "You remember the blood that was on me. I had my arms around her when she was shot!"

"Sure, I remember the blood," Red said, his lip curling, "and I know how you got it. Ash said you grabbed her when she started to fall. That's when he jumped in and slugged you. He heard Dorene tell you to get out of there, heard her scream. He made a run for the door, but you fired just as he got to it. He saw you shoot her!"

"That's a lie!"

"He isn't the one who's lying." Red's hatred was turning his voice rough. "You were drunk—"

"I hadn't had a drink."

"Bah! When you were backing away from us behind that damn gun, you were so drunk you could hardly stand up."

"I wasn't drunk. I was about two-thirds out. Ash hit me—"

"You're a liar, Kendall, and a filthy, stinkin' snake. You killed my sister because she wouldn't let you make love to her, and I'll see you stretched out dead if it's the last thing I ever do!"

Rock pulled in a breath that hissed through his clenched teeth. An almost irresistible craving for violence drove through him, but he couldn't take it out on Red.

He said harshly, "If Ash is so honest, why'd he run away and change his name?"

"Because he was the only eye witness to that murder. He figured you'd come back to kill him and you did, just as soon as you could."

"I went back, all right," Rock agreed grimly, "but sure not to kill him. I need him alive—and talkative."

"Bull!" Red burst out derisively. "You'll never get anybody to believe a story like that about Ed Claiborne, and you'll never get to him. I don't know what your idea is, coming up with a lie like that after all this time, but it won't get you anywhere, Kendall. Ed Claiborne's so far above you that you can't touch him!"

A sense of savage futility washed over Rock and he said abruptly, "Saddle my horse."

As Red moved to comply, Rock stepped back against the wall and, with his left hand, pulled a coiled rope off a peg. He shook out a loop, keeping both his eyes and his gun trained steadily on Red, who was watching him covertly, waiting for an unguarded moment. When the saddling was finished, Red stepped slowly out of the stall and stopped, watching Rock with hard defiance.

Rock flipped the loop over his head and jerked it tight around his upper body, pinning his arms.

"Turn around," he commanded, "and keep on turning till I tell you to stop."

Red's eyes flared with a fresh hatred but he obeyed, winding himself up in the rope. Only when there were four tight coils around his body did Rock sheathe his gun. He trussed the cowboy clear to his knees, then stuck a foot behind him and laid him down on the straw, kneeling beside him.

"I've told you the truth, Red," he said evenly. "If I live long enough, I'll *show* you what kind of a man Ash Carlton is."

"You won't," Red said flatly. "You won't live long enough to do anything, only I hope to God nobody else gets to you first."

"You want that thousand bucks yourself, huh?"

"All I want," Red said through his teeth, "is a chance to cut the heart out of you!"

"Well, you better hustle," Rock said dryly. "From the way that pack was howling tonight, I'd say the competition was going to be pretty keen."

He gagged the cowboy with his own neckerchief, then led his horse out of the stable, picked up his gear and turned south; but he still wasn't leaving town.

"In this game," he told his horse grimly, "you always want to do what the other fella is damn sure you *won't* do."

At the edge of town, set back away from the main road leading south, Rock found a small frame house with a neat sign tacked up beside the door: Mrs. Nash. Clean rooms and home cooking. He pulled up, studying the darkened structure, wondering whether Mrs. Nash had been at the dance. Gambling that she hadn't, he dismounted and knocked. A light went on almost immediately, and the door was opened by a big gray-haired woman with a kindly face and shrewd gray eyes. She held her wrapper close about her with one hand while she held the lamp high with the other, subjecting Rock to a critical inspection.

Rock grinned. "No," he said, "I'm not polluted. All I want to sleep off is a hard day's work."

Mrs. Nash smiled, a warm motherly smile that made Rock like her at once. "All right, cowboy," she nodded. "Stable out back. I'll unlock the back door for you."

The woman had evidently gone back to bed by the time Rock entered the house, but she had left the lamp burning in a small bedroom just off the kitchen. It was a pleasant room, with a clean spread on the bed and a gaily colored rug on the floor. Rock closed the door behind him and tossed his hat onto a chair. It was the only article of clothing he removed before blowing out the lamp and stretching out on the bed.

It seemed to him that he had no more than closed his eyes when the sound of a man's voice reached him. He sat up, instantly wide-awake, surprised at the sunlight streaming into the room.

"Here's them eggs, Mrs. Nash," the man was saying. "My wife shore gave me hell for forgettin' them yesterday evening. Say, did you hear the news? Rock Kendall was in town last night."

"Rock Kendall?" Mrs. Nash echoed. "Is that what all the shooting was about?"

"Shore was. Red Mayberry spotted him at a dance."

"Did they get him?"

"Nope, but Lackey winged him."

"Well, forevermore," breathed Mrs. Nash indignantly. "He had his nerve, going to a dance that way."

"Ahuh, and he still had it with him when he left," the man agreed grimly. "I didn't know who he was when he come bustin' out of there with them two guns, but I just naturally didn't like the looks of him."

The man made a shivering sound, and Rock came off the bed in a silent glide, poised and tense.

"Well, forevermore," Mrs. Nash repeated. "Is the sheriff out after him now?"

"Him and nine thousand other fellers, and I hope they get him. I didn't like the looks of that feller a-tall."

"Hmph!" Mrs. Nash snorted. "I'd like to get a look at him, but I suppose all anybody'll see now is the tail end of his horse."

The man shortly took his leave, but not for several moments did Rock ease out of his strained position, his mind fixed on this and examining it from all angles. The sheriff and nine thousand other fellers, but not Ash Carlton! Ash would be in his hotel room, thinking it a sanctuary while waiting and hoping to hear that his enemy had been gunned down. And he might be alone.

With a sudden cheerful grin, Rock turned to rumple the bed so that Mrs. Nash wouldn't know he had slept on top of the spread. Then, with the aroma of coffee and frying bacon sifting into him from the kitchen, he went out.

Mrs. Nash, her face flushed from the heat of the stove, gave him a cheery greeting. "You wash your paws in a hurry, young man," she ordered. "My biscuits are about done."

"Yes'm," Rock said with a meek grin and hurried to obey. He sensed the woman's friendly interest and felt the need of establishing himself in her confidence. Watching himself in the mirror as he combed his hair, he said casually, "Sounds like I missed some excitement last night."

"Didn't you go to the dance?"

"I'd figured on it," he lied, straight-faced, "but those rascals that brought the new herd in all took off and I got stuck out there."

"Too bad," Mrs. Nash said bluntly. "Maybe you could have shot straighter than old Sheriff Lackey. As if this country wasn't tough enough without having a wolf like that Rock Kendall drift into it!"

Rock grinned. "You'd like to get a look at him, huh?"

"I would. I'd like to bash his head in with a frying pan. And to think Kathy Sinclair went ahead and pulled out with that lobo running loose!"

Rock swung to face her in feigned consternation. "Pulled out?"

"Sure did. She and three or four cowboys rode by here at least thirty minutes ago, headed for Clear Springs."

"Well, doggone," Rock said plaintively, pocketing his comb. "I hope I don't get fired again."

Secretly he was highly pleased with the information. Hell was apt to pop down at the hotel, and for some reason it relieved him to know that Kathy wouldn't be on hand to view it.

Mrs. Nash accepted him without question as a Triple X man and, when he left, cordially invited him to come back any time he was in town.

"I'll sure do it," he promised, wondering as he said it whether he would live long enough to need another meal.

The streets were practically deserted, and he gained the business district without attracting attention. Turning into the alley behind the Town House, he dismounted and left his horse ground-hitched between a stable and a storage shed. He hesitated only briefly, eyeing the back entrance to the hotel as he loosened the gun in his holster. Then, with a tight-drawn breath, he crossed the alley and let himself into the dim, narrow hall leading to the lobby.

He was gambling that not too many people had actually seen his face in the confusion at the dance and that those who had seen it would be assuming, as Mrs. Nash had, that he was still making tracks toward the mountains, fast and far between. At the entrance to the lobby he paused, scanning the room with apparent idleness. There weren't over a dozen loungers present, and none of them gave him more than a passing glance.

With his heart thudding dully against his ribs, Rock stepped out of the hall and sauntered toward the stairway tacked against the wall near the door to the dining room. He had no idea which room Ash occupied, but if he could get upstairs without being detected, he would find it. He had just reached the foot of the stairs when Ash appeared suddenly at the head of them, his head turned back as he spoke to someone behind him. Rock had a flashing glimpse of Jud Moore and the cowboy called Hank. Then he ducked swiftly out of their range of vision and put his back to the staircase, flattening himself as he heard them start down.

A flashing survey of the room told him that he couldn't get out of it before they would spot him. He was caught, and tension gripped him, cold and breathtaking, as he heard the three men reach the foot of the stairs.

# CHAPTER FOUR

ASH WAS a little in the lead as they stepped away from the stairs and headed for the desk. They hadn't noticed Rock—yet, and a wild idea came to him. Without hesitation, he stepped away from the stair casing and called in a clear, surprised voice that would carry throughout the lobby: "Ash Carlton!"

Ash spun as if he'd been shot, his eyes popping with incredulity. Before he could collect himself, Rock stepped forward, grinning and extending his hand.

"Howdy, Ash," he drawled coolly.

Ash backed away, astonishment robbing him of his usual poise. Without taking his eyes off Rock, he flung his hand imperiously toward the two men with him.

"That's Rock Kendall!" he blurted.

Jud, who had been frowning in uncertainty, took an involuntary step backward, a look of shock springing to his face. Hank, however, made a desperate grab for his gun. Rock swerved away, throwing his gun with lightning speed and firing even as he jumped back against the stair casing. He saw the slug hit, high, spinning the lanky cowboy half around; and he swept his gun menacingly over the other men in the room. They appeared frozen, stunned. The only sound in the room following the crash of the shot was the drag of Hank's boots as he staggered, then the solid thud of his body as he hit the floor.

"What the hell's the idea?" Rock demanded hotly of Ash. "You trying to get me killed?"

Ash was as gray as granite, his hands trembling. "How'd you get in here?" he asked hoarsely.

"Walked in," Rock snapped. "These men didn't know me, wouldn't have known me if you'd kept your mouth shut. That's a hell of a thing to do to an old pard."

Ash was still badly shaken, his mind groping with the impossibility of this. "I thought—"

"You thought I was on the run, huh?" Rock grinned tightly. "You should know me better than that, friend Ash. Or had you forgotten you owe me several thousand dollars?"

"I don't—" Ash broke off. Then, slowly, a dull red flush crept up out of his collar to stain his neck.

Rock knew from the strained hush in the room that he had accomplished his purpose and it was time to go. He looked Ash over with only a narrow contempt, hiding the driving hatred he felt.

"I should have known," he said coldly, "that Ash Carlton wouldn't play square, even with an old friend, but this isn't the end of it. I'll see you again, *pardner!*" He swept a warning glance over the other men in the room. "Unless you gents are equipped with cast-iron corsets, you better sit pat till I get out of here; and you, Ash, if you make a try for that hideout gun you're packin', I'll shoot your damned arm off."

He slid away from the stair casing, moving sideways and holding his gun cocked but unaimed as he headed for the hall. He backed into it, moving slowly and listening intently for any sound of movement in the lobby. He heard none. He reached the door, paused for a flashing glance at the alley, then stepped out, leaving the door wide open and watching it closely as he crossed to his horse. There still was no sign of activity in the hotel when he mounted and lifted his horse into a gallop out of town.

Nor was there any pursuit. Apparently every man who was interested in chasing him was already out with the sheriff. Half a mile from town, Rock pulled up, turning in the saddle to look back.

"Now then, damn you," he said harshly, "explain that to your friends."

It wouldn't, he figured, be easy to do. To those stunned men in the lobby, it must have been perfectly obvious that their revered Mr. Claiborne had at one time been associated with a notorious outlaw and had, for some reason, changed his name.

"And that," he told his horse pointedly, "is something honest men don't do, unless they're cowards."

Rock headed east at a mile-covering jog, his mind busy with the challenging future. It had been a small thing, this first blow at Ash, prompted by Red's statement that no one would believe his story; but Rock found some satisfaction in it. If, as now seemed evident, he couldn't buck Ash's present power, then he would destroy that power; and he had already cast the first shadow on the man's impeccable reputation.

Rock put fifty miles behind him before stopping, then rested only a few hours before riding on, still toward the east. Only when he felt sure he ran no risk of meeting Lackey and his posse did he turn south, working his way as rapidly as possible up into the mountains. The sage gave way to stunted junipers and cedars. Then came the pines. The brooding peace of summer lay over the desert, but at this height the air was brisker, filled with the exhilarating tang of evergreens.

Rock met only one rider during that wide circle. From him he obtained directions as to how to reach Kathy Sinclair's Clear Springs ranch and dawn of a clear, crisp day found him on a vantage point above the spread, watching it with hawk-eyed interest.

It was, indeed, a beautiful spot. From the timbered knoll where Rock lay concealed, he could look down onto the neat log buildings, arranged with care among the towering pines. A creek, stemming no doubt from the springs that gave the ranch its name, cut through the place, setting the main house apart from the bunkhouses and corrals beyond.

Smoke was already emerging from the chimney of the cook shack when Rock arrived, riding lazily in the still morning air. Very shortly a fire was started in the main house; and a chunky Mexican woman came to the back door, threw a pan of water off the porch and disappeared again. The wrangler came in with the horses, penned them, then headed briskly toward the cook shack. One by one, the cowboys appeared; Rock counted eleven of them, including the man who had done the wrangling. Even from a distance, he could see that they were a salty-looking bunch, all of them armed and all of them moving with a direct-ness that suggested confidence and ability.

Rock waited with scant patience while the men made their preparations to ride out. He glanced frequently at the main house, wondering whether Kathy intended to ride with them this morning. He saw nothing of her; he got his answer when one of the men, evidently the foreman, rode to the house, disappeared inside for a brief moment, then rode back to the corrals. After a short consultation, the cowboys pulled out, passing from sight into the timber to the east.

Rock slid back from the edge of the knoll and stood up, strid-ing rapidly to the thicket where he'd left his horse. He swung into the saddle, circled the knoll and turned down toward the ranch house, aware of an unaccustomed tightness in his chest. He was gambling again, gambling that Kathy had not seen him at the dance and that Sheriff Lackey had not had time to mention that he was after a man who had introduced himself as Jim Rocklin.

"If she knows me," he told his horse grimly, "she's almighty apt to reach for the rollin' pin."

He came in behind the house, leaving his horse by the neatly stacked woodpile and approaching the back door with a slow, almost reluctant, stride. He had done a good deal of thinking on his way out from town, and a lot might depend on whether or not

Kathy knew who he was. He stepped up onto the porch, hesitating as he lifted his hand to knock. Then abruptly he balled his fist and rapped his knuckles hard against the door.

Kathy herself opened it, looking fresh and dainty in a printed cotton dress. Rock reached for his hat, holding his breath as the look of calm inquiry in her eyes brightened into recognition. Then a quick smile wreathed her face.

"Well, good morning!" she said, a happy lift in her voice. "I was wondering what had happened to you."

She was undeniably glad to see him and Rock grinned, letting his breath out carefully and running a hand over his rumpled head to hide the embarrased relief he felt.

"Nothin'—yet," he drawled.

"You decided to take the job?"

"Well—" Rock hesitated, his grin fading. "I'd like to talk to you a little bit more about it. I've got a hunch or two that might be worth something."

"Come in," she invited, stepping aside.

Rock stepped into the warm kitchen, noting the gaily colored oilcloth on the table, the crisp curtains at the window. The Mexican woman was washing dishes in a large pan on the stove, and she gave him only one glance out of unreadable black eyes.

"Had breakfast?" Kathy wanted to know.

"Yes, thanks," Rock replied, failing to mention that it had been only a handful of jerky some time before daylight.

"But you'd like a cup of coffee. Sit down, Mr. Rocklin."

Rock eased into a chair, feeling awkward and uncomfortable. He dropped his hat on the floor and reached for tobacco, thought better of it and shoved the sack back into his pocket.

"Go ahead," Kathy prompted. "John smokes. In fact," she added with a laugh, "if there's any comfort in it, I may take it up myself before long."

She seemed perfectly at ease, gracious and self-assured, and Rock relaxed somewhat. Her presence, as she leaned over to pour his coffee, was a disturbing force; but Rock held his attention to the rolling of his cigarette, not looking at her fully until she had set a clean china ash tray beside his cup and taken a chair opposite him. Then he saw the nervous tension that she had been concealing behind a cheerful manner. Her hands were clasped tightly, propping her chin, and her eyes were fastened on him with an unsmiling regard that seemed to go clear inside of him.

That look had a stilling effect on Rock. He knew before she spoke that trouble had struck her and struck her hard.

"I'm awfully glad you came," she said, her voice low and vibrant with feeling, "and I hope you stay."

"Those rough times arriving?"

"Done arrived," she corrected. Anger flashed in her eyes, a helpless anger that gave Rock a brief but revealing glimpse of the strong emotions that ran close under her control. "There was a raid on the cattle while I was in town, a bad one. One of the boys tried to trail them and was shot off his horse."

"I see," Rock murmured and glanced uneasily at the Mexican woman, not liking the presence of this third person.

"I guess," Kathy said, "that I shouldn't have let any of the men go to town. But they can't work all the time, and we were only in for three days." She paused, watching Rock closely for his reaction. "You see, I meant it when I said we needed men."

"Sure."

He shifted, still not liking the presence of the Mexican woman. He glanced at her, then looked back at Kathy with significant directness.

"Maria," Kathy said promptly, "straighten up the living room, will you, please? I'll finish those dishes later."

Without a word, Maria dried her hands and left the room, and Rock felt a quick easing of tension.

"Thanks," he said with a grin. "I never could get my tongue to work when an outsider was listening in." He paused, his attention held for a moment by Kathy's understanding smile. Then he said, "Now tell me."

Kathy pulled in a deep breath and seemed to plunge, speaking swiftly. "There's always been rustling out here, but it's been mostly small, scattered bunches. Lately they've been running off bigger herds, and this time they made off with at least a thousand head."

"Woosh!" Rock breathed.

"And they did it so fast!" Kathy frowned, as if she still doubted that it could be done. "Other times when we've lost big bunches, we've figured they were driven to the railroad somewhere. This time the boys feel sure they were taken down into the basin, possibly on to the mining towns south of here."

"And that's a new angle, huh?"

"This whole business is new," Kathy said grimly. "It's just too slick. The boys think there's some new gang working out in here, some outfit that's well organized and has plenty of brains at the head of it. They certainly seem to know what they're doing."

"Ahuh." Rock didn't show his growing satisfaction. He had decided on the way out from town that maybe these rustlers *were* his business. Now he was growing steadily more sure of it. "Any idea who they are?"

"Not the slightest." Kathy shook her head in tight-lipped denial. "It's no secret that some of the homesteaders living down under the rim help themselves to our cattle now and then. We've always figured they were the ones who were doing the petty rustling, but the boys say that none of those pack rats have brains enough to be doing this."

"No," Rock agreed, "but they could be helping with it."

He looked down at his cigarette, remembering that at least one bunch of the pack rats had not been at home when this raid was pulled off. The Ballards. Rita had said her brothers were gone, which didn't prove anything but which did, in the light of her recognition of the murdered lawman, give rise to some mighty strong suspicions.

"I'm worried," Kathy said nervously. "We're overextended and can't stand many like that. I sent a man into town yesterday to wire John to come home."

"Yeah," Rock said softly and continued staring at his cigarette. He was thinking of the vehemence with which Rita had spoken of Jud Moore and the Kid. She knew them well enough to hate them thoroughly, which indicated to Rock that these two Bar Circle men were no strangers in what was very likely a rustler hangout. He was thinking of something else, too: the queer light that had sprung into the Kid's eyes at mention of Billy the Kid.

"Anybody drifting in here from New Mexico that you know of?" he asked.

"Not that I know of, no, but it's a cinch there are some. Those men that got out of the Lincoln County War had to go somewhere."

"Yeah," Rock agreed and looked once more at the smoke curling from his cigarette.

The Kid had looked complimented, almost smug; and, with the hunch growing in him, Rock would have bet that the little gunman was visualizing himself as the Billy the Kid of this new war that was building up. It was entirely possible that either he or his bunkie, Jud Moore, had been connected with the Lincoln County War. They could have helped start this herd before riding to town—and they could have been the ones who led the lawman's horse down out of the mountains.

"I understand," Kathy said, "that there are a lot of questionable characters hanging out down around Skeleton Creek. Maybe they're from New Mexico. Maybe they're our rustlers." She shrugged her shoulders with an impatient gesture. "I don't know, and I don't know how to find out."

"What you need," Rock said slowly, "is somebody to ride down there and put his brand on those jokers."

Kathy laughed, rather shortly. "Yes," she agreed, "but I'm afraid that's out of the question. Those brakes aren't safe for an honest man."

*But Ed Claiborne had ridden into them!* To see Rita Ballard. Rock's blood began to pound as the hunch gripped him tighter and tighter. Neither Jud nor the Kid had the brains to run such an outfit as Kathy had described, but Ash Carlton *did* have the brains.

"Well, there it is," Kathy said flatly. "I haven't tried to brighten the picture. It's dark and it's going to get darker, and we'll need all the men we can get. What do you say, Mr. Rocklin? Will you ride with us?"

"On one condition."

Rock looked up with a direct, piercing glance that startled her.

"Condition?" she echoed uncertainly.

"Yes," he said, putting force into his voice. "I'll ride for you on the condition that you don't tell anybody I'm doing it. If you do tell, you'll be buying me a bullet in the back."

Kathy slowly stood up, eyeing him with puzzled doubt. "I don't understand you."

Rock stabbed his cigarette into the tray and shoved to his feet, grinning in reckless anticipation. "I'm going after your rustlers," he announced.

"Going after them?" she repeated, frowning. "How do you mean?"

Rock shrugged. "Like I said a minute ago, what you need is somebody to ride down there and put his brand on those jokers. Reckon I'm the man."

"You mean you want to go down into the brakes?" she asked incredulously.

"Sure."

"Why, no." Kathy lifted one hand in complete dismissal of the idea. "Heavens, no! You'd just be killed."

"That's possible," Rock conceded, "but that's my worry. All I want is your promise not to tell anybody I'm riding for you."

It wasn't the bullet in the back that was worrying him. It was the fact that too many people, including Sheriff Lackey, knew that Mr. Rocklin had some more to his name—Kendall. If Kathy didn't mention Mr. Rocklin to anyone, perhaps no one would think to tell her.

"But that isn't a one-man job," she protested.

"One man will have to do it," Rock said, "if it's ever done. I'm a stranger around her, Miss Sinclair. Those fellas down in the brakes won't know but what I'm from New Mexico myself. If I slide down there easy, maybe I can find out something."

"But supposing you do find out something? Those rustlers are killers. They—"

She broke off, her glance flashing to his gun. Rock went very still, unbreathing as he waited out her inspection, feeling a tightness form in him. Then she looked up again, and color flooded her face.

"Excuse me," she said hastily. "I didn't mean—But it seems so dangerous!"

"That," said Rock carefully, "is what will make it interesting. Is it a deal?"

"A deal? O-h-h!"

Kathy was suddenly distressed, her face clouded, her breath coming fast and tight. Rock could see in her eyes the harried rush of her thoughts, her desperate desire to grab this chance for help struggling with the fear that she would be responsible for his death. *If she knew,* he thought narrowly, *she'd set the dogs on me herself.*

He waited in silence, letting her fight it out and becoming, in that moment, vitally aware of the depth of her character and the compelling force of her personality. This was no willowy girl with fly-by-night whims but a strong, self-willed woman. The kind of a woman, he thought in sudden, bleak loneliness, who could mean the beginning of life to the right man—or a quick death to the wrong one.

She was searching him to the core, seeking the measure of his strength and the temper of his will; and gradually the anxiety in her eyes faded before a glow of suppressed excitement. She pulled in a deep breath, then abruptly stepped around the table and held out her hand.

"It's a deal," she said fervently.

Rock clasped her hand, vibrating to the warm grip of her slender finger. Her nearness quickened his blood, and Kathy herself grew suddenly short of breath. She tightened her grip for a fleeting instant, as if wondering what she held, then hastily withdrew her hand.

Rock stooped abruptly to pick up his hat, conscious once more of that strange tightness in his chest. "Reckon I better be riding."

"Yes. Will you—will you need any supplies?"

"Store at Skeleton Creek?"

"I think so."

Rock grinned and shook his head. "That's where I'm heading."

She walked with him to the door, then hesitated. Rock, stepping outside and putting his hat on as he strode toward his horse, was aware that she followed slowly, as if hypnotically drawn. He tightened his cinch, then leaned into the horse while he rolled a cigarette, wondering how far he dared go. He had made her aware of him, and he wanted to strengthen that interest.

"Seems to me," she said suddenly, "that it's time I started calling you something besides Mr. Rocklin."

"Jim," he said without looking up.

"Jim," she repeated, as if weighing the word.

Rock glanced up as he licked his cigarette, noting the sober, thoughtful light in her expressive eyes. Irresistibly he looked at her lips, richly warm and full of promise, and he wondered if her kiss would be as stirring as her smile. Abruptly he lowered his glance, with the stabbing thought that Ash Carlton knew.

He lit his cigarette, then glanced at her again, this time with a faint teasing grin. "You made up your mind yet about marrying Ed Claiborne?"

Kathy caught her breath, and her eyes popped wide with shock. "How did you know about that?"

"I was out there, having a smoke, and got caught in a corner when you folks came out. Figured I'd embarrass you less if I just stayed there and kept still."

Kathy's cheeks were growing hot as she realized what he had witnessed, and her eyes took on a snap of anger. "You might," she said emphatically, "have embarrassed me less if you had kept on keeping still."

"Reckon so, and I'm apologizing." Rock placed his boot over a clod of dirt and smashed it, then looked up again, unsmiling. "But I'm still curious."

Kathy looked suddenly away, her face tightening, her hands clenching into little fists. "I don't know," she said, her voice low and tense. "He was over here the other evening, terribly upset."

"Oh, yeah? How come?"

"He—it seems that his real name is Ash Carlton." Kathy still wasn't looking at Rock and seemed reluctant to speak, but apparently the pressure inside her was too great. "He used to be in partnership with that Rock Kendall."

"The devil he did!" Rock blurted and didn't need to feign his surprise. He hadn't expected Ash to admit that because of the stigma of cowardice attached to his running away, and now a chill apprehension was rising in him.

"Yes," Kathy admitted. "Kendall laid for him in the hotel Sunday morning and called him by his real name, apparently trying to embarrass him or get money from him or something. I don't know. Wounded one of his men."

"Good Lord," Rock breathed, ducking his head to hide his eyes.

"Ed—" Kathy hesitated, then corrected herself. "Ash told me all about it. He was engaged to marry the girl Rock Kendall killed. He was a witness to the murder and figured Kendall would try to kill him, so he left Texas and changed his name."

"Scared?" Rock asked sharply.

"Oh, no! He figured if he stayed there, he'd have to kill Kendall and he didn't want to. After all, they'd been partners for years."

"I—see," Rock murmured. He saw it, all right. Ash playing the part of a bereaved lover who had pulled out rather than be forced to kill his ex-partner. A noble attitude!

"I—felt sorry for him," Kathy said constrainedly. "He was so upset. Said he should have told me sooner that Claiborne wasn't his name, but he hated to do it while Rock Kendall was still alive." She lifted an appealing hand toward Rock. "Why, the man must be mad! Tracking Ed down after all this time, to kill him!"

Rock knew then, beyond a doubt, that his first move against Ash had backfired on him. Far from undermining the man's position, it had strengthened it, gaining him sympathy and support that he probably would not otherwise have had.

He felt the bite of a nagging disappointment, but he kept his eyes on the ground and put out a feeler that might yet do some good.

"Dunno," he said thoughtfully. "Since you mention Ash Carlton, reminds me—I met a cowboy one time who knew both of those fellas down in Texas. He claimed that Carlton was the one who killed that woman. Said Rock Kendall had been framed."

"Well, that's an idiotic idea!" Kathy burst out indignantly.

Rock tipped his head dubiously. "Not so sure. If Kendall wanted to kill him, why in the devil didn't he do it there in the hotel?"

"He couldn't have got away with it," Kathy said flatly. "Right there in town?"

"Did they get Kendall?"

"No, he got away."

"Ahuh," Rock grunted. "And he probably could have got away just as easy if he'd put a slug in that fella first."

"Maybe," Kathy said, but she obviously couldn't accept the idea. "Maybe that's his idea of torture, to let Ed think about it awhile before he tries to kill him."

"Yeah," Rock said dryly, "or maybe he won't try to kill him at all. If that cowboy had it straight, I reckon Kendall would rather force the truth out of him than kill him."

Kathy gave him a look that bordered on anger. "If you knew Ed Claiborne," she said evenly, "you wouldn't even consider an idea like that."

"Reckon not." Rock flipped his cigarette away and grinned cheerfully. "I've heard a lot about that man since I hit the country. Sure hope this Rock Kendall doesn't lower the boom on him before I get a chance to meet him."

"What you'd better hope," Kathy retorted pointedly, "is that nobody lowers the boom on *you*."

Rock laughed. "That would be kind of disgusting, wouldn't it?" he drawled. "Especially now." He didn't wait to see her reaction, but turned to pick up his reins. He swung into the saddle, then paused, looking down at her and involuntarily registering every detail of the picture she made. And he saw that her attention was once more fully on him, intently focused. "I'll keep you posted on my progress, Little Boss—if I make any."

She colored at the familiar term but her gaze held steady on his, her eyes deep-shadowed and worried.

"Do be careful," she said earnestly. Then, at his reassuring nod, she smiled, lifting her right hand with fingers crossed and waving it in farewell. "Good luck."

Rock touched his hat brim, then reined away, turning back up the knoll down which he had come. When he reached the top of the ridge, he looked back to see that Kathy had not moved. Again she waved and Rock lifted his hand, then held his horse steady, watching as she turned back toward the house. Not until she had disappeared did he turn on up the ridge, pulling in a breath that swelled his chest and left him vaguely uncomfortable.

He had aroused her interest just as he had intended, and he had done it with cold, dark purpose. Ash Carlton, he knew from experience, did rash things when he was jealous and Rock wanted to use his jealousy as a weapon against him. Perhaps he could do it, but he knew now that if he were not very careful he would be falling into his own trap.

# CHAPTER FIVE

ROCK RODE at an easy pace, paying careful attention to the rough-timbered country through which he was passing and making note of all outstanding landmarks. He climbed out presently onto a broad, fairly open ridge and followed it for perhaps two miles before coming, with breathtaking suddenness, to the edge of the rim. He pulled up, whistling his appreciation of the vast expanse of country spread out before him. Far beyond he could see the hazy outline of mountains, but it was the broken, heavily forested basin below that took his breath.

The wall here was a sheer cliff, dropping down several hundred feet to the floor of the basin. On either side of his position were shoulders reaching out, jagged, unscalable, with shrubs and struggling trees clinging precariously to tilted ledges. The floor of the basin itself was a tilted landscape, the green carpet broken by irregular ridges and shadowed, twisting valleys. A pleasant breeze blew up over the rim, stirring the pines and taking the heat out of the morning sun.

For several minutes Rock sat immobile, scanning that wild country, trying to map it in his mind. "One awful big country," he murmured, and wondered if he would be able to find anything down there except his own grave.

He turned east, following the irregular line of the rim, watching it closely for trails leading down. He found several but he kept on, spotting the huddle of gray buildings that he took to be Skeleton Creek and continuing on until he found, in the head of a steep, brush-choked canyon, where the cattle had gone over.

Here he turned down, riding with a slow caution and ranging his eyes constantly through the timber ahead of him. When he reached the floor of the basin he tried to determine how many riders had been with the herd but found it impossible. The broad trail angled a little to the east, and Rock followed it for several miles, crossing a rocky summit and dropping, some time in early afternoon, into a second valley. Here the tracks turned down a creek flowing toward the south, and Rock pulled up.

"Ahuh," he grunted with satisfaction. "They went on to the mining towns, all right; and now, bronc, let's get out of here before somebody catches us snoopin'."

He had found out all he wanted to know about the stolen cattle for the present. Now he wanted to learn something about the men who had stolen them, and he was aware of a rising impatience that was not all due to his desire to get at Ash Carlton. In spite of the singleness of his purpose in braving this country, he felt an involuntary anger toward these men who would steal from a woman.

Shadows were growing long by the time he reached Skeleton Creek, hot, dusty and hungry. It was, he found, even grayer and less inviting than it had appeared from the rim. The Skeleton Creek Store, a frame building with a rickety porch, stood on the north side of the dusty road, flanked by a number of weathered, nondescript shacks. On the south, scattered hit or miss through the brush and timber, were several old log buildings, dominated by a two-story structure that Rock took to be a saloon and gambling hall.

Except for three saddled horses, two dogs and a few wandering chickens, the place appeared to be deserted. As Rock approached, however, a boy darted from behind the saloon and ran out to intercept him. He was a towheaded youngster, perhaps fourteen, dressed in a patched collection of garments that were too big for him.

"Stable your horse, mister?" he asked eagerly.

Rock pulled up, looking skeptically at the dilapidated shed and corral set back in the brush behind the saloon. "Got any grain?"

"Got a little corn," the kid said proudly. His eyes were a bright sparkling blue, and they missed nothing as they traveled admiringly over the brown Morgan. "He's made quite some few tracks today," he observed.

"Yeah." Rock glanced at the three dark shaggy horses, at the dusty packs and at the carbines stuck into saddle boots. He knew, before he ever saw them, what kind of men owned those outfits; they were the kind of men he wanted to meet right now, provided they were not the Ballards. He said, "How far to the Ballard place?"

" 'Bout five miles, on down the creek."

"They been in lately?"

The boy shook his head. "Not for quite awhile. You know 'em?"

"Some of them," Rock said and started to turn toward the stable.

The kid reached for the reins. "I'll take care of him, mister. You go on and get a drink."

Rock looked again at the baggy overalls, at the faded shirt that hung loosely over the thin frame. Then he looked back at the eager brown face and couldn't help grinning.

"All right, Bud," he said, swinging off and handing over the reins. "Don't need to unsaddle him. Just give him a good feed of corn."

"You can stay all night if you want to, mister. Got beds upstairs here."

"Say," Rock blurted, with a laugh, "how much of a commission do you get out of drumming up trade this way?"

"Well," the kid said, jerking his head toward the saloon, "they feed me."

"Oh," Rock murmured, with sudden understanding. He asked softly, "What's your name, young fella?"

"Jimmy."

"Jimmy, huh?" Rock dug into his pocket for a dollar. "Well, Jimmy, this old pony may be dry. Lead him down to the creek and let him water out before you feed him, will you?"

"Gee!" the kid breathed, his eyes shining. "Mister, I'll lead him plumb down to the river for a buck!"

He turned away, leading the brown, and Rock looked after him for a moment, held by a curious and sympathetic interest. Then, with a faint shrug, he turned to the door of the saloon.

It was a dim, ill-smelling place, with a few poker tables and a rough pine bar; its only customers were the three dark-garbed men whose horses stood outside. They turned at Rock's entrance, their bearded faces noncommittal, their eyes veiled as they looked him over.

Rock returned their careful scrutiny, noting the bulge of a second gun under one man's jacket. He nodded to them without speaking and sauntered to the far end of the bar, leaning into it and shoving his hat back with a grateful sigh.

"Whisky," he said to the lanky, gray-haired bartender, "and a drink for these gents if they'll take one with a stranger."

He glanced at them inquiringly, got their reserved nods and laid the money on the bar. Then he took keen but unobtrusive note of the bartender, a hard-faced man who carried a revolver shoved down inside his belt and who walked with a decided limp. He poured Rock's drink in silence, showing no interest either in his customer or in the job he was doing.

Rock said experimentally, "Awful long ways between drinks in this country."

"Not so far," the barman said, "if you've got friends."

"Yeah." Rock let go a discouraged sigh. "Kind of hard to make friends, though, when you—like to travel."

One of the men gave a harsh, jeering laugh, and Rock grinned in rueful admission of a lot of crimes he had never committed.

"Got a good horse, stranger?" the man asked, his voice a subtle taunt.

"Awful good horse," said Rock, "although he's gettin' a little leg weary."

"This is a good place to rest him up."

"Yeah." Rock twisted for a look at the poker tables. "Get some pretty good games going once in a while?"

The barman nodded. "You got some money you want to throw away?"

"Dammit, no," Rock retorted. "You just described the other fella."

The rider laughed again and, with a pseudo-amiable atmosphere thus established, Rock turned his attention to the rolling of a cigarette. A number of names were running through his mind, men he had heard of in connection with the Lincoln County War. Richards, who had vanished into thin air after being charged with murder. Anderson, wanted for rustling. Two or three others that he knew had stolen horses. He dared mention none of them since he didn't know these men, but he wondered if any of those names would fit comfortably on Jud or the Kid.

He lit his cigarette and inhaled deeply before lifting his squinted gaze to the barman. "I'm looking for a pard," he said seriously. "Cowboy from New Mexico. I thought he was heading this way, but I haven't been able to get a line on him."

"Oh yeah?" The bartender was cautious. "He got a name?"

"Yeah, he's got one, but he might not thank me for usin' it." Rock waited a moment for that dry remark to take effect, then kept his glance fastened on his drink, as he described Jud Moore. "He—isn't exactly a friendly cuss," he finished, looking up with a faint grin. "Got a face like a cross between a hard night and a good scrap lookin' for a place to come off."

Rock was watching the proprietor, but the man's face revealed nothing. He merely shook his head curtly, and Rock glanced at the three riders to see the one who had laughed tip his hat forward and scratch the back of his head thoughtfully.

"There's a feller," he said slowly, "riding for Bar Circle up on the rim, fits that description. Hails from New Mexico, too."

"You know him?" Rock asked with a quick, tight interest.

"Not personally, no. Seen him a couple times, and that's enough." The rider grinned crookedly. "You weren't kiddin' when you said he wasn't a friendly cuss, and I'd hate like hell to gab about him to the wrong man."

"I'd hate to have you," Rock said promptly. "In fact, I'd just as soon you'd be a little careful who you gab to about *me*."

The rider laughed, evidently reassured that his first impression of Rock had been right. "Well, cowboy, I reckon this is your pard, all right. He's calling himself Jud Moore these days."

"Jud Moore," Rock repeated, fighting down his hard, biting eagerness. "That name means nothin' to me. He got any others that you know of?"

"One, anyhow." The rider hesitated, eyeing Rock with a final, calculating survey. Then he said softly, "Richards."

Richards. The man who had fled New Mexico ahead of a murder charge. Rock pulled in a chest-swelling breath and grinned broadly.

"That's him," he said with vibrant satisfaction, and lifted his glass. "Here's a go, gents."

It wasn't conclusive. The fact that Jud Moore was a graduate of the Lincoln County War didn't prove that he was involved in the rustling here; but it did prove, at least to Rock's satisfaction, that he had been right in his deductions about the Kid. The man was an apt and deadly impersonator of Billy Bonney.

Rock took the time for a meal of cold meat and beans, served by the sullen, black-eyed wife of the bartender. Then, impatient to follow up his lead, he bought a sack of tobacco and headed for the stable.

He found Jimmy in the stall with the horse, scratching the animal's ears and talking in a soft, crooning voice. The boy looked up with a wistful grin as Rock entered.

"Gee," he said, "he sure is nice."

"Yeah," Rock agreed. "He's a friendly sort of a jigger." Thinking that friendliness was something this boy might find rare, he jerked his head toward the saloon and said, "You live with those folks?"

Jimmy quickly shook his head. "Sometimes I sleep here, if there's any horses in; but I got a little cabin over here. Dad built it a couple years ago."

"He had a wreck, huh?"

"Yeah. He rode out one time—" Jimmy looked down at the floor, his small face tight. "They—said he was stealing cattle."

"Aw, don't you believe it," Rock said gruffly. "Folks'll say anything, Jimmy, if they think it'll hurt somebody."

The boy looked up, and the wonderful light that came into his eyes told Rock that he'd made a friend. The knowledge warmed him and he grinned, ruffling the towhead before leading his horse outside and mounting.

"You comin' back?" Jimmy asked, obviously disappointed but trying to appear nonchalant.

"I hope so," Rock replied, and grimly meant it.

He was thinking of the lawman, lashed belly down over a horse, with powder burns on the back of his vest. He was thinking, too, of dark-eyed Rita Ballard, who would offer to kiss a man—and then sell him to the highest bidder.

"I hope so," he repeated, and turned down the creek toward the Ballard ranch.

It was, he found, much like the few homesteads he had seen around Skeleton Creek. Two cabins of bleached logs, connected by a porch and covered by one long rough-shingle roof, stood at the edge of a forty-acre clearing. Ugly black stumps dotted the neglected fields of corn and beans, and the sheds and corrals behind the house appeared to have been thrown together with whatever materials happened to be handy.

Although strong light still shone on the red and yellow walls of the rim, the sun had set down here in the canyon, bringing a welcome coolness. Rock turned in through the broken gate, noting that the corrals were empty. However, smoke issued from the chimney of one of the cabins, and he rode up to the porch, dismounting and throwing the reins.

Except for the clear call of birds and the faint murmur of a breeze in the timber, the place was quiet. Rock glanced sharply around the clearing before stepping up onto the porch, shifting his gunbelt and briefly touching the black butt of the gun. The door of the cabin on the left, from which the smoke came, was wide open; Rock moved slowly toward it, the clink of his spurs sounding inordinately loud.

He stepped into the dim room, taking swift note of the battered range, the rough board table and benches, the cluttered cupboard. A stall-like partition reached nearly across the room, leaving only a narrow passageway into the second, smaller room beyond. Rock could see a box in the back corner, holding an unlighted lamp, and the edge of a deerskin thrown on the floor.

He twisted for a quick look behind him. Then, his eyes on that aperture, he called, "Anybody home?"

He heard a rustle of movement, a quick, light footstep. The next moment Rita Ballard stepped into the opening, her lithe figure clad in buckskin, her dark hair disheveled. She stopped short at the sight of Rock, her eyes widening with a wild, trapped look. Then, before he could speak, she darted to the cupboard, jerked open a drawer and whirled with a gun lifting.

With a startled curse, Rock lunged at her, swerving desperately as the gun swung toward him and exploded. The crash of the shot was deafening, and powder smoke stung his nostrils as he grabbed for her. She dodged him, twisting away and firing again, so close to his face that the powder burned his cheek. Half blinded by the flash, Rock threw himself against her, grabbing her arm and shoving it down as she fired the third shot.

The force of his charge knocked her back onto the table. Rock, still hanging onto her arm, stumbled hard over a bench and fell into her, making a grab for the edge of the table with his free hand. He couldn't connect and rolled off, dragging her down with him.

The gun was knocked out of her hand as they went down but Rock hit the floor solidly on his back, a jarring fall. Rita, as lithe and supple as an Indian, twisted out of his grasp and bounded to her feet, her eyes darting feverishly in search of the gun. She spotted it and made for it, ignoring Rock's frantic yell.

"Wait!"

In desperation, Rock threw out a leg and tripped her, causing her to fall heavily against the cupboard. He rolled to his knees, struggling with a riot of conflicting emotions. He'd never fought a woman before, never had to, and he couldn't fully believe the deadliness of her intent. Then he was on his feet, grabbing for her arms as she regained her balance and whirled.

She was too quick for him. Darting inside his reach, she lifted her hands to claw at his face like some crazed animal. Rock knocked her hands aside, tried to grab her, but again she eluded him. She was fighting silently, her lips drawn back from her sparkling white teeth and her eyes glittering wildly.

"Rita!" he gasped. "For God's sake, quit it!"

His words had no effect on her, and Rock lunged against her, pinning her against the cupboard. Only for a moment. As he tried once more to get hold of her, Rita ducked her head and sank those sparkling white teeth into his left wrist, biting down with a savagery that sent pain shooting clear to his shoulder.

Rock swore viciously. A white-hot anger roared through him and he grabbed her by the hair, jerking her head up. Sight of the blood on her chin, the feel of the warm blood running down his hand, further maddened him. She was clawing at him again, trying to kick, and the last of Rock's restraint vanished. Letting go of her hair, he swung his arm in a back-handed slap that knocked her spinning. She slammed into the cupboard, cracked her head solidly against the edge of its work table and hit the floor in a loose, unmoving heap.

For perhaps ten seconds, Rock stared down at her, his fists doubled and his breath coming hard. Then he swung away, picked up the gun and threw it savagely out the window into a thick tangle of brush.

He went out, sweeping a hot glance over the clearing and seeing no one. He kicked open the door to the second cabin and stood spread-legged in the doorway, surveying the one murky room. There were three unmade beds, the quilts rumpled and dirty. Extra clothing, all belonging to men, hung from nails on the wall or lay wadded in corners along with boots, spurs and other gear.

Without bothering to close the door, Rock went back to the first cabin, noticing then the trail of blood he was leaving. His face seemed on fire from several gouges, and he could feel the blood running down his jaw, dripping onto his shirt. His arm still throbbed, and a strange nausea writhed in him.

He passed Rita, huddled on the floor with her face hidden under the tousled mass of her hair, with hardly a downward glance, and went to the bucket by the wash stand. It was nearly empty. He dipped his bandanna in the water, wrapped it around his wrist. Then, with the anger and the sickness still in him, he picked up the bucket and strode to Rita. He leaned to grab her arm and pull her over on her back, then hesitated, studying her face. It was pale except for a blotch on her temple that was swelling and turning dark. Her lashes lay thick and black against her cheeks, giving her a look of serenity and innocence that had its effect on Rock. Shame stirred in him but served only to augment his unreasoning anger. Clamping his jaw, he straightened and emptied the bucket of water over her head.

She gasped, instinctively lifting her hands to shield her face. Then her eyes opened and fastened on Rock with a dull, listless stare. He lifted her to her feet, holding her tight as she swayed drunkenly against him. After a moment, he helped her to a bench where she dropped, clinging blindly to the table. Rock waited, aware of a queer aching tightness in his chest. He figured he'd been justified in hitting her, but the sight of her, bruised and trembling, got under his hide.

"Come out of it," he said curtly.

Slowly she lifted her head, staring at him for several moments before she really saw him. Then she gasped, her eyes popping wide with swift, stark terror. Her obvious thought stung Rock.

"If I was the kind of a man who could kill a woman," he said coldly, "you'd be fifteen minutes dead!"

She didn't immediately grasp the significance of his words. Her eyes clouded, then closed and, with a low moan, she dropped her head onto her arms and started to sob.

Rock left her like that and went out, striding swiftly along a well-worn trail that he knew would lead to spring or creek. Darkness was rapidly closing in and the birds had quieted, leaving an eerie hush over the thick timber along the trail. He found the spring, a deep pool lying under a towering granite boulder, and filled the bucket.

The walk cooled him, bringing some relief from the grip of his strange emotion. Rita had not moved when he returned. She had quit crying, although she still breathed with a soft moaning sound. Rock set the bucket down and turned to eye her without sympathy.

"Kinda sick, huh?" he said coolly. "Maybe you'll remember that the next time you get a yen to throw a gun on somebody."

"You scared me," she mumbled, her voice little more than a whisper. "I was afraid you'd—kill me."

"Just because I'm Rock Kendall?"

Rita didn't answer, and that further eased Rock's disturbed feelings. It wasn't his reputation that had caused her to fight so desperately. It was the fact that she had betrayed him to Red and had feared his vengeance.

Abruptly he went back outside to care for his horse. He led the animal into the lean-to barn, unsaddled him and found corn and wild hay. Then he carried his saddle and blankets around behind the corrals and left them in the shelter of a dark thicket, thinking that he would sleep out tonight and he wouldn't care to have anybody know where he was doing it.

Afterward, he rolled a cigarette, inhaling with deep, relaxing breaths and staring at the dark bulk of the rim. Stars were coming out, white and clean and sparkling, but Rock found no comfort in them. Never had he felt so utterly alone. Memory of the clear-trusting light in the blue eyes of Kathy Sinclair only accentuated the feeling, reminding him as it did that he was an outcast. Rock Kendall, he thought bitterly, didn't even belong in the brakes, with the Rita Ballards and the cold-eyed drifters that hung around the Skeleton Creeks of the West.

By the time he went back to the cabin the second time, Rita had lit the lamp and was rummaging in the cupboard for something. She had, he noticed, washed the blood off her face, but she was still a bedraggled individual. He noticed, too, that the wash pan, now filled with clean water, had been moved to the table near the lamp.

Rita didn't look up as she turned from the cupboard, a bottle of turpentine in her hand. "Did I—bite you pretty deep?"

"Deep enough," he said bluntly, regarding her with deep suspicion.

"Sit down," she whispered, her face coloring. "I'll fix it."

Rock circled the table before sitting down, his back to the wall, his face toward the open door. Shoving his sleeve up and removing the soggy bandanna, he laid his arm on the table and looked up with hard challenge.

Rita didn't meet his gaze, keeping her head lowered as she slowly approached and dipped a clean white cloth into the water. She washed the double wound carefully, almost solicitously, but Rock had no illusions about this seeming change of heart. Rita Ballard would be looking out strictly for herself. She knew when she was whipped and she would try now to buy his forgiveness with docility and tender regard; but Rock could feel the rebellion in her, seething and frustrated.

He wondered suddenly whether the lawman had been here, perhaps sitting at this very table when he was murdered, and he said, "Where's all your folks?"

"They haven't come yet."

"They haven't?" he echoed in surprise. "Where the devil did they go?"

Rita shot him a sidelong glance. "I don't know," she said evenly.

Rock knew she was lying, but he didn't press the point. He would get nowhere if he antagonized this girl. It was possible he would get nowhere even if he tried to make friends with her, but it was worth a try.

"Well, golly," he said. "Must be kind of hard on you, having them gone for a week or so like this."

"Hard, hell," she retorted. "There's more work for me when they're here, the lazy hogs."

Her callous statement jarred Rock, and he said constrainedly, "I take it you don't care much for them."

"I don't. I wouldn't care if they never came back."

"That's a heck of a way to feel about your own brothers. What's the matter with them?"

Her only answer was a sullen glance. Rock looked down at her hands, small and brown and shapely but roughened by hard work, and he sensed the harshness of the life that had molded her. She tied off the bandage on his wrist, then looked at his face, hesitating.

"Yeah," he said dryly. "My face caught some of it, too."

She flushed, but he gathered that it was from resentment rather than embarrassment. She wrung out a fresh cloth and bent over him, washing the scratches with the same care she had used on his wrist. Rock sat very still, his eyes playing over her face. Her mouth had a sulky look to it; but her lips were full, red, and their nearness bothered him.

He looked up into her eyes and said, "You got three brothers?"

"Two. Buck and Cherry."

"Who uses that third bed?"

Rita tossed the cloth on the table and reached for the turpentine. "Tonto," she said without interest.

"Who's he?"

"Cowboy."

"Only one riding for you?"

She turned, the bottle in her hand, and paused to eye him with the beginning of doubt. "What difference does it make?"

"Maybe none. Maybe quite a little." Rock shrugged, then added dryly, "As you may know, some folks prefer to look at me over a gunsight."

Rita smiled, not in humor but in provocative challenge. "He's the only one," she said, "and I doubt that Tonto would be afraid of you."

"Maybe," Rock said evenly, "Tonto wouldn't have any reason to be afraid of me."

Her smile faded as she searched him. Then, a guilty flush rising into her cheeks, she stepped forward to dab the turpentine on his face. As she finished the job and turned away, Rock stood up, reaching out deliberately to grab her arm and jerk her back around. His action frightened her, and he gave her no chance to recover.

"How many times has Red been down here to see you?" he demanded.

"He's never been down here."

"Where'd you meet him?"

"In town—that day."

Rita was answering hastily, watching him with wide-eyed apprehension, and Rock knew she was telling the truth. That let Red out, as far as any rustling tie-up was concerned. The fact pleased Rock, but he didn't show it.

"So," he said grimly. "You sold me out to a stranger. Why?"

"Why not?" she retorted. "You're an outlaw."

"You've got no love for the law!"

"Maybe I haven't, but you killed Red's sister."

Rock shook her, none too gently. "You didn't do it out of sympathy for him, either. Now answer me. Why?"

"All right." Rita's chin came up. She was still afraid of him, but she was suddenly, brazenly defiant. "I wanted that reward."

"Would you have got it?"

"Yes. I offered to tell him where he could find you for half of it, but he said I could have it all. All he wanted was your dead carcass, and I'm sorry he didn't get it!"

"So," Rock said again. "I *was* right." He knew now what had angered him so: the thought that a girl he believed to be living outside the law would betray one of her own kind just for the money involved. He swept a harsh glance down over her and said caustically, "What would you do with a thousand bucks?"

Rita's breast heaved with sudden passion. "I'd get out of these goddamned brakes!" she said hotly. "I'd have a decent place to live, and I'd have something decent to wear!"

"Nothing wrong with this cabin," Rock said. "Nothing wrong with that buckskin. It fits you."

"The hell it does! I hate it. I hate this country, and I hate everybody in it!"

"Including your own brothers."

Rita's eyes were a blazing affirmative, but she had no more to say. Rock sensed the dullness of her existence, the loneliness that was driving her, and an involuntary response stirred in him. His grip on her arms tightened.

"You're alone too much," he murmured.

"I can't help it," she snapped. "I sneaked off for that dance, but if Buck ever finds it out he'll beat me half to death."

"Was Red worth it?"

She gave him a sharp glance that gradually brightened. Rock waited until the smile started to form on her lips. Then he pulled her into his arms and kissed her. And he had a feeling, even as her hands crept up around his neck, that if she had a knife in one of them she would use it.

# CHAPTER SIX

FROM A high, timbered butte, rocky and steep, Rock looked down for the first time on Ash Carlton's Bar Circle ranch. The sturdy log buildings stood at the head of an ever-widening green valley surrounded by pines. A creek, winding through the spread, sparkled merrily in the noonday sunlight.

Rock cast a sidelong glance at Rita, sitting her shaggy bay mustang beside him. She rode astride, with only a blanket strapped to the horse's back, and she seemed unaware of the picture she made. Her buckskin blouse was low at the throat, her skirt well above her knees. With her loose-flying dark hair, her slim brown legs and moccasined feet, she looked as wild and untamed as the country itself.

Rock twisted for a look at the jumbled country through which Rita had led him. They had left the trail at the foot of the butte, but Rock estimated, even with this extra climb, that they were not more than twelve or fifteen miles from the Ballard homestead. He looked back at Bar Circle and said idly, "Awful handy to the brakes, isn't it?"

"If I had his money," Rita said sourly, "I'd get out of this damned country."

Rock turned to look at her fully, but for a moment his thoughts were not on her. He was remembering the sparkle in Kathy's eyes as she described this beautiful land, her laugh when she admitted she loved it. The memory roused him and he said with sudden, strange jealousy, "Reckon Ash rides down pretty often, doesn't he?"

"Ash who?"

"Carlton. Your Mr. Ed Claiborne."

Rita's eyes grew instantly veiled. "Why call him Ash?"

"That's his name," Rock said bluntly. "Didn't he ever get around to telling you that he committed a murder down in Texas?"

Rita looked down at the buildings and said nothing, but her mouth had taken on a sulky look. Rock noted, however, that the statement that Ed Claiborne was capable of committing murder had not surprised her.

"Guess Jud and the Kid know this trail, too," he went on, prodding her. "They come down pretty often—running errands for the boss?"

Rita flashed him a hot, resentful glance and abruptly reined her horse around to start back. Rock let her go while he tarried for a last look at the ranch spread out below him, noting the comfortable size of the house, the maze of corrals, the horses and cattle grazing down the valley. Longing rose in him, a feeling that was akin to homesickness. This was a good layout and should one day be his—if he could stay alive long enough to prove Ash's guilt.

The trail led along the rim for some distance before tipping off into a timber-choked canyon. The descent was winding and they rode single file, in silence. Not until they had gained comparatively level ground did Rock trot his horse up beside Rita, to see that she was still sulking.

"Appreciate your taking me up there," he said gruffly. "Sure a big country for a stranger to find his way around in."

"Why did you want to see it?"

"Just curious." Rock pulled out his tobacco sack and started a cigarette. "For a man in my position," he added with a grin, "it's a good idea to scout out the country *before* you have to hightail through it."

"Yeah," she agreed, a challenge in her voice. "Did you notice all those fresh tracks up there?"

"Uh-hum. Somebody been doing a lot of ridin'."

"Posses out looking for you!"

"Possible," he admitted dryly.

Rita turned to look him over with sultry speculation. "Wonder how you'd look with your shirt all bloody."

"And my eyes glassy?" Rock laughed at her. "You're a cheerful cuss."

But Rita was not to be joked out of her mood so easily. She was still studying him, her eyes narrowed, as if she were visualizing his death and finding a satanic pleasure in it.

"How long do you expect to live?" she inquired, as if she were talking about the weather.

Rock lit his cigarette and inhaled deeply before answering. "I'm gonna live to the ripe old age of ninety-three," he drawled then. "I'm gonna get married and have fourteen kids, and every one of them is gonna have fourteen more. How many grandkids will that give me?"

"Too many," she said, with a sudden giggle, "if they're all like you. Who are you going to marry?"

"That," said Rock, "is an awful good question. You, maybe."

"Like hell," she snorted. "When I get married, it'll be to somebody who can get me *out* of the brakes, instead of nailin' me in 'em."

"Yeah," Rock said, a little wearily. "When you reckon your brothers will be home?"

She shrugged. "Hard to tell."

"They ride off and leave you like this very often?"

"Not often enough."

The answer did Rock no good at all. He took a drag off his cigarette and asked lazily, "You folks run cattle?"

"We're just homesteaders."

"And hire a cowboy?"

She gave him a startled glance, then looked quickly away again. "I didn't say we hired him. He just—stays there sometimes."

"And rides out with your brothers," Rock drawled significantly. "Honest, don't you know where they went?"

"What do you care?"

"Well," he said, with a misleading grin, "if I knew where they went, I could maybe figure out when they'd be coming back. That gun-slingin' habit of yours run in the family?"

Her only answer was a long searching stare. Then she looked away again; and Rock, though galled by delay and inaction, let it ride. The girl baffled him, professing to hate her brothers but still shielding them. Rock felt sure that she was shielding them, and he wondered whether it was because her hatred couldn't reach as deep as the blood ties that bound her to them or whether it was because she feared their punishment. He couldn't be sure and he decided abruptly that, until he was sure, he would make no further attempt to pry information out of her that might condemn her own brothers.

Back at the cabin, he made himself useful, thinking to show Rita that he was not just another "lazy hog" and perhaps to ease the strain he still felt between them. The girl was changeable, as moody and unpredictable as a desert storm. Rock wondered, frankly, whether her confidence or friendship could be won, but he was determined to try.

After caring for the horses, he filled the water buckets, then went to the woodpile. And he was very careful to work facing the open window of the cabin. He hadn't seen any rifle in the cabin, and he didn't believe Rita would risk attacking him again even if she had one; but he wasn't taking any chance on her that he could possibly avoid. The pain that grew in his sore wrist as he wielded the axe was enough to remind him that Rita Ballard was two-thirds wildcat.

He chopped enough wood to last her for several days. When he carried an armload of it into the house, he saw that his efforts were having some effect. Rita did not look up from her biscuit dough when he entered, but she had, he noticed, combed her hair carefully, tying a red ribbon around it to hold it in place.

With that to spur him, Rock went after his razor. The mirror hanging above the men's wash bench on the porch was cracked and dirty, but it revealed his image plainly enough. He looked, he thought ruefully, like he'd gone down in front of a mild stampede. His face was spotted with short scratches and gouges and one, on the left side, reached from his cheekbone clear to his chin.

Shaving was a painful job, but it did make him look considerably less battered. A clean shirt helped, too, and it was with a feeling of eager confidence that he went in to dinner a little after sunset.

Rita had it on the table waiting for him. Rock saw at a glance that it was a simple meal of beans, salt pork, biscuits and coffee; but it smelled good.

"Work up an appetite?" she asked; and her manner, almost cheerful, gave Rock renewed hope that she was beginning to feel a genuine warmth for him.

"Just stand back," he replied with a grin, "and I'll show you."

They had barely sat down, however, when Rock heard horses approaching. He was on his feet at once, stepping to the window and involuntarily reaching a hand to touch his gun. Three riders, mounted on shaggy, rangy-looking horses and driving a pack horse, were just entering the clearing from the east. Rita's bitter curse told Rock who they were, and he experienced a sharp disappointment. Her softened mood, which might have meant so much to him, was gone.

"You'd better eat first," she told him irritably. "After those hogs get in here, there won't be anything left, and I'll be damned if I'm going to cook any more tonight."

"I'll wait," Rock said briefly.

He stepped back a little from the window, but he continued to watch with cold, hard interest as the riders approached the cabin. They were a rough-looking outfit. Rock would have known anywhere that they were not ordinary range riders, and they certainly didn't look like homesteaders. The one in the lead especially held Rock's attention. He was dressed like a cowboy except that he wore a fringed buckskin shirt on the outside of his overalls, held down by a heavy, sagging gunbelt. This, Rock guessed instinctively, was Buck Ballard.

The other two were dressed in customary range garb; but, as they neared, Rock had no trouble telling which was the second Ballard. He was even darker of face than Buck, with coarse, ragged black hair showing under his high-crowned sombrero. He had the look of an Indian, and Rock wondered.

The third rider was a big man with several days' stubble of black beard on his face, the only one of the trio who didn't carry a rifle.

The distance, the hats pulled low, the uncertain light of dusk, all combined to prevent Rock from seeing their eyes; and it was the eyes mostly by which he judged the danger in men. As they passed from his view to dismount at the porch, he drew away from the window, turning casually to put his back to the partition. Just as casually he lifted his left hand to hook a thumb in his belt, directly over the butt of the second gun.

Rita was re-setting the table, slamming the three extra tin plates down with a vicious clatter. She glanced once at Rock, a mere flashing of angry eyes that gave him the impression she was blaming him for this homecoming. Then she lit the lamp and sat down on a bench next to the wall.

The sudden flaring of her nasty temper rubbed on Rock's nerves, but he was coolly ready when the jangle of spurs sounded on the porch and Buck Ballard stepped into the room, followed closely by Cherry and Tonto. They stopped at sight of Rock, their hands hovering over their guns, their eyes fastened on him with quick, hostile suspicion.

Those eyes told Rock all he needed to know, and he tensed at the grim awareness that a wrong word or move here could cause an explosion. The eyes of the two Ballards were as shiny black and hard as wet coal, with a glitter that carried a threat of cruelty.

Rock felt their cold impact, and an instinctive animosity rose in him. Nor did he have any further doubt as to the ancestry of this family. Cherry Ballard, in the revealing light of the lamp, definitely showed a strain of Indian blood, and he carried a sheathed knife as well as a gun.

Tonto was a tight-lipped man with narrowed, piercing gray eyes.

Rock nodded to them without speaking, but his greeting was not acknowledged. Buck Ballard threw a questioning glance at Rita, who leaned one hand on the bench as if about to lie down. Rock was aware that she smiled, a cold, crooked little smile. Then she spoke, her voice a malicious, taunting dare.

"That's Rock Kendall, gentlemen!"

Rock felt the leap of a flaming wrath. Then he froze, strung taut, his hands quivering. He saw shock ripple through the three men he faced, followed by a strained, breathless rigidity. He was aware that Rita still leaned on the bench, ready to duck; and his fury at her malevolence filled him with a violent urge.

"Look out, *gentlemen!*" he warned through stiff lips.

They were hesitating, their doubts and their desires plain for him to read. They knew how much he was worth, and they wanted to collect. They could collect if they all drew at once, but they'd pay for it and they could see that. Rock saw them flicking sharp, hungry glances at his hands, knew they guessed he had a second gun inside his shirt.

That was too much for Tonto. With infinite care, he lifted his hand and took a slow, guarded step to the side.

"Not me, Kendall," he said flatly.

Rock kept his eyes on the Ballards, daring them now to try it. Cherry was the last to give it up. Not until Buck had turned back out the door, brushing past him, did the tension leave him. Slowly he eased up, his black eyes playing over Rock without any visible emotion. Then he, too, went back outside. Tonto hurried after him.

In one long stride Rock reached the girl and jerked her to her feet, grabbing her arms in a steely grip that made her wince.

"What the hell was the idea?" he demanded harshly. "Inviting them to draw on me like that?"

"Bah!" she burst out, evidently angered by his roughness. "They're afraid of you!"

"Ahuh! But if they ever get a chance at my back, I'm just a thousand bucks, cold."

Rita's eyes narrowed as she looked him over with taunting speculation. "I might stick a knife in you myself for a thousand bucks."

"You'd stick a knife in me for less than that if the notion struck you." Deliberately, Rock folded one hand around her throat, bending her head back so that he could look straight down into her eyes. "Watch yourself, kitten," he said through his teeth, "or you're going to get that lovely neck of yours wrung!"

He held her like that until fear closed in on her and she cringed away from him. Then he gave her a shove back onto the bench and stalked outside. The men were at the corrals throwing packs and saddles; and Rock rounded the cabin, keeping out of their sight as he strode rapidly away into the woods.

Rage still possessed him. He remembered the one flashing glance Rita had given him before she lit the lamp and knew that she had been deliberately setting the stage. Her treachery was staggering to Rock. She was, he thought furiously, as elemental and as cold-bloodedly selfish as the cat he had called her, purring under a man's hand one minute—and ready to slash at his throat the next. Rock didn't doubt that she had hoped he would kill her own brothers before he went down.

He gained the shelter of the trees but still he kept on, penetrating a hundred yards before slowing his savage pace. He'd had no idea when he left the cabin except to get out of that lighted room while the men were outside; but now it occurred to him that he had left his saddle in the shed, his saddle bags and his rifle still on it. Immediately he swung to circle and come in behind the corrals, approaching the edge of the clearing with all the stealth of which he was capable. Unless he missed his guess, those two Ballards would have the keen senses of a pair of killer lobos.

He saw the men while still some distance back in the brush, hunkered by the corral, smoking. Rock didn't need to hear their words to know what they were discussing, but he wanted to know how the discussion was going. Cautiously he circled toward the shed, wondering whether they knew he was not in the cabin. It was almost dark now, and he gained the shed without attracting their attention. He eased into it and moved away from the door, crouching and straining to hear.

For several moments there was utter silence, and Rock was beginning to think they had left when a voice he took to be Buck's broke out harshly.

"Hell! I ain't lost no thousand bucks, not when it'd come that hard. Besides, the boss may want to use him."

"That's the way I figure." The words were spoken in the drawl of a Texan, and Rock pegged the speaker as Tonto. "Anyhow, the Kid'll be down tonight after their divvy. We can talk to him about it."

"Yeah, and in the meantime, Cherry, you hold your elbows in close or you'll be headin' for hell on a hot slug. That jigger'll kill you!"

Rock heard a belligerent grunt, then a straining of poles as the men shoved to their feet. He remained motionless, listening to their footsteps fade out toward the house, staring blankly at the wall of the darkened shed as he thought of their words. Evidently Cherry wanted to jump him, but that wasn't what took the breath out of Rock. It was the fact that the Kid would be riding in here tonight. Rock knew with quick, stabbing certainty that the little gunman would be carrying a message from Ash, warning these men against Rock Kendall. If that message were delivered, Rock would be licked before he could even get started.

Slowly he shoved to his feet, his jaw set. He knew now, from what Tonto had said about the Kid coming after their "divvy," that he had been right about the activities of these men and their connection with Bar Circle. The Kid was a rustler, and the certainty of that erased any restraint Rock might have felt. *That message would not be delivered!*

Rock waited until he heard the clatter of a washpan on the porch. Then he got his saddle and blankets and carried them to the dark thicket in which he had hidden them the night before. Then he lingered, smoking a cigarette and enjoying the brief security this thicket offered. The coming night was soft, quiet, soothing; and Rock took advantage of its cloak for a moment's relaxation. He knew that when he stepped out again, he would be carrying his life in the palm of his hand, for anyone to grab.

It was fully dark by the time he re-entered the cabin to find the men already eating. Rita stood sullenly by the stove but, when Rock entered, she pulled his heaping plate from the warming oven and handed it to him. Evidently, she had decided once again that she would gain more if she behaved herself. Rock thanked her gruffly and went on to the table, noticing, as he sat down, that a platter of sidemeat and a big bowl of gravy had been added to the meal. He wondered again whether Rita had a fondness for her brothers that she wouldn't admit or whether she toed the mark in fear of them.

She poured Rock's coffee before she sat down and then attended strictly to the food before her. The men, too, kept their eyes on their plates, eating in strained silence, and Rock took the opportunity to look them over more carefully. Tonto, he decided, was just a cowboy gone wrong, a dangerous man but not a particularly vicious one. The Ballards, however, were bad to the core. Rock would have bet on it, and it made him increasingly aware of his precarious position here.

One by one, the men finished eating, shoved their plates back and rolled cigarettes. The fact that they did not leave the cabin told Rock that they didn't care to arouse his enmity or suspicion, but they were remaining aloof, as coldly alert as a pack of hunting wolves. In spite of their recent decision, Rock knew that they'd take him if they got a chance.

Rolling his own cigarette, he said casually, "Saw Ash in town the other day."

Buck Ballard looked up with narrow, reserved interest. "Ash who?"

"Carlton. Hell," Rock said in disgust, "I can never remember. It's Ed Claiborne now."

The name had the same effect on these men that it had had on Rita. They grew very still, their dark faces inscrutable, their eyes carefully noncommittal.

"You know him?" Ballard asked presently.

"Oh, hell, yes. He and I've been pards for years." Rock saw the startling effect of his statement and he proceeded to enlarge on it, speaking in the same easy manner. "We had a ranch down on the Pecos for awhile, until Ash had to get out of the country. The K Bar C. It was a dandy spread, but it looks like this Bar Circle is a better set-up."

The three men exchanged quick, questioning glances, then looked back at Rock with sharper interest. Rita was watching him, too, although she showed no surprise and but little interest.

"He couldn't have chosen a better location," Rock went on. "Handy as a pocket in a vest. I scouted the layout today but—" He grinned ruefully. "Wasn't sure Ash would appreciate having me drop in to say hello."

Tonto gave him only a blank stare. The Ballards did not change expression, either, but Rock sensed that some of the tension was easing out of them. They were accepting him, which strengthened his belief in the hunch he was playing. He took a drag off his cigarette, managing to retain a matter-of-fact air when excitement was growing in him.

"I didn't get to talk to him very long there in town," he said regretfully. "Somebody spotted me and I had to hit for the tall timber, but what little I did hear sure sounded interesting."

He waited, looking hopefully from one to another of the men, but they didn't respond to his invitation to supply further information. Again they exchanged glances, then looked back at Rock only briefly before looking down to show an unusual and elaborate interest in their cigarettes.

It wasn't much but it was enough for Rock, and he looked down at his own cigarette to hide the fierce elation that surged through him. He was sure now. Ash Carlton *was* the leader of this rustler gang, although getting the proof might not be easy. Ash undoubtedly didn't ride on any of the raids, and the men who did do the riding undoubtedly wouldn't talk unless pressure could be brought against them. And it would have to be deadly pressure.

Rock was turning the problem over in his mind, wondering how to go about it, when the sound of a horse directly outside the cabin startled him. The others showed no concern, twisting around to look at the door but making no move to rise. Rock, however, slid off the bench and stepped instantly back against the partition, facing the door but still commanding the table.

He heard the thud of boots hitting the ground, the rattle of spurs dragged across the porch. Then the Kid stepped into the room, the buckle on his belt picking up a quick light from the kerosene lamp. He didn't notice Rock, his attention on those at the table as he stepped indolently away from the door. Before he could speak, Rock took a short step away from the wall and stopped, balanced and ready.

"Evenin', sonny," he drawled insolently.

The Kid jerked around, then seemed to freeze, a look of shock on his thin face. "You did make it down here!" he exclaimed.

"Sure," Rock said in derision. "You didn't think that sheriff could stop me, did you? Like he stopped you!"

That scorn had its effect. The Kid pulled in a quick breath that flared his nostrils, the indication of fury that Rock well remembered, and he leaned forward a little. His voice had gone flat.

"The sheriff saved your life that day."

"Oh, sure," Rock agreed sarcastically. "Kept me from going into that nameless grave. Well, you know my name now, sonny. Put it on the headstone—if you can!"

Rock felt nothing now but a cool detachment. He was aware that the Ballards and Tonto were sitting rigidly tense, their hands gripping the edge of the table; and he wondered whether they would hold fast when the shooting started. He saw the one flicker of doubt that crossed the Kid's eyes and was gone. Then the man's hands stabbed down toward his guns.

Rock drew and fired in one swift, effortless motion, the crash of the gun resounding against the walls of the cabin. He saw the bullet strike, dead center on that left shirt pocket, jarring the Kid. Blood spurted out to drench the man's shirt as his hands jerked once, convulsively, at the guns that were only half out of their holsters. Then, a look of pained surprise coming to his face, he took a faltering step into the room and collapsed.

Before he hit the floor, Rock swung his gun toward the table, but the Ballards and Tonto were still petrified, their wide eyes glued on the Kid. Rock saw their stunned, incredulous expressions, sensed that they had respected the Kid's prowess with a gun. Before they could recover, he threw a baited hook at them.

"That bunkie of his," he said tightly, "must have done too much talking about Billy the Kid."

"Yeah," Buck Ballard agreed, his voice hushed. "Richards is always spoutin' off about the Lincoln County War."

Rock felt a rush of exultation he could hardly conceal. That dragged Jud Moore into this right by the boot straps; and Rock thought, *Your foreman, Ash!*

# CHAPTER SEVEN

Rock, knowing this would require an explanation, looked down at the sprawled body of the Kid and said tersely, "We tangled in town before I found out he was riding for Ash, but it wouldn't have made any difference. He and I could never ride in the same outfit."

He waited with a tight hope, but no one spoke. The men were watching him now, eyeing him with narrowed uncertainty. Rock had the feeling that they were backing up, taking new and wary stock of him, and he knew it was time to quit. Abruptly he sheathed his gun and gave a crisp order.

"Pack him out and tie him on his horse. I'll take him back to the ranch and see what Ash has to say about this."

He stalked outside, his breath coming quick as an idea grew in him, a way of using this that might, if it worked, strike a crippling blow at Ash. He'd take the Kid's body back to Bar Circle, all right, but he wouldn't stop to see what Ash had to say about it. Not right then, anyway.

As he was striding away, Rock heard Tonto's awed voice: "My God! Did you *see* that?"

This time there was not even a belligerent grunt from Cherry, and this further added to Rock's sense of keen satisfaction and growing excitement. They'd seen it, all right, and never again would they consider drawing on him, at least when he was facing them. They had watched the Kid try his luck, and any curiosity they might have had was fully satisfied. Moreover, Rock knew that by riding boldly out of here with the Kid's body he would allay any doubts they might have left about his relationship with Ash Carlton.

His groundwork was well laid. Given a few days to think it over, these men should accept him and open up to him. In the meantime he would see to it that Ash was too blasted busy to be sending out any more messengers.

He saddled his horse, then found a burlap sack and helped himself to enough corn for two or three good feeds for the animal. As he was tying the sack to his saddle, Rita approached, her steps dragging. She stopped a few feet away. Rock finished the tying before turning to face her, his left hand on the work of his saddle, his right on his hip.

"What's on your mind now?" he asked gruffly.

"Rock, I—" Rita looked down at the ground, worrying a tuft of grass with one moccasined foot. "Rock, I'm sorry I did that."

She sounded genuinely ashamed, but Rock's suspicions were deep-rooted.

"Who all," he asked deliberately, "were you trying to get killed?"

She looked up quickly, her lips parted as if to protest. Then she looked back at the ground and shook her head. "I'm hateful," she said miserably.

"You can be," he agreed and let it ride there, wondering whether she could be anything else.

"I felt mean, nasty, but I shouldn't have taken it out on you. You've been nice to me."

"I wasn't very nice when I hit you."

"Yes," she said, "you were. You took a lot before you did that, and you wouldn't have done it at all if I hadn't given you away—" She broke off, shaking her head. "That was awful of me."

"No," Rock said, a little surprised at himself, "it wasn't. It made me sore to think you'd sell me out like that but—" He shrugged, then added bitterly, "I'm fair game."

"Oh, no."

She moved up to him quickly, her hands lifted; but then, without touching him, she folded them at her breast, clutching at the neck of her dress. Her face, in the uncertain light of the stars, appeared pale and her eyes were black, unreadable.

"Are you really going up there onto the rim?" she asked hesitantly. "With all those posses?"

"I reckon."

"What—will they do if they catch you?"

"Bloody my shirt, probably. Or hang me."

He spoke with an even challenge, and he saw her cheeks darken before she lowered her head.

"That was a terrible thing to say," she whispered. "I don't know why I'm so mean, but I—Rock, before you left, I wanted you to know you're the only man who ever chopped any wood for me or anything like that."

Suddenly stirred, partly by pity and partly by a rough anger, Rock folded his hands over her shoulders and pulled her up against him. Her body was soft and yielding, the touch of her hands quick and tight on his arms. He still couldn't read her eyes, but her lips were parted, inviting him.

Rock kissed her, harshly, with an increasing pressure as he sensed the willingness of her response. She was, for this moment, warm and sincere, making amends in the only way she knew. When Rock finally raised his head, she lifted her hands to his cheeks and peered up at him intently.

"Will you be coming back?" she asked.

"Barring accident," Rock said, "I'll sure be back."

"Be careful, Rock!" she said fervently, then slipped out of his arms and ran for the cabin.

For a long moment Rock stared after her, standing very still, prey to a number of conflicting emotions. Yes, she could be something besides hateful—when her own desires demanded it. Rock's distrust in regard to women was a deep-lying thing, curbing him, making him wary; he wondered now whether Rita was capable of any genuine, lasting affection. He doubted it, very much. Instinct warned him that both her remorse and her evident concern for his safety were whimsical at best.

Abruptly he turned to swing onto his horse and reined around toward the front of the cabin. He saw at a glance that his orders had been carried out. The Kid's slender body was lashed firmly across his saddle, face down, and Tonto stood holding the lead rope, waiting. The two Ballards sat on the edge of the porch, in the full flood of light that poured out of the kitchen. Rock nodded his thanks and, without a word, took the rope Tonto held up to him and turned out of the clearing.

He rode slowly, saving his horse, and it was considerably after midnight when, in the light of a pale, distant moon, he reached the timbered butte above Bar Circle. He dismounted short of the top, cramped and stiff, and tied the Kid's horse in a thick clump of trees. The brown he left free to graze, reins dragging, while he himself stretched out for a few hours' rest.

He slept fitfully, constantly disturbed by the stamping and shifting of the Kid's horse. The animal was tiring under that dead weight, but Rock knew that a few hours of it wouldn't hurt him and he had no intention of unloading that body only to load it up again. He got up at dawn, tied the brown and gave him a good feed of com. Then he climbed to the top of the butte on foot, found good cover and waited with a cool patience until the Bar Circle men, twenty strong, mounted and rode out.

Ash himself was in the lead, sitting his horse with a square-shouldered arrogance that kindled the fire of hatred in Rock. The cavalcade headed toward the east, toward Clear Springs; Rock thought bleakly, he's going to combine business and pleasure. Involuntarily, his gaze centered on the man's broad back, and he could not help the darkly insistent thought that a .30-30 slug could reach him, even from here.

Not until Ash had disappeared in the trees did Rock turn his attention to Jud Moore, riding a little behind. The man was slouched, his body thick and heavy in the saddle but his head lifted as he scanned the country lying toward the rim. Apparently he was wondering why his bunkie had not returned. Rock could see the man's throat, leather-brown at his open shirt collar, and he wondered if Jud dreaded the hangman's rope as much as he did himself. For a brief moment he felt a touch of pity, a sort of chill sympathy for a kindred spirit. Then he shrugged off the feeling. Jud Moore had picked the crooked trail he was riding, and he had known when he did it what the consequences would be.

One other man in the group caught Rock's attention. Red Mayberry. Just as Rock spotted him, the young cowboy pulled his rifle from the scabbard, checked it carefully and shoved it back, a significant move that brought a grim smile to Rock's face. These men weren't looking for cattle. They were looking for Rock Kendall, and Red still cherished the hope that no one would get ahead of him.

When the men were well out of sight and hearing, Rock went back after the Kid's horse. He led the animal to the top of the butte, found a trail leading down to the ranch. There he tied the reins to the saddle horn and gave the horse a whack on the rump with his hat. As the snorting animal moved out, Rock went back after his own horse, made a wide circle around the ranch and headed for town, knowing that Ash and Jud would be in before the day was over.

"I don't reckon," he murmured, "that they'll think it's so funny when one of their own men comes in that way."

Rock rode leisurely, sparing his horse and keeping a sharp watch for posses or stray riders. A feeling of jubilation rode with him. The game was on in earnest now, and for once Ash was not holding all the aces. Rock could easily beat the Bar Circle men to town since the cook wouldn't ride out after them and they wouldn't return to the ranch at least until noon. But then they would come fogging in, and Rock found himself grinning at the prospect.

"The Campbells are coming," he told his horse, "and we'll see to it that Sheriff Lackey is right on hand to greet 'em."

The sun had set and a reassuring gloom was settling over the land by the time he rode in at Mrs. Nash's, wondering whether that good woman would greet him with a batch of biscuits or a heavy iron frying pan. It was unlikely, he thought, that she could have found out he was anything but just a Triple X cowboy, and he needed both food and shelter.

He dismounted at the back door, pausing for a brief look around before knocking. He heard the clang of a stove lid, a heavy tread. Then the door opened and Rock reached for his hat, grinning experimentally.

"Evenin', Mother Nash," he drawled.

"Well!" Her quick smile suffered a severe check. "Whatever happened to your face?"

Rock lifted a hand self-consciously to his jaw. "I tangled with the wrong filly," he said.

"Drag you?"

"No, just—threw me—gently."

The woman laughed at his discomfiture. "Well, I'm glad to see you anyway, although you're back sooner than I expected. I hope you didn't lose your job."

"No, ma'am. I'm just in town on an errand."

Her eyes were twinkling. "Hungry?"

"Worse than that," he said with a laugh. "I haven't eaten since last night."

"Well, forevermore," she said indignantly. "Whatever is the matter with that Kathy Sinclair, anyhow? You get your horse put up, young man, and then wash your beat-up face while I throw a meal together."

"Yes'm," Rock said and felt good all over.

He was relieved to find the small stable empty, which probably indicated that the woman had no other boarders, although he had the sobering thought that Mrs. Nash was probably hard put to it to make ends meet. After he had cared for his horse, he carried his pack into the same room he had used before, then hastened to obey the second of her commands. Mrs. Nash was bustling and had the meal on the table by the time he had finished.

Her friendliness was infinitely warming to Rock. Thrown as he was most of the time with hard, dangerous people, he found it exhilarating and at the same time saddening to sit in her kitchen, listening to the run of cheerful, harmless gossip, hungrily drinking in the cozy atmosphere of a wholesome household. It was something he had almost lost the feel of.

He thought of the sparkling clean kitchen at Clear Springs ranch, with its crisp curtains and gay, spotless oilcloth, and an unfathomed restlessness swept through him. He straightened to drain his third cup of coffee and reach for tobacco, saying reflectively, "I noticed a dust as I was coming into town. Riders?"

"Lackey," she nodded, "and one of his posses."

"Oh, yeah?" Rock kept his voice casual, but he thought, *This hand is mine, Ash!* He said, "Looked like they were riding pretty slow."

"Give out," she snorted. "That poor old man's been runnin' the legs plumb off his horse trying to find that Rock Kendall."

"No luck, huh?"

"None at all. He can't find hide nor hair of that hellion."

"Well," Rock said with a dry humor, "he'll bump into him unexpected one of these days." He lit his cigarette and stood up. "Reckon I'll amble downtown a bit."

Mrs. Nash looked up at him with the beginning of disapproval.

"On business," he said pointedly and grinned. He held up his right hand. "I guarantee not to come home plastered."

She laughed. "All right, cowboy. If you're not too late, I'll have a piece of apple pie and a glass of milk with you."

Night had fallen, black and comforting, by the time Rock stepped out. He hesitated, glancing at the darkened stable, hating to move into the town on foot. But the brown horse needed rest. He had covered a good many miles in the last two days and might, if something went wrong, have to cover a good many more, and fast.

With a shrug, Rock flipped his cigarette away and turned up the street. It was a quiet time of evening, the time when most people were indoors relaxing from the strain of the day. Rock didn't hurry but he cut across vacant lots and through alleys, heading as directly as he could toward the sheriff's office in the eastern part of town. Ash and Jud could be expected at any time now.

As he passed a small saloon on a side street, he noticed a couple of saddled horses, reins dragging, beside the building. Quietly, without hesitation, Rock borrowed one of them. He led the animal into the cluttered alley behind the sheriff's office and paused, squinting up at the one small, barred window in the back of the adobe building. A glow of light showed there, assuring Rock that someone was in the office out front.

Another building crowded the adobe on the west, but on the eastern side was a vacant area that still held a number of large sage bushes. Rock left the horse near the back corner of the building, the reins knotted and dangling in a bush. Then, with a tight eagerness swelling up in him, he moved cautiously to the dusty window and peered into the office.

Lackey was there, seated at a battered, untidy desk directly under a hanging lamp. And he was alone. Rock noted the deep lines of weariness in the man's face, the grim set to his mouth as he labored over a writing job. He glanced once at the gun showing under the tail of the sheriff's coat. Then, his own jaw clamping in implacable determination, he ducked under the window and moved to the front of the building. The street was quiet, seemingly deserted, as he strode boldly to the door and stepped into the room, gun in hand.

Lackey glanced up inquiringly, then turned as still as stone, his eyes wide and incredulous. Carefully Rock closed the door behind him and stood against it, seeing the officer's shock give way to a breathless apprehension.

"Take it easy," Rock said evenly, "and keep your hands on the desk. I just came to palaver a little."

"Palaver?" the sheriff echoed. He studied Rock for several moments, doubtfully. Then a dull red flush crept into his face as the enormity of this struck him. "Where in the hell have you been?" he demanded.

"Who, me?" Rock said innocently. "I been ridin' around, admiring the scenery. Why? Somebody been lookin' for me?"

The sheriff started to flip his hand but froze the gesture in mid-air, his eyes darting to the gun in Rock's hand.

"Ahuh," Rock said. "You hold those hands still. I'm a nervous sort of a jigger, and it'd be kinda difficult to give this information to a dead man."

"What information?"

"You heard of a gent named Richards who's wanted for murder over in Lincoln County?"

"Sure." Lackey was feeling his way cautiously, his eyes narrowed. "What about him?"

"If you got a chance to pick him up, you'd do it, wouldn't you?"

"You're damn right!"

"Well, he'll be in tonight. He's using the name of Jud Moore."

"Jud Moore!" Lackey's eyes popped wide with disbelief, then squinted again uncertainly. "What makes you think so, Kendall?"

"I don't think it," Rock said flatly. "I *know*."

He waited, watching the officer closely, giving him time to get used to the idea.

"How'd you find it out?" Lackey asked presently.

"From Buck Ballard."

That told. Rock could see that the Ballards were no strangers to this sheriff and he drove ahead, speaking deliberately.

"I was down there the other day, Lackey. Met the Kid—and tangled with him. You know the Ballards. Tougher than hell and poison mean! Doesn't it strike you kind of funny that a Bar Circle man would be on friendly terms with them? And doesn't it strike you even funnier that they'd know the Bar Circle foreman well enough to know his real name? Both of those men belong to this new gang of rustlers that's giving you a bad time."

"Can you prove that?" Lackey snapped.

"No, I can't," Rock said, "but you can."

"How?"

"Slap Jud in the hoosegow and send a wire to the sheriff of Lincoln County. It's a cinch Mr. Richards would rather talk about rustlers in Arizona than be extradited to face a murder charge in New Mexico, and I got a hunch some of his information would surprise you. You're straight, Lackey. You want to get these rustlers and you want to get the scum that's drifting into your territory, including me. Maybe it takes a killer to catch a killer, but I'm not guessing about this and you know it."

The sheriff didn't answer. His craggy face was set in hard lines, his narrowed gaze fastened on Rock with obvious anger and distaste.

"Your Mr. Ed Claiborne," Rock added deliberately, "*may* be a nice fella, but he's sure had a couple of hard cases working for him."

"He is a nice fella," Lackey said, his voice rough. "And if Jud Moore is this man Richards, then I reckon Ed—Ash doesn't know it."

"The hell he doesn't," Rock retorted. "I got a hunch that's why he hired him."

"What do you mean by that?" Lackey demanded angrily. "What are you trying to do, anyway?"

"I'm trying," Rock said evenly, "to clear my name. I didn't kill that woman, Lackey. I've been outlawed for three years for a murder Ash Carlton committed."

"He committed! You trying to tell me he killed Red's sister?"

"He did. And I hope to make him admit it. That's why I'm taking the trouble to dig the skeletons out of his closet."

"Well, for hell's sake!" Lackey spat scornfully. "That's the damnedest bunch of hogwash I ever heard of."

"Sure," Rock said, unruffled. "Nobody can believe their Mr. Claiborne is a double-crossin' skunk—yet. But you might take a good look at the people he runs around with after dark!"

Lackey started to rise and thought better of it, but he did lean forward over the desk, his hands clenched. "Kendall, if you think I'm going to help you annoy—"

"I'm not asking you to help me," Rock interrupted curtly. "But you *will* arrest Jud Moore because you know I've told you the truth. He and Ash will be in pretty soon, rearin' about their little two-gun playmate." He felt for the door knob with his left hand. "Reckon that's all, Lackey. Unless you want to get a leg shot off, you better sit pat till you hear me ride away from here."

The sheriff remained rigid in his chair, but his face twisted with rage at his helplessness. Carefully Rock pulled the door open behind him and stepped backward onto the walk, his gun still trained on the officer's chest. He could not restrain a grin.

"Hell of a thing to do to a man, isn't it?" he drawled.

Then he closed the door and moved swiftly but silently around to the side of the building. He heard the crash of the chair as the sheriff got up, then a string of lurid, impotent curses. He reached the horse, hooked the knotted reins over the saddle horn and spooked the animal into a wild run down the alley. Then he dove flat beside a shed, shielded from the alley by a collection of old packing boxes.

Lackey, however, didn't even come outside, evidently feeling that it was hopeless. Rock tilted his head to examine the window in the back of the jail, finding, as he had expected, that there was no glass in it. Satisfied that he would be able to hear what was bound to be a heated conversation, he stretched out comfortably, relaxing against the ground and waiting with an eager anticipation.

He did not have long to wait. He had been there only a few minutes when he heard a number of horses pound up to the front of the sheriff's office, then the harsh rap of boots on the wooden floor inside. Lackey's voice came to him clearly, tight with constraint.

"Evenin', boys."

"Howdy, Sheriff."

It was Ash, all right, and the sound of his voice sent a tremor through Rock. He tensed, his breathing shallow and inadequate as he listened.

"What's happened?" Lackey asked.

"The Kid's been murdered. Came in this morning tied over his horse just like that lawman was."

"Oh, hell," Lackey said wearily. "I figured he was dead. Kendall was in here a minute ago."

"Kendall?" Ash echoed, and he sounded shocked. "He was in here?"

"Yeah. He said he and the Kid had tangled, and he said you'd be in—"

Jud Moore interrupted him, his voice raw. "You had Rock Kendall in here?"

"He had me," Lackey retorted bluntly. "Came in with a gun in his hand."

"How long ago?"

"Five, maybe ten minutes."

A general clamor sounded from the building, pierced by Ash's excited voice.

"Let's get after him! He can't be far!"

"You can't find him at night," Lackey protested angrily. "Hell! I can't even find him in the daytime!"

There was a moment of silence. Then Ash said, with a triumphant ring, "I knew he was the one who killed the Kid. Sent him home—Lackey, he murdered that lawman, too."

"Maybe," Lackey said, but he sounded skeptical.

"What was his idea coming in here? Not just to tell you he'd committed another murder!"

"No."

Again there was silence, and Rock could well imagine the piercing gaze the old sheriff was directing at Jud Moore. He'd have a hand mighty close to his gun, too.

"He came in," the sheriff said slowly, "to tell me who you were."

"Me?" Jud blurted.

"Yeah. Don't move, Jud."

There was another silence during which Rock heard a guarded step and figured Jud was being relieved of his hardware. A fierce satisfaction rose in him, along with an ungrudging admiration for Sheriff Lackey. He'd had the lawman figured, right down to the ground.

Then Ash burst out indignantly, "What's this all about?"

"Can't be sure," Lackey replied, and he sounded relieved. "I'm sorry about this, Ed, but Kendall claims this man is wanted for murder over in New Mexico. Name of Richards."

Jud's denial was prompt and harsh. "That's a damned lie!"

"Maybe," Lackey conceded, "but I'll have to run you in, anyway. Kendall sounded like he knew what he was talking about."

"You can't lock me up on the word of a killer!"

"Yes," Lackey said, "I can. At least until I wire the sheriff over there. Come on, Jud."

"Wait," Ash protested. "Lackey, this is ridiculous."

"Maybe," Lackey said again, and his voice was growing edged. "If it turns out that way, I'll be glad to apologize. In the meantime—move into that cell, Jud."

There was a marked hesitation before Ash said, in a calmer voice, "Go ahead, Jud. I reckon that's best."

"Best, hell!" Jud exploded. "Ash, if you—"

"Now take it easy," Ash said smoothly. "This can all be cleared up. I'll back you to the limit, Jud. You've got nothing to worry about, and a day or two in jail won't matter."

"I'll kill that—"

Jud choked off the last of his savage utterance and moved into the cell with an angry rap of boot heels. Rock heard the door clang shut, then Ash's voice, smooth and hard.

"Kendall lied to you, Lackey. That's obvious, although I don't blame you for protecting yourself this way. He's after me, striking at me through my men, and no telling who he'll attack next. He's mad, I tell you, and a killer wolf. He's got to be destroyed!"

"Yeah," Lackey agreed grimly. "I'll destroy him if I get a chance, but—"

"But what?"

There was a slight pause before the sheriff spoke flatly. "Nothin'. I'll get him, Claiborne. Come on, I'll buy you a drink."

For a long time after they had left, Rock lay rigid, thinking. He heard Jud pace his cell restlessly for several minutes before throwing himself down on the bunk with a vicious curse. Rock's mind registered this, just as it registered the satisfaction of having hit Ash twice in the past twenty-four hours. But it was Lackey's strange hesitation that held him.

What was going on in the old lawman's mind? Was it possible that he was beginning to wonder? Rock dared to hope that it was. It seemed reasonable that the sheriff would have his doubts, since the man he hunted had twice had him under a gun—and had held fire.

With this thought adding to his buoyant optimism, Rock finally crawled out of his hiding place and turned back toward Mrs. Nash's, striding swiftly and with a spring in his step. However, he had covered no more than two blocks when a shot sounded behind him, muffled and dull. A man's scream shattered the night, stopping Rock in his tracks. Then the gun boomed again, and an ominous hush settled over the town.

# CHAPTER EIGHT

WITH THE blood seeming frozen in his veins, Rock turned and started back. He knew those shots had come from the jail, and he knew what they meant even before he saw the crowd gathering around the back of the building. The light of a lantern bobbed fitfully in the center of the group, throwing grotesque shadows against the wall.

Pulling his hat low over his face, Rock eased up to the edge of the crowd and stretched to see over the shoulders of intervening men. He saw the sheriff just straightening from an inspection of the ground while Red held the lantern. Then Ash moved into his range of vision, his hat shoved back on his handsome head, his leather jacket making him look even bigger and more forceful than usual.

"Stood on a packing box," Lackey said grimly. "Shot him in the back, then through the head."

"Rock Kendall!" Ash bit out, and Rock turned cold all over.

"Hell," Lackey said angrily. "If he wanted to kill him, why did he go to all the trouble of having me lock him up?"

"You forget, Lackey," said Ash, in a hard voice, "that it's me he's hitting at. Just killing Jud wouldn't have hurt me except for losing a good man; but by leading you to believe that I'd hired a murderer, he figured to cast a shadow on my reputation."

"It's Ash he's hittin' at, all right," Red said flatly. "Hell, he had nothin' against Jud."

"They had a fight," Lackey pointed out, "first day he hit town."

"Yeah, but Kendall whipped him. He wouldn't hold a grudge over that."

"Don't you see?" Ash spoke up, with an angry impatience. "It's all just a damnable maneuver to deprive me of two good men and make people doubt my honesty. His claim that he found the Kid at the Ballard place is a damned lie. He met him out on the range somewhere, killed him, then hatched this lie about Jud, all just to strike at me!"

"I don't know," Lackey said uncertainly. "Sure seems like a roundabout way of goin' at things. I was going to send a wire—"

"And he didn't dare wait for it," Ash interrupted. "He knew Jud would be cleared. There's no sense in sending that wire now."

Lackey sighed wearily. "Reckon not."

Rock knotted his fists as a queer sickness stole into him. He could see Ash clearly in the full glow of the lantern, his face gray and tight. He appeared high-strung, and Rock wondered with a fresh surge of hatred whether he had fired those shots himself. As if in answer to his question, someone spoke.

"Were you here when it happened, Lackey?"

"No. I'd gone up the street with Ed. After I left him, I stopped in to buy a cigar and was just comin' out when I heard the shots." The sheriff swore. "And I was beginning to think maybe Kendall had a streak of decency in him!"

"Decency!" Red echoed hotly. "After what he did to my sister? And what he did to Jud here tonight? Hell, Lackey! There isn't a bone in him that isn't rotten!"

"I can see that now." Lackey twisted his head to spit angrily. "I got to thinkin' after he was in here awhile ago. It's a cinch I can't arrest him, and I can't kill him in a fair fight. I got to thinkin' that he wasn't the kind of a man I'd like to shoot in the back, somehow, but I'll take him now—any way I can get him!"

Rock turned away, his jaw clamped against the glittering triumph in Ash's eyes. He felt sure that Ash had committed the murder himself, had, in fact, intended doing so when he told Jud so smoothly that it could all be cleared up. But there was no way in the world to prove it, and Rock Kendall was now wanted for murder in Arizona as well as in Texas.

"They can't hang me but once," he muttered, but there was no comfort in that bleak thought. He knew that the feeling against him, fanned white hot even before he arrived by sympathy for Red, would now rise to a new intensity. His chances for survival had grown infinitely slimmer because of this night's work.

With a heavy stride, he returned to the rooming house and let himself into the lighted kitchen. He tossed his hat into the bedroom and was just turning when Mrs. Nash appeared from the front part of the house.

"Well!" she greeted him bluntly. "You look about as cheerful as a room full of mourners."

Rock managed a painful grin. "Thinking does that to me," he said ruefully, "but I reckon the pie will fix it."

"Sure." She nodded in emphatic agreement. "Fillin' a man's stomach always empties his head. Sit down, cowboy. I'll fetch the cow juice."

Rock sank into a chair and rested his elbows on the table, staring blankly at the printed oilcloth. He was aware that Mrs. Nash set a big wedge of applie pie and a glass of milk before him, but he didn't rouse himself until she sat down opposite him. Then he saw that she was eyeing him with frank curiosity.

"What was the shootin' awhile ago?" she asked.

Rock picked up his fork and cut a bite of pie, not looking at her. "Somebody lowered the boom on Jud Moore."

"On Jud Moore?" she echoed with sudden, sharp interest. "Kill him?"

"Deader'n hell," Rock said grimly. "He was in the cooler, and somebody let him have it through the window."

"Well, forevermore," breathed Mrs. Nash, aghast. She laid her fork down and leaned back, staring at him in incredulity. "I thought that was the Bar Circle outfit that rode past awhile ago but—you say Jud was in jail?"

"Yeah."

"What for?"

Rock speared a bite of pie before answering, wondering whether he could do it without letting this woman know who he was. She was keen, missing very little that went on around her, and she was also talkative. Any rumors that he planted with her would be sure to fly—if he didn't tip his hand during the planting.

Rock had little faith in himself on this night, and he had no stomach for this kind of fighting. Every impulse in him drove him to go after Ash, with a gun or a knife—or his bare hands. But he had to take it slow. Ash still held all the aces, and if Rock tried to crowd the game he would only destroy himself.

"It seems," he said slowly, "that Rock Kendall told the sheriff Jud was wanted for murder over in New Mexico. So Lackey locked him up, intending to wire the Lincoln County sheriff to come take a look at him."

"When," Mrs. Nash asked pointedly, "did the sheriff ever do any talking to Rock Kendall?"

"This evening."

Rock jerked his head toward the center of town, and Mrs. Nash's incredulous stare grew wider.

"Is that hellion in town again?"

"Well, he was, anyway," Rock said dryly. "I reckon he's fannin' the breeze again now."

"Well, the nerve of him!" the woman burst out indignantly. "Following Ed Claiborne right into town. If old Lackey doesn't get off his haunches and do something, Kendall will kill that man yet!"

"Dunno." Rock paused, his fork poised in mid-air. "Something funny about this business, Mother Nash. You heard, I suppose, that Claiborne's real name is Ash Carlton."

"Yes, but I can never remember to call him that."

"Nobody can. He's been Claiborne around here too long. But I met a fella one time—" Speaking slowly and in apparent perplexity, Rock repeated the "rumor" he had told Kathy about his having been framed. "You'd think," he'd finished dryly, "as handy as Rock Kendall is with a gun that if he'd wanted to kill that jigger he'd have had the job done before this. Because he surely knows he can't last, the way things are goin'."

For a long moment Mrs. Nash stared at him, her mind on his words. Then, in the thoughtful silence, she picked up her fork and began working absently on the food before her. Rock finished his pie and shoved the plate back, squinting at it reflectively.

"Here's another funny thing," he said slowly, encouraged by her reception. "The Kid was killed yesterday, down at the Ballard ranch."

Mrs. Nash looked up in surprise. "Those no-good homesteaders?"

"Ahuh, and the way I got it he was on friendly terms with them. You know, the rustlers have been hitting our outfit pretty hard and I rode down into the brakes one day, snoopin' around. I didn't like the looks of that Ballard outfit a-tall, and I'm kinda curious as to why a Bar Circle cowboy was hobnobbin' with 'em."

Mrs. Nash accepted that in silence, too, watching him with sharp attention.

"And then as soon as Jud gets his tail in a crack—" Rock snapped his fingers. "Most folks seem to think that Kendall killed him, but I can't believe it. Looks to me like he and the Kid were mixed up in the rustling that's going on around here, and *somebody* was afraid Jud would talk."

"Well, do you suppose?" the woman murmured. "I've heard there was a new gang working out in there."

"That's the way we figure it," Rock nodded. "It's a hell of a thing to say about your neighbors, but I'm betting those two

Bar Circle men were members of it. And I can't help wondering whether or not it stops there."

"What do you mean?"

Rock met her gaze squarely, and he showed her his hard speculations. "I'm new in this country," he said slowly, "but I do hear tell that your Mr. Ed Claiborne has made a hell of a lot of money since he came here."

He let it ride there but he saw, with grateful certainty, that the shrewd woman was involved in a good many deep speculations herself. Which might not do any good, but Rock knew that if a rumor were repeated often enough, a number of people would eventually regard it as the truth.

Rock went to bed, but not to sleep. For a long time he lay staring wide-eyed at the darkened ceiling, struggling with his thoughts. His hunch about Jud and the Kid had led him right up to pay dirt, then had exploded in his face. Not only had this latest move increased the enmity against him, but it had also wiped out two possible witnesses against Ash, the two that Rock felt would have been most likely to break under pressure. He thought of the Ballards, dark, inscrutable; and he realized suddenly that he had heard nothing from Cherry except that one belligerent grunt. He thought of Tonto, cold-eyed and tight-lipped, and he wondered what in the cowboy's past had driven him to outlawry. Perhaps there was something there that would make the man talk, but the thought of further dragging inaction maddened Rock.

Abruptly he came off the bed and stalked to the window, staring out at the silent, moonlit street. It was late, possibly two o'clock. Ash would be in his room at the hotel, perhaps gloating over the clever way in which he had parried the thrust of his enemy. Rock could see clearly the triumph that had been in the man's eyes, could hear the smooth run of his lying voice; his hatred became all at once unbearable. He had to get his hands on the man. With the thought of doing it, Rock became suddenly very still, cool and withdrawn as he examined an idea that had just come to him.

It would be reckless, perhaps disastrous, but Rock had meant it when he said he knew he couldn't last much longer. He had to end this thing, and maybe he could do it tonight. He couldn't hope ever to get to Ash out at the ranch, surrounded by his cowboys, but here in town the man might be alone in his room. Alone and perhaps asleep.

With abrupt decision, Rock swung away from the window, and he realized then that his jaws were aching from the restraint of the past few hours. He grabbed up his hat and spurs, the only things he had removed, and let himself silently out of the house. As he headed for the stable, his mind was racing, picking up the details, but he knew what he was going to do. Or try to do.

He saddled his horse with swift, sure hands, then rummaged through the stable until he found an old rope. He dug out his pocket knife, cut the rope into convenient lengths and looped them over his cartridge belt on the left side. He pulled a couple of extra bandannas out of his pack and rammed them into a pocket for use as gags. Then, with the drive of a long-frustrated desire, he led his horse outside, mounted and turned toward the center of town.

The streets were quiet, so quiet that even the soft plop-plop of his horse's hoofs in the dust sounded loud. The town was sleeping, evidently satisfied that their current scourge had pulled out, but Rock knew they would have made their plans for the morning.

He came in behind the Town House, hungrily eyeing the darkened windows in the second story. There was no back stairway, and Rock looked critically at the one-storied, flat-topped building that crowded against the hotel on the east, its roof scant feet below the level of the windows. But he still didn't know which room Ash occupied and might, he knew, create an unholy bedlam if he disturbed the wrong person.

A private stable loomed across the alley from the hotel, dark and quiet. Rock eyed the small window in the end of the building, knowing it was in the hostler's quarters; and he dismounted, removing his spurs and hanging them over the saddle horn. Leaving the brown with reins dragging, he quietly approached the wide door of the stable.

It was open and Rock slipped in, feeling rather than seeing the presence of horses as he made his way cautiously through the blackness. His eyes were becoming adjusted to the deep gloom by the time he reached the door at the end of the stalls, and he paused to listen intently. A faint sound reached him, a gentle, steady snoring. Rock tried the door, finding that it gave readily to his hand, but it creaked protestingly as he shoved it open. The rhythm of the snoring broke, and in one long stride Rock reached the skinny little man lying on the cot, his grizzled face clearly visible in the moonlight streaming through the window. His eyes were just opening sleepily when Rock slapped his left hand across the fellow's mouth and rammed the muzzle of his gun into the man's ear.

"Don't move," he hissed, "and you won't get hurt."

The man jerked convulsively as his eyes popped wide. Then he grew rigid, staring up at Rock with naked terror. Rock shoved his gun back into the holster, then snaked out one of the bandannas and gagged him. The little fellow offered no resistance as Rock rolled him over, bound him hand and foot and tied him to the bunk.

Back out in the stable, Rock swiftly saddled a horse, picking one at random in the dark and helping himself to the gear hanging on the wall. He led the animal outside, got the brown and took both horses into the deep shadow at the far end of the stable. Not knowing how well broken the borrowed horse was, he knotted the reins and hooked them over his own saddle horn. The brown, he knew, would stand right there until he came back. If he came back.

Only briefly then did he hesitate, wiping his clammy hands on his pants as he once more eyed those second-story windows. Then, with long strides, he crossed the alley and let himself into the back door of the hotel.

The hall was in darkness, even the lobby ahead appearing dim. Evidently only one lamp was burning and, thus reassured, Rock moved slowly and silently up the hall. He paused at the entrance to the lobby, sweeping it with a glance. The only person in sight was the night clerk whose brown head was bent over the desk as he studied some papers. Rock had never seen the man before and, pulling his hat down low over his eyes, he stepped out of the hall and sauntered toward the desk.

He was almost there before the clerk heard him and looked up, startled. Rock took note of the blue eyes behind thick glasses, the thin, pale face; he nodded and smiled pleasantly.

"Evenin'," he drawled and covered the last few intervening steps. While the clerk was still eying him in uncertainty, Rock reached out a swift left hand to grab his shoulder at the same time that he flashed his gun over the desk, its muzzle centered on the man's wishbone. "If you yell, you're a dead man!"

The clerk gasped, his eyes riveted to the gun, and he cringed under Rock's clutching hand. Rock gave him no time to recover from the shock. He shoved him along the far side of the desk until they reached the end of it, then stepped around it, shoving his gun into the man's stomach.

"You won't get hurt," he said evenly, "if you do exactly what I tell you."

"Are you—are you—"

"Yeah," Rock said, "I am. And if you're thinkin' Ash might be sore about this, I can tell you right now that he won't hurt you half as bad as I will. Turn around and lie down on your belly."

For a second the clerk hesitated, his face twisted with anxiety and uncertainty, but apparently he saw something in Rock's eyes that convinced him. With a harried sigh, he turned and lay down. Rock gagged him first in case the fellow should change his mind, then tied his hands behind his back and trussed his legs. Afterward he rolled the man back under the desk, out of sight, and eased the bandanna across his mouth.

"What room is Ash in?"

The clerk pulled his breath in sharply, his eyes clouded by his torturing thoughts. He was, Rock could see, an honest, decent man torn between fear and an admirable sense of duty.

"Look, fella," Rock said softly. "I'm not going to kill him. I want to talk to him. Tell me now. Which room?"

"Twenty-seven," the clerk said, and he sounded as if he were strangling. "At the left end of the hall."

"You got a master key?"

The clerk nodded jerkily toward the desk above him. "In the drawer."

Swiftly Rock tied the gag back into place and rose, getting the key and rounding the desk with a long tight stride. He could feel the eagerness knotting up inside of him, bunching in his chest and making his breath come hard. With quick stealth he climbed the stairs and paused at the top for a careful survey of the dim, carpeted hall. Somewhere a man was snoring with a heavy rhythm and a clock was ticking, muffled and sounding far away, in one of the rooms. These were the only sounds, and Rock saw no one.

Moving deliberately now, setting his feet down with great care, he turned down the hall, his eyes flicking to the brass numbers on the door dead ahead. Twenty-seven. The hall curved there, turning to serve the rooms over the dining room, and Rock eased up, hesitating for one glance down this side areaway. The window at the end of it was open, the curtain ruffling in a slight breeze. That was the only movement.

Quickly Rock stepped over to Ash's door. He tried the knob, turning it silently, but as he had suspected the door was locked. He knelt before it, holding his left hand against the door as a steadying guide as he eased the master key into the lock. He figured Ash would have left the key in the door and he soon found this to be true, but slowly, with infinite care, he pushed it out. He felt rather than heard it drop, a tiny thud on the carpet inside, and for a moment he froze, every sense strained. Not a sound could he hear from the other side of the door, and he wondered in sudden panic whether someone had seen him coming. Maybe there were other men in there with Ash, waiting breathlessly in the dark, their guns cocked and trained on the door.

For a second Rock wavered. Then, clamping his jaw, he stood up, laid quiet hold of the knob and, with the same slow care, turned the key in the lock. There was a faint click, barely audible. Gripping the knob with a tight pressure, Rock turned it, eased the door open. It was the corner room, and the little patch of moonlight brightening the floor under the back window reassured him. He slid into the room and a flashing glance showed him only one man: Ash Carlton, sprawled on the bed flat on his back, his mouth sagging open in sleep.

Rock paused for one brief instant to gaze down at his sleeping enemy. Ash wore nothing but a pair of shorts, his fine-muscled body clearly visible in the light from the moon. His big chest lifted and fell with slow regularity, and his hands, stretched above his head, dangled past the brass bedstead. His blond hair curled and shifted lazily in the slight wind coming through the eastern window; but his face, Rock noted, wore a slight frown, as if he were having a bad dream.

Rock thought with a grim eagerness, Not as bad as it's going to be.

With his breath shallow and tight in his throat, he turned to take his key out of the door, closing it and locking it on the inside. Maybe he could do this without causing a commotion, but maybe he would need more time than an unlocked door would give him. He had it mapped in his mind: knock him out, gag him, tie him, then bring him to and march him out of here.

After that, fear for Ash would keep the hounds off his trail until he could figure some way to force the confession he needed.

Rock's hopes were riding high, but as he turned toward the bed, a board creaked under his boot. Instantly Ash's eyes popped open, and for a split part of a second Rock held the man's startled, incredulous gaze. Then, as Ash twisted to slide a hand frantically under his pillow, Rock dove at him over the foot of the bed.

His chest slammed hard into those smooth shoulders, flattening Ash, shoving his hand away from the gun he was reaching for. Rock heard it clang against the bedstead, then thud to the floor, and he started to reach for his own gun to knock the man out. Before he could get it, Ash heaved up under him, twisting, throwing him off. Rock tried to hang on, but that bare, hard flesh slid through his fingers and he toppled over the edge of the bed with Ash rolling to fall on him. Rock got his hands and one leg up and flipped Ash off before the big man lit on him, but he couldn't avoid those long grappling arms. As he was pulled away from the bed, struggling to free himself, Ash let out a wild yell for help.

Cursing, Rock twisted over and drove his knee into the man's stomach, eliciting a grunt out of him but not breaking that steely grip on his arms. He got one leg under him and threw himself over on top of Ash, slamming his head into the man's jaw. For a second the grip loosened and Rock got his hands on the floor and lurched to his knees, wrenching free. He could hear men running in the hall now, excited voices calling out, and he staggered to his feet, once more reaching for his gun. He was off balance and stumbled against the washstand with a force that momentarily numbed his right wrist. Then Ash was on his feet, lashing out with a big right fist.

Rock jerked his head aside, feeling the blow graze his neck as he grabbed Ash around the body. Ash yelled again, a thick, breathless cry, and like an echo came a pound on the door, the rattle of the knob. The sound shot through Rock like an icy wind, and he hurled Ash away from him and smashed his left fist hard into the man's face. Ash slammed back into the bureau and bounced away from it, again grabbing Rock's arms. He wasn't trying to fight now but only to hang onto Rock, to hold him until help came. He was heavier than Rock, longer of arm, and there was no clothing to slide and give on his smooth, hard body.

Rock was wrestling to free himself when a heavy weight drove into the door. The whole room seemed to shudder, and in desperation Rock twisted his body and lunged sideways at Ash, knocking him back. Again that weight crashed into the door, and Rock heard the shivering of wood. He stepped in fast and brought one heavy boot stamping viciously down on Ash's bare foot. Ash jerked convulsively and a strangled groan came out of him. Instinctively he let go of Rock and started to bend over, and Rock stepped back, grabbing for his gun. This time his aching fingers closed around the butt, and he swung the weapon up and down in a short, savage blow that caught Ash on the back of the head.

The man dropped without a sound, but Rock knew it was too late now even to use him as a shield. Those men in the hall would shoot before they'd listen. He had to get out of here and, knowing that, he spun toward the window, gasping painfully for breath. He was aware of the clamor in the hallway, beating against his throbbing head, and he heard another heavy blow hit the door. It splintered, and Rock knew that one more drive would break it in. He grabbed the window sill and jackknifed, vaulting through it and landing on the roof below—directly in front of Red Mayberry. Rock caught just a glimpse of that freckled face, of the gun in Red's hand. Then, with the momentum of his jump, he brought his knee up and his left fist around in a smashing attack that sent the cowboy sprawling.

Staggering to catch his balance, Rock drove on, running for the far edge of the roof. He was only halfway there when he heard the door crash in behind him. At that same moment he noticed the top of a ladder that had been thrown up against the far side of the building and, just as the sight registered, a man popped into view, a gun in his hand.

Without hesitation, Rock swerved aside and fired. He saw the man double over, the gun dropping as he grabbed for the ladder with both hands. He missed his hold and slid from sight, yelling with the fear of a fall. Rock could hear the yells of other men, too, down there on the ground. Then a shot blasted out from the hotel; and Rock, dodging aside and whirling, had the cold, numbing thought that he was trapped.

# CHAPTER NINE

Rock saw the flash of guns back in the darkened window, and he slammed a shot at them. A curse, high-pitched and agonized, broke on the night, and Rock heard the mad scramble as men shoved to get back away from that window. Ducking low, he ran for the front of the building. There would probably be more men on the street than in the alley, but at least there was an awning there to break his fall and he had to get off that moonlit roof.

A bullet burned his leg as he reached the parapet and dove over it, grabbing it with his left hand to swing his body around and keep himself from going headfirst down that slanting roof. His legs hit hard on the crude roofing four feet below. He let go of the parapet and tried to flatten himself for a slide, but he couldn't do it and started to roll, holding hard with his arms and legs in an effort to slow himself. As he reached the edge of the porch, he got a grip on the boards that momentarily checked him and he swung off into space feet first.

His legs buckled when he hit the street, dropping him into smothering dust, but he scrambled up and jumped under the awning as the first man appeared at the edge of the roof. He could hear the wild yells, directions being bellowed to other men; but Rock didn't take the time to survey the street to see who was in sight. Still acting on the theory that it was best to do what the other fellow was sure he wouldn't do, he dashed down the walk and darted back into the lighted hotel.

There were three men on the stairs, bounding up toward the sound of the excitement, and Rock was almost across the lobby before the last one spotted him. The fellow tried to stop, turning; but Rock fired a swift shot at him that sent him scrambling on to the top with a startled yell. Then Rock was legging it down the hall with a grim hope that his horse had not been discovered—and moved.

He burst out the door just as two cowboys were starting to enter. The one who had been reaching for the knob was knocked spinning, but the other jumped back, his gun lifting. Rock shot him, a pointblank range that couldn't miss, and as the man dropped back in the moonlight, Rock recognized a cowboy he'd seen riding with Bar Circle.

Even before the man hit the ground, Rock had leaped past him and was running the last few yards to the spot where he'd left the brown. The horse threw up his head and jumped as Rock bolted around the corner, then stood steady, bracing himself against the lunges of the other animal like a good cow horse. Those reins broke just as Rock approached and, as the frightened horse shied clear, Rock vaulted into his saddle and wheeled him away from the alley.

He heard the yell that went up behind him, knew that the second Bar Circle cowboy was giving the alarm, and he let the brown have his head for three pellmell blocks. Then he pulled him out of his run, holding him to a nervous, springy walk as he approached Mrs. Nash's. He was still half a block away when he heard the first of the riders pounding out behind him, but still he held the horse in, not daring to awaken the woman who was innocently giving him sanctuary. Perhaps the shooting had awakened her. Perhaps she was watching him now, wondering, but he had to risk that.

As he turned into her yard, he glanced back, caught a flash of movement beyond trees. Then the house intervened and he looked to the stable, fighting the desire to jump his horse toward it. The thunder was growing closer and he knew the men had turned into the street running past the house, but he held steady until he reached the stable. Then he jumped to the ground, swung the door open and shooed his horse inside. He had barely closed the door to the merest crack when the riders came in sight, flashing past to go on into the desert.

Rock leaned weakly into the wall, aware for the first time that he was wringing wet and heaving like a wind-broken horse. He lifted an arm to mop his face and discovered then that he still held his gun. Automatically he ejected the empties and thumbed fresh cartridges into the cylinder, wondering how many men he had killed. At least one, he knew—that Bar Circle cowboy. More murder charges, he thought, and felt suddenly, unutterably tired.

The brown horse nuzzled him, and Rock lifted a hand to that silky neck.

"Kinda close, wasn't it, old fella?" he murmured.

The brown, with almost a human sigh, stuck his face under Rock's arm. For a brief moment Rock buried his face in that thick black forelock, and the bleak thought crossed his mind that this was the only friend he had in the world.

Rock was up early the next morning but he killed time, shaving, lingering over his breakfast, waiting for the posse that he felt sure would be riding out. He wanted those men ahead of him rather than behind him.

His strategy in approaching the house quietly, he found, had paid off. Mrs. Nash had no inkling that he had ever left his room. When he first appeared in the kitchen while she was getting breakfast, she expressed a curiosity that she obviously expected him to share.

"Wonder what all the shootin' was about last night."

"Shootin'?" Rock echoed blankly.

"Didn't you hear it?"

"After I ride all day," he said pointedly, "I go to bed to *sleep*."

"Well, Lord," she grunted. "You must have been plumb unconscious if you didn't hear that racket. I heard it but didn't get up to look until a bunch of riders tore past. Wonder who they were chasin' this time."

"Prob-ly the same wolf," Rock said with a shrug, and sat down to his breakfast.

He was savoring his third cup of coffee when he heard the riders coming, and he stepped to the front window to peer out. There were at least forty men in the group, a number of whom he recognized as Bar Circle cowboys, and they were a grim-looking lot. Ash rode with Lackey at the head of the cavalcade and he rode in silence, his face set, his eyes fixed straight ahead of him. Rock found a savage pleasure in the thought that the Bar Circle owner would be nursing one hell of a headache.

"Goodness," said Mrs. Nash beside him. "I'd hate to be in Rock Kendall's boots."

"Yeah," Rock murmured. "His boots are damned apt to get planted—with him still in 'em. Lackey doesn't go down into the brakes much, does he?"

"Never does him any good. That country's too big and too rough. The advantages are all with the outlaws down there."

"Yeah," Rock said again and wondered whether the posse would go down there this time. Rock had admitted hanging around the Ballard place. His story had been discredited in the eyes of the sheriff, but Ash knew it was true and might persuade the posse to make a sweep through the brakes. At least, Rock thought, with that many men around, Ash wasn't going to be holding any private confab with Buck Ballard.

Abruptly he went back to the kitchen, finished his coffee and went after his horse. When he returned for his pack, he found that Mrs. Nash had fixed a lunch for him and wouldn't let him pay for it.

"You tell that Kathy Sinclair," she said gruffly, "that she's got no business sending a man plumb into town on an empty stomach."

"Yes'm," Rock said with a grin.

Then he hesitated awkwardly, wanting in some way to tell her how much her kindly regard meant to him. He couldn't do it. Touching his hat in careless farewell, he reined abruptly away, wondering, in case he didn't come back, whether she would ever find out who it was that she had befriended.

He swung a little to the east as he rode out of town, figuring the posse would be bearing west toward Bar Circle. The brown was well rested, eager to travel, but Rock held him to an easy jog. He couldn't risk approaching the Clear Springs ranch until after dark, anyway.

Lamps had been lit by the time he topped the ridge behind the spread and pulled up for a brief inspection of it. He could see men moving past the lighted windows of the bunkhouse, could hear one whistling out near the corral. The place appeared cozy, peaceful, with the homey smell of wood smoke hovering in the night air; but Rock was not lulled into any sense of security. He looked narrowly at the lighted windows of the main house, wondering whether Kathy had by any chance learned his identity. If she had, he might be sticking his neck into a noose by going down there when the crew was in.

Again he looked at the bunkhouse, at the shaft of light streaming from the open door. A man came to lean in the doorway, one shoulder tipped against the casing as he stared out at the night.

"And if he heard a horse sliding down off this mountain," Rock murmured to himself, "he'd come take a look-see."

Abruptly he reined back over the ridge. He found a sheltered thicket for his horse, slipped the bridle and tied the animal with his rope. He loosened the cinch, hooked his spurs over the saddle horn. Then, leaving the horse with a feed of corn to work on, he turned back over the ridge on foot, his nerves humming. It was risky, getting that far away from his horse; but at least the animal would be rested and ready to travel—if Rock could get back to him.

He picked his way down the slope carefully, coming in behind the house and pausing by the woodpile for a study of the windows. He could see the Mexican woman working at the stove. He caught no glimpse of Kathy, but he felt sure she would be here and he hoped, fervently, that she did not have company. Involuntarily, he touched the butt of his gun. Then, with a tight breath, he stepped away from the woodpile and strode up onto the porch to knock.

Maria opened the door, her black eyes sweeping over him with noncommittal recognition. Then, without a word, she stepped back out of his way and Rock moved into the kitchen, hat in hand. The odor of roasting meat came from the stove; and the table, he noted, had been set for two. He glanced apprehensively at the door to the living room just as Kathy stepped into it, one hand lifted to brush a strand of hair off her forehead.

She stopped short at sight of him, her eyes popping wide as she caught her breath. Rock seemed to freeze, his body rigid, his breath stuck in his throat. *She knows me,* he thought; but no sooner had the thought crossed his mind than Kathy stepped on into the kitchen, smiling a little uncertainly.

"Hello!" she said, a queer catch in her voice. "I wasn't expecting you back so soon."

"I—got a little news," he said.

Not immediately could he dispel the icy tension that had gripped him, nor could he get his eyes off the girl who was approaching him. The color was high in her cheeks, as if she'd been riding, and her hair had a soft, loose look as it curled around her face. Her dress was as blue as her eyes, snug-fitting through the bodice, the collar open at the throat.

She stopped a few feet away, her eyes flicking with quick concern over his battered face. She didn't ask any questions, but Rock felt the heat of blood in his cheeks. He grinned painfully.

"Rough country down there," he drawled.

"Apparently," she said, with constraint. Her glance darted to the windows, and she added quickly, "Come on into the living room. I'll pull the shades."

Rock followed her slowly, still feeling awkward and uneasy. He sensed a tension in her, a restraint she had not shown him before, and he wondered whether it was due to the fact that he was calling in the evening—or to the fact that she had been thinking about him.

He paused in the doorway, watching her quick, light movements as she moved from one window to another. The room was a pleasant one, with a big stone fireplace, Indian rugs on the floor, heavy leather furniture. Only one lamp was burning, near the couch which extended out from the far side of the fireplace, and the soft light gave the room a pleasant, homey feel.

"Sit down," she invited, with a graceful little gesture that urged him to take his pick.

He waited until she had seated herself on the couch, then eased into a chair opposite, still holding his hat and turning it uncomfortably in his hands.

"News," she said with a smile. "Got those rustlers yet?"

"Well—"

Rock pulled in a deep breath and held it, thinking that he would have to do this very carefully. He didn't dare admit any part in the events of the past two days since the town knew that both the Kid and Jud Moore had met their downfall at the hands of Rock Kendall.

"No," he said slowly, "I haven't, but there's been a little excitement. Jud Moore was killed last night."

"Jud Moore?" she echoed, startled. "Who did it?"

Rock shook his head. "The sheriff seems to think Rock Kendall did it, but I can't believe it."

"Rock Kendall," she repeated, her eyes intent with a close, sharp interest. "What happened?"

"Quite a bit," he said grimly. "Seems that Kendall hunted the sheriff up and told him that Jud was a man named Richards who was wanted for murder over in New Mexico. One of those Lincoln County jiggers we were wondering about. So Lackey jailed him. Then somebody shot him through the bars of his cell."

Kathy frowned. "And they think Kendall did it?"

"Yeah, they do." Rock lowered his head and ran a hand down the back of his hair, not trusting his eyes. "I heard the shots and went to see what had happened. There was quite a crowd. Ash Carlton was there and he claimed that Kendall had lied, had just framed the whole thing to cast a shadow on his honesty."

"Well, they could find out. Wire for someone to come and identify the body."

"Sure, but they decided that wasn't necessary. Lackey accepted Carlton's explanation of it." Rock looked up, his voice suddenly hard. "But I sure can't accept it. I don't think Rock Kendall would have risked his neck in town unless he knew what he was talking about."

Kathy looked down at her lap, frowning again. "It—doesn't seem so," she admitted. "Then—what do you think?"

"I think," Rock said deliberately, "that somebody was afraid Jud would talk, and they weren't worrying about the Lincoln County War, either!"

"You think he was involved in this rustling here?"

"Yes, ma'am, I do. In fact, I'm sure of it, although I can't prove it. Another thing. Kendall did kill the Kid the other day, down at the Ballard ranch."

"At the Ballard ranch! What was the Kid doing down there?"

"That," said Rock, "is an awful good question. The way I got it, he was on friendly terms with them; and I happen to know," he added with hard significance, "that the Ballards just got back from a week-long trip."

Kathy went very still, hardly seeming to breathe, her eyes fastened on him with burning concentration. "Are you sure," she asked slowly, "about the Kid and the Ballards?"

"I saw him ride in down there," Rock said evenly. "I've been shadowing that place."

A moment longer Kathy stared at him, her face strained. Then she looked down at her hands, clenching them tightly in her lap. Rock could see her breast and shoulders lift with a deep, labored breath, and he knew that she had accepted his statements with all their shocking possibilities. When she finally spoke, her voice was muted, tight.

"Do you think either the Kid or Jud could have been the leader of that gang?"

Rock shifted in sudden discomfort. "Possible, I suppose," he said gruffly.

"But you don't believe it."

Her head came up sharply, her gaze boring into him, digging for the naked accusation he didn't want to make. He looked down at the floor, shaking his head with a faint reluctance.

"No," he admitted, "I don't."

"Nor the Ballards?"

"Nor the Ballards."

Kathy abruptly stood up and whirled toward the mantel, gripping it with white-knuckled fingers. "Rock Kendall," she said, her voice tight with agitation. "He's out to ruin Ash, isn't he?"

The starkness of her remark jolted Rock. The thought that he was hurting her knifed into him, and he shifted again, worrying his hat. "He's—after him, anyway, I reckon."

"He's making Ash look like a rustler!" Kathy spun toward him, lifting one hand in appeal. "I—I can't believe it!"

Rock dropped his hat and came out of his chair, irresistibly reaching for her. His hands closed over her arms, pulling her away from the mantel, turning her squarely to face him.

"Are you in love with the man, Kathy?"

"I—" Kathy faltered, her lips quivering, her eyes clouding as she struggled with her emotions. Then her head dropped. "I don't know," she said miserably. "I don't know how I feel or what to think. I've known Ed—"

She broke off, swallowing hard, and Rock felt an almost uncontrollable desire to pull her into his arms. It had never occurred to him that a girl like Kathy Sinclair could be lonely, but he knew at this moment she was. Dreadfully alone and frightened. He wanted to say something, to comfort her; but the certainty that her pain had just begun tied his tongue. Whether Ash lost this fight or won it and married her, only for her to find out later—either way Kathy was going to be hurt.

"He was over again the other evening," she said, lifting her head and showing him a troubled gaze. "Told me to stay home while that woman killer was loose."

Her words hit Rock like a blow in the face, slugging him with the full, bitter meaning of his identity. He let go of her and stepped back, his fists doubled, his voice rough with a dull anger. "Going to?"

"I've got a ranch to run." She shook her head, then pulled in a sudden deep breath and let it out in a derisive little snort. "I doubt," she said dryly, "that Mr. Kendall would take a shot at me, anyway, unless I shot at him first."

"But he might try to rope you," Rock said significantly.

Her head came up again, her attention centering on him with swift, probing speculation. Rock's steady gaze was even more significant than his words had been, and it brought a slow sweep of color into Kathy's cheeks. For several moments she stood absolutely still, her glance locked with his while a strange, intent light came into her eyes.

"What part of Texas are you from?" she asked suddenly.

Her question startled Rock, jarring him into instant wariness. Casually he leaned to retrieve his hat, then turned it slowly in his hands, staring at it with fixed attention. "Pecos country."

"Oh? Is that where your folks live?"

He shook his head. "I'm kind of low on folks." He didn't want to say any more, knowing they were on dangerous ground, but Kathy's expectant silence drove him on. "Got a couple of brothers somewhere, but I haven't seen them since I was twelve."

"And don't even know where they are?"

"No idea." He glanced up just long enough to catch the light of a keen personal interest in her eyes. "One of them said he thought he'd go to Montana but—" He shrugged. "There wasn't much to hold us together after Mother died."

"Was she—a widow?"

"Yeah." The sudden tenderness in Kathy's voice tugged at Rock, leading him on in spite of his growing uneasiness. "I don't remember my dad much. I was just a little shaver when he left for the war."

"And didn't come back," Kathy murmured.

She was silent for a moment, but Rock could feel her gaze on him, digging for his thoughts. He kept his eyes on the hat he was methodically crushing and then smoothing, dreading her questions but powerless to change the subject.

"From something you said in town," she went on, "I gathered that you had run cattle at some time or another."

Rock put a very careful crease in the crown of his hat. "Yeah," he admitted, "I had a bunch of cattle once. Lost them."

"How come?"

"Bad luck."

She waited, once more expectant, but Rock had no intention of going any further in that direction. He poked out the dent he had just made, then promptly made another, his hands gradually tightening under the pressure he was fighting not to show.

"Well," she said finally, her voice a little grim, "I happen to know that bad luck isn't hard to come by in the cow business. Did you own your own ranch, too?"

"Half of it. I had a pard." Rock looked up with a sudden, rueful grin. "He was a disappointment."

Kathy smiled in quick appreciation, but there was a strange thoughtfulness in her eyes that was vastly disturbing to Rock. He was trying to fathom it, scrutinizing her narrowly, when she suddenly stepped up to him and put her hands on his arms, her fingers closing in a warm, intimate grip.

"And now," she said wonderingly, "you're chasing somebody else's rustlers. Jim, will you stay and have dinner with me?"

Rock was floored. He flashed a dismayed glance down over his rough clothes, at his hands. A protest flew to his lips, but Kathy gave him no chance to voice it.

"Sure you will," she said brightly. She stepped back but left one hand extended. "Give me your hat, cowboy, before you ruin it completely."

Rock had the feeling all at once that he ought to get out of there, but it was too late now. Kathy had taken his hat and was pulling out a small table at one end of the living room, starting to set it. Suddenly restless, he strode back into the kitchen, found a wash basin and carried it out to the back porch. The silent Maria brought him a towel and he cleaned up as well as he could, brushing the dust from his clothes and smoothing his hair.

Afterwards he rolled a cigarette and stood at the edge of the porch, staring at the stars, fighting his dark thoughts. This was what he had wanted, the confidence and friendship of Kathy Sinclair; but the knowledge that he had won them tightened his throat and left him strangely upset. A slight wind was blowing down from the ridge, setting up a low moan in the pines. It was a lonesome sound, and it added to Rock's feeling of restless disturbance. That's where he belonged, he thought grimly—out there in the night.

At Kathy's call, however, he flipped his cigarette away and went in, able to show her a cool front. And the thought that Ash Carlton had stood here, holding her chair for her, forcibly reminded him that the game was not over yet. He accepted her smiling thanks with a slight bow and went on to his own place, the scent of her lingering in his nostrils.

Kathy was a gracious hostess, but she was also a range-bred girl who understood that cowboys came to the table to eat. She saw to it that Rock's plate was well-filled, then turned her attention to her own food in discreet silence. Rock, too, looked dutifully down at the savory meal before him, but he couldn't immediately bring his thoughts to bear on it. Kathy had placed a couple of candles on the table, now the only light in the room. Their flickering glow touched her face with a mellow light that affected Rock powerfully. Long after he had picked up his fork and started to eat, he was still seeing the smooth line of her throat and the soft curve of her lips.

That dinner was one of ever-increasing tension for Rock. Kathy watched over him with a woman's jealous solicitude, fore-seeing his wants, keeping his coffee cup filled. Her eyes were constantly seeking his, sometimes pensive and speculative, sometimes brightly alive with the secret they shared. Rock wondered whether his own tumultuous thoughts were showing. The loneliness of the past three years was closing in on him, driving him in spite of the maddeningly insistent voice deep inside him that kept telling him that was wrong.

When he finally cleaned his plate and reached for tobacco, Kathy asked quickly, "Had enough?"

"Plenty," he said, battling a constraint that made speech come slow. "I can't tell you what this has meant to me."

"It's meant just as much to me," she said, giving him a level glance. Then suddenly she smiled, her eyes lighting with a pleasant memory. "What was it you said in town that day? I got my money's worth."

Rock lowered his glance abruptly to his cigarette. She *had* been thinking about him, and for some reason the knowledge hit him with a stabbing reminder that he was Rock Kendall, a man branded and despised. A man who had to lie to enjoy the company of a good woman!

"This has been awfully nice," Kathy said with feeling, "and I really appreciate your staying. This old house gets awfully big sometimes when John's gone."

"Reckon it does." Rock stood up, pulling in a deep breath that crowded rather than cleared the tight congestion in his chest. "I've heard it isn't polite to eat and run, but my old pony's standing out there."

"Of course." She came to her feet, then hesitated. "I don't suppose you'd want to stay here tonight, in the bunkhouse."

"No, thanks."

"I didn't think so," she said with a smile, "but I wanted you to know you were welcome."

She fetched his hat and Rock headed for the back door, knowing he had to get out of there. Not until he reached the porch in comforting darkness did he pause, but even then he was intensely aware of the compelling warmth of her, there beside him.

"I'll come again," he said gruffly, "when I know anything worth telling."

"All right." She hesitated, peering up at him, trying to read his face in the dark. "Do you have any place to go?"

"You mean to spend the night?" Rock looked up at the stars, remote and twinkling with a devilish nonchalance. "I've been sleepin' under them for a right smart spell."

"Jim." Impulsively she put a hand on his arm, gripping it tightly. "I'm sorry I got upset tonight. I had no right to do that. The future of this country is worth more than any one person's life. Even mine. It's just—"

She broke off, and Rock knew she was thinking of Ash. Again he sensed her loneliness, her desperate need of someone to confide in and to trust for guidance. He looked narrow-eyed up at the darkened ridge and said, "Maybe it'll all work out."

"Sure it will," she said, "and I had no business blowing up like that. I don't think a woman can ever fully understand the hard side of life that a man has to face, and—well, I hope I didn't add to the problems that were already worrying you. I appreciate what you're doing, Jim, even if—if—These turbulent times can't last forever!"

The fervency of her voice and her implied faith in him were too much for Rock. Irresistibly he swung to face her, his arms closing around her shoulders to draw her up close. For only a moment he gazed down at her, the outline of her face pale and indistinct in the starlight. Then he was kissing her with all the hard, hungry passion that was in him.

He felt her hands on his shoulders, pressing at first, then clutching with all the strength of her slender fingers. The touch of her lips, soft and yielding, fired him; and a surge of feeling deeper and richer than anything he had ever known threatened to overwhelm him. This was real. He knew it and was reveling in it when the very sweetness of her response hit him like a hard fist. Rock jerked his head up, staring down at her and seeing the shaken expression in her eyes. Suddenly, uncontrollably, hot shame poured through him and he swung away, his fists doubled and his breath clogged in his throat.

He knew now what had been bothering him all evening. He had led her to this—just to make Ash jealous! His reasons for arousing her interest in the first place seemed all at once damnable; and an urge, as strong as the pound of his heart, rose in him—to tell her who he was, to come clean with her and put this on a decent basis. But the thought of her inevitable reaction was unbearable, and he couldn't do it.

"I shouldn't have done that," he said harshly.

"I guess I—wanted you to."

The muffled sound of her voice, faltering and stricken but yet honest, stung Rock and he turned back, reaching for her.

"Kathy—"

He checked himself, stopping short. She hadn't moved except to lower her arms, but her face, it seemed to him, had turned ghost-white. Slowly Rock straightened, dropping his hands with a restraint that made him ache.

"You don't know," he said tightly, "and I can't tell you, but I had no right—I beg your pardon, Miss Sinclair."

With a slight, stiff bow, he left her, plunging off the porch and striding blindly toward the ridge. Behind him, in the darkness, he thought he heard a muffled sob.

# CHAPTER TEN

Rock didn't find it easy to go to sleep that night. Long after he had put his horse out to graze in a grassy hollow, he lay wide-awake, staring at the star-studded sky, taking stock of himself.

The feeling of sordid guilt that he had carried away from Kathy's was still with him, riding him unmercifully. He'd had no right to drag her into this, to use her feelings for his own selfish purposes. Her own sincerity and straightforward honesty shamed him into realizing what a hard and ruthless act it had been. He'd been thinking of Ash Carlton—and of no one else. Even his willingness to run down the rustlers had been based solely on his desire to break Ash. And Kathy was grateful to him!

Not once had Rock considered the service he could render to the good people who were trying to build this country. He had been submerged in his own dark schemes, working strictly for Rock Kendall. But Kathy believed in him, just as she believed in the job he was doing and the stark necessity for its being done even if she herself got hurt. Her faith was like a tonic to Rock, pulling him out of his morbid loneliness, and for the first time he realized the scope of his undertaking. This was a vast new country that could build to prosperity or be wrecked in its infancy. Its future right now seemed to be in his hands.

The knowledge brought Rock an exhilarating sense of his own worth. No one but a Rock Kendall could do this job. However Lackey and Mrs. Nash and Kathy Sinclair might feel about his name, they needed him as a man; and suddenly Rock felt a stirring desire to live up to Kathy's faith, to sweep this range clean and make it safe. One sobering thought came to him, that the job might entail hurting still another woman. Rita Ballard.

Without wanting to, Rock found himself comparing the two women. One as bright and sunny and clear as a day in spring. The other as dark and wild as a stormy night. Both of them inextricably involved in this turmoil that could ruin their lives, and Rock squirmed at thought of the position he was in. Getting Kathy's rustlers would perhaps mean heartbreak for the simple, thwarted girl in the brakes, but maybe the blow could be softened ....

Rock was in the saddle before dawn, climbing the timbered butte above Bar Circle, and he was viewing the country with a new perspective. This could be his range no less than it was Kathy's, and the sense that he had aligned himself with something big and decent made him feel good.

He watched with a keen, cold interest as the Bar Circle outfit came alive, and he detected a new, grimmer purpose in the movements of the men. There seemed to be no time wasted on talk or idle motions as they caught and saddled their horses. Rock knew that, with the deaths of at least three members of the outfit to spur them on, every man would be after him in earnest now, with murder in his heart and blood in his eye. Rock watched them narrowly, wondering whether any more of them were involved in the rustling or whether the others were, like Red, honest cowboys who were probably unaware of the set-up. Maybe, he thought with a faint hope, Ash had lost his last messenger.

The men were mounted when Ash appeared from the main house, striding with a swift and angry determination. He mounted the horse that had been saddled for him, jerking the animal around and spurring him viciously. Taking it out on his horse, Rock thought with contempt, and watched with hard restraint as the men rode out and disappeared to the east.

He waited several minutes longer, watching the place, wanting to make sure. A horse, alone in the far corral, let out a shrill whinny that was answered far down the valley. Rock could hear a bull somewhere, growling as he headed in for water, but aside from these natural, reassuring sounds of the range the ranch was quiet. Finally a man emerged from the cook shack, bare-headed, a flour sack tied around his middle. Unhurriedly he walked to the back door of the main house and disappeared inside.

Satisfied that Ash had taken every man except this cook, Rock got his horse and turned him down off the butte, approaching the ranch with a strange tingle in his blood. It would be the first close-up of the place that might one day be his home. He came in behind the sturdy pole corrals, noting that they were in good repair. The buildings, too, showed evidence of being kept up, and they looked as if they'd be snug in the wintertime. The main house faced down the valley, and Rock could visualize the view that it must command of the lower range. It was an ideal spot. He approached it with a queer sense of coming home at the same time that he felt his status as an outcast more keenly than ever.

He rode boldly up to the back porch and dismounted, leaving his horse with reins dragging as he stepped up to the open door. The kitchen was untidy, but it was a large, light room, well furnished. Rock noted instantly the one dirty plate and cup on the table, the ash tray overflowing with cigarette stubs. Ash, apparently, had eaten in solitude probably wanting to think; obviously his thoughts had not been comforting.

The cook, a pudgy little man with a stubble of gray whiskers, looked up from the work table he was clearing and eyed Rock with only a mild curiosity. There was no recognition in his glance and no suspicion. Evidently it had never occurred to him that Rock Kendall would have the gall to ride in here.

"Howdy," Rock said with a grin. "How's chances for a handout?"

The cook shifted his cud, squinting at him in disgust. "You couldn't a got here fifteen minutes sooner, could you?"

"I was humpin'," Rock said. He glanced at the slab of bacon the man had been wrapping, laid a hand over his stomach and sighed dismally.

"Oh, hell," the cook grunted and turned to pull a frying pan to the center of the stove. "Get you a cup, cowboy. The coffee's still hot."

"All right," Rock said, but he ambled instead toward the door leading to the living room.

"Where you goin'?" the cook demanded quickly.

"Got something for the boss," Rock told him and kept on walking.

The cook stood silent a moment, uncertain about this. Then, mumbling incoherently to himself, he turned his attention to the slab of bacon.

Rock stepped into the good-sized living room and paused, sweeping a critical glance over it. It bore ample evidence that this was a bachelor outfit. Chaps, spurs, a coiled rope hung from pegs on the wall at one end; and both the mantel and the big desk in the far corner were cluttered with a collection of miscellaneous objects, including a number of loose cartridges. The rugs scattered over the floor were not too clean, and the once-bright curtains had a bedraggled look.

Rock could not help the strangely sickening thought that if Kathy married Ash she would hit this room like a tornado.

Flicking a glance over his shoulder to be sure the cook had not followed, Rock crossed to the desk and began methodically going through it. Knowing Ash, he felt sure the man would have a considerable sum of money stashed away here somewhere, and Rock could use it to good purpose. He went through the drawers with quick care, making as little noise as possible, and glancing frequently at the kitchen. The cook, however, seemed to be going ahead with his breakfast.

In the bottom drawer, under a collection of tally books and ranch records, Rock found what he was looking for—a fair-sized roll of bills. He didn't stop to count it, and he felt no guilt in helping himself to what he considered rightfully his, anyway. He just slipped the rubber band, flattened the roll and shoved it into his hip pocket, thinking of a dark-eyed girl who wanted pretty clothes and a decent home. A girl who had never had anything to offer except her lips to gain the things she wanted out of life.

Rock still wasn't sure how Rita felt, and he had no thought to bribe her for information that would hang her own brothers. He only knew he couldn't go ahead with this unless he could offer some security for the girl's future.

Afterward he paused to scan the room more carefully, consciously seeking something that had been brought from the old home on the Pecos. The old clock, perhaps, or a picture. But he saw nothing familiar. Apparently Ash had fled with only what he could carry in his saddlebags, and Rock went back to the kitchen with a queer, empty feeling.

His breakfast was on the table, hotcakes, bacon and coffee, and Rock sat down to it. He cast a covert glance at the cook, who was once more starting to clear the work table, working in a silence that was neither friendly nor hostile. Rock thought of the work that must be waiting for him over at the cook house, and he asked casually, "The boss eat alone like this very much?"

"Naw." The cook aimed a stream of tobacco juice at the wood box. "Been kinda upset the last couple days."

An idea popped into Rock's head, and he promptly acted on it.

"Well, I can savvy that. Jud and the Kid getting killed that way left an awful hole in the gang."

"Yeah," the cook said, shaking his head. "They were good men."

"Awful good men," Rock agreed. His first bait had not been taken, so he threw out a second morsel. "It's not going to be easy to replace them, but Buck's got a couple of ideas. That's why he sent me up here."

The cook looked up, still with only a mild curiosity. "Buck who?"

"Ballard," Rock said, as if surprised that the man hadn't known whom he meant. He noted the cook's perplexed frown, and he went on smoothly, "Buck didn't want to say anything to these two fellas, of course, until he found out what Ash thought of them; but Buck figures they'd make good men."

The cook turned fully to face him, his frown deepening into an alert suspicion. "What's Buck Ballard got to say about who we hire?"

"Why, hell," Rock said, as if that should have been obvious. "He'd be working with them. Why shouldn't he have something to say about it? We get a couple of knuckleheads in there, we'll all get our necks stretched."

"Our necks stretched?" the cook echoed blankly. "What the devil are you talking about?"

Rock looked up, a bite of hotcake poised above his plate. Carefully he looked the man over, his eyes narrowed with speculation.

"Maybe," he said slowly, "I'm talking too much. I supposed you knew Ash and the Ballards—Hell! You didn't think he made all his money off his own cows, did you?"

He broke off, then abruptly lowered his head and went on with his breakfast, aware that the cook was standing rigidly still. Trouble with his indigestion, Rock thought with diabolic glee. He had not come here to plant any rumors, but he could not overlook the possible chance of getting some of those men off his trail. He knew that no honest cowboy wanted to be caught working for a questionable outfit; and if the cook accepted his statements, perhaps added to them, some of Ash's men might get fiddlefooted and pull out on him.

Rock finished his breakfast in satisfied silence. Then he rolled a cigarette, noticing that the cook was wrapping the bacon but staring beyond it. At some mighty distressing ideas, Rock thought. He lit his cigarette and asked idly, "When'll the boss be back?"

The cook answered without looking up. "Don't know."

Rock nodded. "I'll be back later. Thanks for the breakfast."

He got up and ambled to the door, pausing for a moment to gaze out into the brilliant sunlight. A flash of movement at the corner of the house caught his eye and he whirled toward it just as a bullet zipped past his head, so close that he instinctively ducked. In the split second after that shot crashed out, Rock recognized a man that he should have remembered and taken into consideration. The wounded Hank. A white sling encased the cowboy's right arm and hand, but his left held a gun that was leveling for another shot.

With a quick shove against the casing, Rock cleared the door just as Hank fired the second time. There was in Rock a strong repugnance toward killing a crippled man even in self-defense, and he held low as the gun bucked against his hand. The sharp-faced cowboy, swearing thickly, stumbled and went down, the gun flying out of his hand—and out of his reach—as he made a grab for the edge of the porch to catch himself. Rock collided with a porch post and grabbed at it, swinging his gun toward the door as the cook appeared, wide-eyed.

"What the hell?" he blurted.

"Hank," Rock said, knowing there was no point in further subterfuge. "Reckon he knew my horse, but he sure as hell shouldn't have tried it left-handed."

Rock saw the comprehension come to the man's round face, followed instantly by a breathless fear.

"You!" he gasped.

"Yeah," Rock said. "Now you stand hitched, cookie, or you won't be in condition to put another patch on that jigger."

He backed to his horse, watching the man closely although he could see that the cook was too nearly petrified to try anything. Hank evidently had fainted. Rock sheathed his gun as he reached for the reins, then swung into the saddle and had just settled himself when the brown horse threw up his head, his ears pointed back toward the butte. For an instant Rock froze, every sense keyed to a new danger, scanning the brush beyond the corral. He saw a vague movement. Then a rider came into view, a rifle in his hands. Rock recognized Ash Carlton at the same moment that he saw the three men behind him, all of them holding their horses to a walk and approaching with furtive stealth.

With instantaneous reaction, Rock whirled the brown, spinning him around and spurring him into a lunging run. A wild yell went up behind him, followed by the crack of a rifle, and Rock saw the bullet kick splinters out of a porch post. He flashed around the corner of the house, passed Hank and jumped his horse over a small creek. The brown was hitting his stride now, and the sheltering timber was close. Rock was almost to the fringe of the trees when he saw the riders spilling down off the ridge directly ahead of him. At least six of them, and they saw him at the same time. Guns blasted, and Rock swerved the brown down the valley, angling toward the timber on the other side and spurring the horse to his utmost.

Rock's first thought had been that they had heard the firing but he knew now that they'd cut his track, then had seen his horse from the butte and had split up, hoping to encircle him. There would be riders coming in behind that far ridge, too, but Rock couldn't see them yet and he dared not stay out in the open. Ash and the three men with him were spurring hard straight down the valley, trying to cut him off; Rock leaned far over his horse's neck, trusting the brown.

He saw the creek flash by, a blur of gray. Then the smooth green floor of the valley was under the horse's flying hoofs, and Rock saw that they'd make the trees a good fifty yards ahead of

Ash. Ash had a revolver in his hand now, and Rock could see smoke blossoming briefly in front of him as he fired. He saw one cowboy pull up and jump off his horse, kneeling to aim his rifle; but the trees were close and Rock flashed into them unscathed.

Immediately the ground started sloping up and it grew rough with rocks, brush, fallen timber. Rock held to his diagonal course, keeping a sharp watch for low hanging limbs and for the riders that he knew were somewhere on his left. The brown was running beautifully, dodging, jumping, maintaining his superb pace as he reached for the top of the ridge. They were still short of the top when Rock glimpsed the other riders, a little behind him but racing their horses in the easier going down the backbone of the ridge.

Rock thought then that he'd never make it, but his only chance was to beat them over this ridge, to outdistance them or lose them in the timber and canyons beyond and thus work his way back toward the rim. If they drove him down into open country, he'd never get away from them.

Then the brown broke into the open on top. Rock had just a glimpse of the men bearing down on him before his horse plunged off the far side; but in that one glimpse he recognized Red Mayberry in the lead, and he was close enough to see the snarl on the flushed face of Dorene's brother. It seemed like an omen to Rock, and his jaw clamped as he faced the tangle of brush and trees ahead of him.

The brown was taking the rough sidehill at a breakneck pace and Rock had to pull him up, knowing he could never keep his feet when he hit the bottom. Lunging and sliding, crashing heedlessly through the brush, they reached the narrow floor of the canyon. Rock turned the horse to go straight across it, but a gun boomed from up the canyon and Rock saw that Red had also reached the bottom, The cowboy had tipped off at the same time he had, deliberately keeping between him and the safety of the rim; and, gritting his teeth in helpless rage, Rock again turned his horse down country.

The brown tried valiantly, but the Bar Circle men were well mounted and gradually, inexorably they forced Rock down toward the desert. The pines thinned, gave way to cedars and junipers. Rocky washes and steep, jagged canyons cut the country, every one a hazard. The hot wind of the chase dried the sweat that was pouring out of Rock's body, tightened his face until it felt like leather. Froth from the brown's mouth was splattering him, drying stiff, and he wondered whether those other horses were beginning to labor.

He saw the break of the canyon coming, and he turned for a swift look behind him. He had distanced Ash and his men, putting them beyond effective rifle range. He had gained a little on Red, too. He glimpsed the cowboy topping a ridge above and behind him, and he turned grimly back to face the canyon. If it angled off away from Red, he would turn up it in a last desperate break.

It did, he saw instantly, and he swerved the brown, throwing one glance at the dark promise of the mountains before losing them from view. The slope was steep, covered with low brush and littered with rocks. The brown took it in stride, plunging for the bottom as if he felt the renewed hope of his rider. He was almost down when something—bush or rock—snagged his feet from under him.

Rock felt the terrible lurch, felt the bottom drop out of his stomach. Then he was being catapulted head first down the last of the slope. He saw the rocky ground coming and threw up his arm, ducking his head and trying to twist to take the fall on his shoulder. He lit with a jarring impact and his body flipped with a force that threw him on, rolling and bounding, toward the bottom of the canyon. Blindly he groped for something to hang onto, to stop his headlong plunge; but a blow struck his forehead, exploding in his brain, and he lost track of his arms. Then something slammed with terrific force into his chest, and everything seemed to stop except his whirling, spinning head.

For a time he made no effort to move, his body completely lost to him. Then a dull sense of urgency crept into him, prodding him. He had to get up, although he couldn't remember why. He opened his eyes, wondering where he was, staring vaguely at the big gray rock that loomed right before his face. He realized that it was pressing into his chest and stomach, that his legs were somewhere on the other side of it; and he thought, That's a damn fool thing to do, wrap yourself around a rock.

He could hear a rumbling in the ground now, working its way through the roar in his head, and his first thought was of a stampede. He struggled up onto his elbows, trying to find his legs, trying to get that damn rock out of his middle. He managed to get his head off the ground and saw his horse, lathered and heaving, standing in the bottom of the canyon. Then he saw riders coming toward him along the floor of the canyon, their horses stretched into a killing run. There were other riders coming down the slope above him, too. He could hear them sliding and crashing, but it was the group in the canyon that held his hazy attention. The rider in the lead had lost his hat, and that red hair, flaming in the sunlight, looked vaguely familiar.

They were close now, close enough for him to see the guns glinting in their hands. It hit Rock all at once, and with a thick curse he shoved away from the rock, fumbling for his gun. His holster was empty. With an icy hand suddenly clutching at his stomach, he grabbed at the rock, pulling himself to his knees. A blind dizziness swept over him, toppling him sideways, but still he groped for the gun in his belt. His shirt had been torn open and the butt was there, hard and familiar in his curling fingers. He got it out, but before he could lift it a smothering weight drove into him. The next instant the gun was wrenched away from him and hard hands closed over his arms to pull him to his feet.

Nausea was writhing in him. For a moment he couldn't locate his legs and sagged heavily in the grip of the men holding him. Then he found them and planted them wide-braced against the ground, lifting his head to stare blearily at the men around him. Their faces were swirling, but one face, flushed and snarling, was directly in front of him. Rock's vision cleared, and he recognized Red Mayberry at the same time that he saw the gun in his hand. It was lifting, centering on his stomach, and the sight jolted Rock wide awake. Instinctively he wrenched at the hands holding him, struggling to free himself. He couldn't do it, and the realization stung him to cold pride. With his fists impotently doubled, he squared back and quit, his head up in scornful defiance.

Red eared back the hammer but before he could fire Ash jumped at him, shoving his arm down. The gun exploded, and Rock felt the jar of the bullet beside his foot. Then Ash and another cowboy were struggling with Red, trying to hold him while Rock watched, unbreathing. Ash got the gun and the cowboy pinned Red's arms behind him, but the redhead wouldn't give up.

"Let me go," he gritted, writhing and twisting. "I'll kill him!"

"Sure, we'll kill him," Ash said grimly, "but not that easy. You simmer down now."

With that he turned, and Rock felt a chilling shock at the light in his eyes. Hungrily he looked Rock over, his glance sliding down over him and then lifting again to linger on his throat. Rock read that look for what it meant and something knotted up in his chest, cutting off his breath. Ash smiled, a twisting of his lips that was as icy hard as the light in his eyes.

"Pistol whip a man, will you?" he said.

Then he struck, a swift blow that caught Rock on the jaw and knocked him backward. His brain seemed to explode again, and for what seemed an eternity he felt as if his arms were being pulled out of their sockets and his neck was breaking. Then they jerked him up and he got his head forward, letting it hang until the ground quit pitching under his eyes. He knew that Ash was watching him, waiting eagerly for some sign of weakness and fear, and he forced his head up, forced his legs to stiffen.

Ash was still smiling, but his expression had hardened to one of stark cruelty. Rock read the desire to torture even before Ash started taunting him.

"You're long-legged enough," he said softly, "to do a good job of kicking."

Rock didn't answer, but a growl of approval went up from the cowboys. Red's voice broke through it, thick and hot.

"Let go of me, damn you! I'll watch him swing."

Dread settled over Rock, cold and sickening. He was aware of the blood running down his face from a cut over his temple, aware of the weakness that still put a tremor in his muscles. He was licked and he knew it, but he managed to keep his gaze steady on Ash, clamping his teeth against the futile hatred that writhed in him.

Ash was in no hurry, savoring this moment, gloating over it. He didn't take his eyes off Rock as he returned Red's gun and asked, "How come you were so far up country, Red?"

"I know this canyon and figured he'd turn up it. I was hoping to get a shot at him as he went past."

"You know this canyon," Ash murmured, with that hungry gaze still on Rock. "Know of a good tree in it?"

"You're damned right," Red said, with a deadly satisfaction. "There's a big old oak down here just a little ways."

"And that," said Ash, "is where Rock Kendall goes to hell."

He smiled again, a mockery that roused all of the flaming wrath Rock had nursed for the past three years. He was aware of the hands on his arms, fingers biting into his muscles. He knew he couldn't do it but with sudden, uncontrollable passion, he tried. Throwing himself violently to the side, he jerked his right hand free and smashed it into the nearest face on his left. The man let go of him, jerking back, and Rock wrenched away from grabbing hands. Savagely he lunged at Ash, relishing the wild fear that leaped into the man's face. He reached for him, got his hands on him, but his strength had not returned and his legs buckled. He stumbled hard, fighting to hang onto Ash, to drag him down. He couldn't do it. Ash whirled, throwing him off, and he had barely hit the ground when someone landed on his back, flattening him out. The next instant, his arms were jerked behind him and he felt the bite of a rope around his wrists.

Rock let himself go, closing his eyes against the certainty that he was going to hang. He wasn't afraid to die, had expected to meet his death ar any moment during the past three years; but the thought of hanging, disgraced and degraded, ate into the very soul of him. The searing desire to take Ash with him in death slowly burned itself out, leaving him cold and utterly desolate.

He offered no further resistance as they pulled him to his feet and boosted him into his saddle. Then they started down the canyon, Ash on one side of him and Red on the other, his rope in his hand and swinging suggestively. Rock was aware that both men were watching him narrowly. He felt as if his insides were shriveling, but he kept his eyes riveted straight ahead of him, kept his head up. They'd get no satisfaction except the pleasure of seeing him die.

They rounded a bend and the tree loomed close ahead, one big limb reaching out high and sturdy. Rock glanced at it only once and did not look up as they led his horse under it and stopped. He heard the whir of Red's rope. Then the honda was dangling in front of him and Ash was reaching for it, working open the noose with tantalizing slowness.

Rock pulled in a tight, painful breath and held it, wondering how long it would take. They'd spook the horse out from under him. Then—a thought, dreary and tormenting, crossed his mind. His dream of a range safe for women and kids had been short-lived, and he wondered how soon Kathy would find another Rock Kendall to do the job.

Ash was smiling again, the smile broadening into a grin of satanic pleasure as he toyed with the rope.

"I'm curious," he said, with a hard amusement. "I sure never expected you to walk right into our hands. What were you doing at the ranch, anyway?"

Rock looked at him, despising him, remembering three years of hell. He curled his lip and said acidly, "I was looking for a picture of Dorene."

Ash's eyes flared. Then, with one savage jerk, he had widened the loop and was urging his horse in closer, crowding up within easy reach of Rock's neck.

# CHAPTER ELEVEN

Rock's heart was hammering, pounding against his ribs and against his temples in a dull roar; and he wasn't sure that it was more than his heart until he heard the excited shout up the canyon. Then he knew that it *had* been partly the pound of horses' hoofs.

Ash flashed a startled look up the canyon, then stood up in his stirrups and lifted the noose with swift, vicious intent. But a yell, flat and authoritative, rang in Rock's ears.

"Hold it! *Ash!* I'll plug you!"

Rock's nerves jumped as he recognized Lackey's voice. Then a tremor of relief shot through him. The next moment the old lawman was beside him, gun in hand, and members of the posse were ringing the cowboys.

"I figured something like this," Lackey said grimly. "I heard that shot awhile ago, then found his hat and gun. Coil that damn rope up and put it away."

An outraged yell went up from the cowboys as they surged forward, their fists raised. The brown horse fidgeted nervously, and Rock wondered with something akin to panic whether Lackey could stop this now. He watched with a chill apprehension as the big lawman stood in his stirrups, brandishing his gun and letting out a roar that brought some measure of silence.

"Back up!"

"Lackey, you keep out of this," Ash said hotly. "We caught him and, by God, we're going to hang him!"

"You ain't gonna do any such damn thing," Lackey shot back. "I'm taking charge of this man."

"But, damn it, we've got a right to him. He's killed three of our men!"

"Sure, and I'd like to see him swing just as much as you would."

"Then get out of the way," Red burst out savagely.

"Not so fast, young feller." Lackey's voice was grimly determined. "I savvy how you feel and I'm not blaming you, but I reckon there's a lot of folks down in Texas—your sister's friends—that feel pretty much the same way. They're entitled to get in on the pleasure of stringin' him up."

"And I guess we ain't," a cowboy said heatedly. "Maybe some of those fellers was lookin' at him, but Jud shore wasn't!"

A concerted, angry growl backed up his statement, and Ash spoke with urgent force.

"Let us finish it now, Lackey. You know the man's dangerous. He might get away and—"

"He won't," Lackey interrupted bluntly. "He ain't goin' nowhere except to jail. Now get out of the way."

A number of the cowboys swore viciously, but Ash let go of the rope and it was snapped back over the limb with a furious jerk. Rock pulled in a deep breath, then lowered his head, fighting back a sudden dizziness. He hadn't realized until now how badly his head ached, nor how hard he'd been gritting his teeth. His jaws hurt, and he made an effort to relax, to conserve his strength for what lay ahead.

Someone jammed his hat down onto his head, a rough action that again turned him dizzy. He swayed, and Lackey grabbed his arm to steady him.

"Had the hell knocked out of you, huh?"

"Part of it," Rock admitted, with a faint grin. "But this is the first time I was ever glad to see a sheriff."

"You'll still get the rope," Lackey told him grimly, "and if I wasn't a sheriff, I'd help pull on it." He motioned for one of the possemen to lead Rock's horse and barked gruffly, "Let's go."

The big group got into motion at once, Bar Circle cowboys mingling with the possemen as they rimmed out of the canyon and headed for town far to the north and east. Rock could hear them going over the details of the chase and the capture, but he had no interest in their words. He was looking ahead, to a ride that he knew would be grueling and to a jail from which no one in the world would help him escape.

Ash and Red stuck close to him, and Rock could feel the bitter disappointment that was riding them. Undoubtedly both men were regretting that Red's bullet had gone into the ground; and Ash, at least, would be nursing a deep-seated worry. Having Rock in jail wouldn't be enough. The man wouldn't be completely at ease until Rock Kendall was dead and buried and he could trample on the grave.

Rock flicked a sidelong glance at him, wondering at his silence. Ash was staring straight ahead of him, his eyes narrowed in thought, a smile, almost tender, playing around his lips. Rock looked at that smile; and suddenly, vividly, he was hearing again the scream that had been torn from the lips of Jud Moore. With the shock of it turning him cold, he looked back at his horse's ears; and he knew then that if he went into that cell he wouldn't live out the night.

Anger rose in Rock, at his helplessness and at the damnable irony of being placed under Ash's gun like a steer at a slaughter house. He was further galled by the thought that if such a murder were committed everyone would assume that Red Mayberry had committed it. Ash would be in the clear, a respected man on his royal way to the governor's chair.

The group was maintaining a steady jog, a pace that was hard on Rock, tied as he was. His arms were getting numb, but the rest of his body ached and burned from the effects of his fall. It was too bad, he thought sourly, that he hadn't broken his damned neck. Then, suddenly, the idea came to him and he glanced sharply at Lackey, riding in tight-lipped silence. The officer was grim and efficient, but Rock knew he was human. If he thought his prisoner was injured, he would slow down; and if they slowed down enough so that it would be dark when they reached town, Rock wouldn't need much of a break.

It was a mighty slim chance, but Rock could see no other. Accordingly, he started feigning a slow-growing weakness. His head bobbed occasionally, although he seemed to be making an effort to keep it up. Gradually he slumped, letting his shoulders droop and bracing his legs less stiffly against the stirrups. He knew when he caught Lackey's attention and he was aware that Ash was watching him suspiciously; but he ignored them, staring listlessly at nothing and breathing with a deep, heavy rhythm. Finally, his chin on his chest and his eyes closed, he swayed in the saddle.

The brown stopped with a suddenness that threw him forward and a quick hand grabbed his arm, pulling him back up.

"Are you hurt?" Lackey demanded.

Rock seemed to have trouble focusing his eyes, but he finally centered them on the sheriff's face, noting the frown of concern. "I'll make it," he said dully.

"Where'd it get you?'

Rock shook his head wearily. "Dunno," he mumbled. "I hit a rock."

"Where?"

Again Rock shook his head, not answering, and a cowboy helpfully supplied the information.

"He was wrapped plumb around a rock when I first saw him, and he must have been shore travelin' when he hit it."

"Prob'ly busted him up inside," someone suggested, without sympathy.

"Unless he's faking."

This from Ash prompted Rock to straighten, although he did it with an obvious effort. He squared his shoulders and lifted his head, holding his breath for a moment as if in great pain. "I'm all right," he said then, coldly. "Let's go."

Such evidence that he did not expect their sympathy had a telling effect.

"We better take it slower," Lackey said uneasily. "Anybody got a canteen?"

The drink was stimulating to Rock, bolstering his strength, but he didn't show it. Rather, as the day wore along he seemed to grow constantly weaker. Several times he would have fallen if someone hadn't grabbed him, and Lackey delegated two men to ride beside him, keeping him on the horse. Progress was necessarily slow, and Red chafed at the delay.

"Hell," he said in angry disgust. "Tie him on the damn thing and let's go on to town."

"We'll get there," Lackey said, but he didn't sound sure of it and that in itself was encouraging to Rock.

Even Ash seemed finally convinced that the injuries were genuine, and Rock played it to the limit. By early dark, with the lights of town showing ahead, he appeared to be barely conscious, his head rolling loosely with the movements of his horse. His arms were paining maddeningly, their circulation partially restored by the jostling of the two men holding him; but a wild hope was growing in him. He'd soon know ....

Black night had fallen by the time they pulled up in front of the sheriff's office. Rock could hear boots thudding against the ground, gear rattling as horses shook themselves; but he kept his head lowered, showing no interest in his surroundings.

"Get the lamp lit, Benson," Lackey ordered curtly. "White, you go for the doc. We'll get him in onto the bunk."

Several hands reached for Rock and he slid loosely into them, letting himself go. His hat was knocked off and his left leg, uncaught, hit the ground hard. Rock roused himself then, opening his eyes and struggling to get his legs under him. It wouldn't do for them to carry him, and he knew they wouldn't if they thought he could walk at all. They pulled him up, holding him a moment while he shook his head and gasped for breath. Then, staggering blindly, tripping at the walk and again at the threshold, Rock allowed himself to be led into the lighted office.

His heart was hammering wildly and his breath was coming hard and fast, which would appear natural enough under the circumstances. He was aware that the men were crowding in behind him, silent and curious, and that suited him perfectly. If his chance came, he wanted them inside. He lifted his head only once, his eyes half closed and veiled. Then he let it drop again, but he had seen the door to the cell yawning wide at the back of the room—and he had judged the distance to the dusty window on the left.

Just beyond the desk, Lackey, who was leading the way, turned and stopped.

"Let's get that rope off of him," he suggested.

Rock's blood leaped but he forced himself to remain limber, sagging heavily into the man on his right. He felt Lackey fumbling at the knots and he rolled his head drunkenly, then let it drop again. Less than ten feet to the window and only two men in his way, the man who was holding him and Ash Carlton, watching attentively.

The rope loosened, fell away, and Rock exploded into action. Jerking away from the man into whom he was leaning, he rammed his shoulder hard into the fellow's chest, knocking him back and breaking his grip. He whirled, again using his shoulder on the startled man who was still trying to hold him. His arms were heavy, his hands swollen, but he didn't rely on them. As the first surprised yell went up, he wrenched free and lunged for the window, smashing head down into Ash. The man went spinning and Rock, his arms thrown over his face, dove headlong through the glass.

The crash of the window was all but lost in the mad roar that went up inside the building. Rock lit on his hands, rolled on his shoulder and came to his feet running as the first shots blasted out behind him. In an instant he was out of the patch of light, legging it for the horses standing out front. He didn't know how many men remained with them, but it didn't matter. If he were going to get away, he had to have a horse.

As he came abreast of the corner of the building, a gun exploded almost in his face. Without slackening his pace, Rock charged into the man holding it, knocking him away and ducking low as he plunged for the dark mass of horses in the street. He had just a glimpse of the jam of yelling, swearing men in the doorway, of the flashes of their guns. Then, with the angry whine of bullets seemingly all around him, he reached the frightened, snorting horses and threw himself into the first saddle that came to his hand.

The horse jumped away, ramming perilously into other animals as he fought to get out of there. Rock leaned far over his neck, fumbling for the dragging reins, swearing at his stiff, swollen fingers. He was spurring the horse mercilessly even before he got them, and the animal was lunging ahead, kicking and striking. Then they were in the clear and the horse jumped into a run.

It was only a hundred feet to the corner, and Rock was relishing a fierce exultation when the horse staggered, came dangerously near going down. Rock hauled him up and spurred him on, knowing he'd been hard hit. The horse rounded the corner, still running valiantly; but Rock could hear the hard pound of hoofs coming behind him and a chill apprehension settled over him. If those men got their hands on him again now, nothing on God's earth could keep them from stringing him up to the nearest telegraph pole.

He dodged into an alley, cut between buildings and came into the main road leading south. He was riding with a tight rein, pulling the horse out of his frequent stumbles, but he had not covered two blocks when he felt the animal's stride breaking. He was starting to falter, badly, and Rock knew he'd never get away on him. As if in echo to his own bleak thought, he heard the bellow of Lackey's voice.

"Scatter out and watch close! That horse won't go far!"

Despair edged into Rock, and he swore viciously. Then the Nash house loomed on his left, the kitchen window glowing with a bright cheerfulness. It seemed like an invitation to Rock. He was coldly aware of the woman's feelings toward Rock Kendall and he knew the chance he was taking, but it was the only chance left to him.

He twisted for one look behind him, but he could see nothing in the darkness. Knotting the reins around the saddle horn, he spurred the horse into a final burst of speed and quit him. He lit on his feet, staggering to keep his balance. Then, ducking low, he made a run for the front door and let himself into the unlighted living room.

He closed the door swiftly behind him, pausing to listen. He could hear nothing except the pound of his own heart, the roar of blood in his head, and he turned toward the kitchen, covering the distance with long tight strides. He stopped in the doorway, seeing Mrs. Nash in the middle of the room, evidently on her way to see who had entered.

She gasped at sight of him and stopped short, staring wide-eyed. Only then did Rock realize what a wild figure he must make. Hatless, with his shirt torn open and the right side of his face and neck stiff with dried blood, he must have displayed all the desperation he felt.

A bunch of horses thundered past out in the street, and Rock clenched his fists, wondering how to tell her. She saw the grip of his tension and stepped toward him hesitantly.

"What's happened? Is someone after you?"

"Yes, ma'am." Rock pulled in a deep breath, then looked her squarely in the eye. "I'm Rock Kendall, Mrs. Nash."

"Rock Kendall!" she gasped. *"You?"*

"Yes, ma'am."

The color drained out of her face, but Rock divined that it was from shock rather than fear and he went on deliberately.

"What I told you the other evening was the truth. I *didn't* kill that woman. I was framed for it, and I've been trying to get to Ash to make him admit it. I ran into the Bar Circle outfit this morning and got caught. I got away from 'em at the jail, but my horse was hit and—"

He broke off as an exultant yell sounded a short way down the street. He knew what it meant, and he looked back at the woman with a tightening urgency.

"They've found the horse," he said. "They'll be coming back in a minute."

She took a quick step toward him, then stopped, clasping her hands to stop their trembling. "What—will they do to you? Send you—"

"They'll send me to hell on the end of a rope," Rock interrupted, his voice breaking into harshness. "They'd have lynched me this morning if Lackey hadn't showed up, but he couldn't stop them now."

He could hear the horses coming back now, scattered, moving slowly. Mrs. Nash heard them, too, and she flashed a frightened look over her shoulder. Then she moved quickly up to Rock, her hands lifted but not touching him as her eyes played frantically over his face. He could see the uncertainty and indecision that were racking her, and he spoke quietly.

"It's up to you, Mother Nash. I've nothing to offer except my word, and if you can't believe me I'll get out of here."

"I don't know," she whispered wildly. "I can't believe—"

The clang of a horse's hoof against stone sounded directly beside the house. Mrs. Nash jumped, and her fingers reached out to touch Rock's throat in an instinctive gesture of horror. The next moment she had shoved him back out of the doorway and was grabbing his hand as she went by him. Her hand was as cold as ice, but the firm grip of her fingers was as warming as a hot drink to Rock.

Swiftly she led him into a front bedroom. It was very dark and Rock could make out the furniture only vaguely, but he guessed that it was her own private room. She swung open a closet door and motioned him inside just as a heavy knock sounded from the kitchen.

"God bless you, Mother!" Rock breathed.

Then the door closed behind him, leaving him in pitch darkness. He heard the click of a key, then the woman's heavy steps receding. Rock felt for the wall and slid down to a sitting position, suddenly aware that his legs were trembling. He sleeved sweat from his face, then froze as voices sounded in the kitchen. He couldn't distinguish the words, but he felt the vibration in the floor as men moved into the house.

He marked their progress into the living room, other bedrooms. They were searching every room in the house, and he knew they'd be doing a thorough job of it. He sat rigidly still, hardly breathing, wondering how Mrs. Nash would manage it. He heard her voice, strained and excited.

"For heaven's sake, look everywhere. I want to *know* that man isn't in here!"

"We're lookin'," someone answered grimly, and Rock heard the bedroom door swing open.

A dim ray of light showed under the door to the closet, and Rock watched it, listening to the steps approaching. The knob rattled suddenly, hitting his nerves. Then a man's voice spoke gruffly.

"Where's the key to this door?"

"In my pocket," Mrs. Nash answered. There was a pause, then, "No, it isn't either. I must have put it up in the cupboard again."

"You keep it locked?"

"Oh, yes. I've got my valuables in there."

"Well, if you keep it locked all the time, it's a cinch he ain't in there. You better lock the rest of your house, too, Mrs. Nash."

"Don't think I won't," she retorted. "You men are the last ones that are going to get in this house on *this* night."

Rock heard the men leave, heard the front door shut emphatically behind them. Then for several moments he waited, listening as Mrs. Nash moved around the house, evidently checking windows and pulling shades. Finally she came back into the bedroom, and Rock shoved to his feet. As the door swung open, he found that, after the total blackness of the closet, the bedroom seemed quite light. Light enough for him to see Mrs. Nash's features clearly.

Rock stepped out slowly, lifting his hands to her shoulders and looking down at her with a gratitude that made him humble. "I don't know how to thank you, Mother Nash."

Uncertainty clouded her eyes. "I hope I haven't done the wrong thing," she said nervously, "but I couldn't bear to see them hang you."

"You haven't done the wrong thing," Rock told her. "Mother Nash, you know what I told you the other night about the rustlers?"

"Yes," she said, watching him anxiously. "I've been thinking about that."

"Then you know who the leader is!"

"Well, I—" She hesitated, evidently not wanting to believe it. "Rock, are you sure?"

"Positive," he said forcefully, "and with any kind of luck I'll prove it."

"It seems awful," she said, shaking her head. "Kathy's fond of him."

"Kathy," said Rock, "is beginning to have her doubts, too."

"Kathy?" Mrs. Nash looked up, startled. "You know her?"

"I'm workin' for her." Rock could not restrain a grin at the woman's expression. "She doesn't know who I am, of course, but she knows I'm after these rustlers. And she's backin' me."

Mrs. Nash's mouth had fallen open at the first of his statement, and it remained open for several moments afterward. Then she lifted her hands to her hips and eyed him up and down in utter amazement. "Well!" she exclaimed. "If you're not absolutely the damnedest man! You come out here in the kitchen and tell me all about it, young feller, while I fix that crazy head of yours and get you something to eat."

The woman did a quick, careful job of bandaging the cut on his head. Then she prepared a hurried meal while Rock relaxed with a cigarette and gave her the information she desired. She did not interrupt him, but the shrewd, speculative gleam that crept into her eyes as he spoke of Kathy made him acutely uncomfortable.

"Soon as I've eaten," he finished, "I'll see if I can scare up a horse and gun and head back out there."

"I'll get your horse," she said surprisingly, "and your guns, too, soon as those hotheads cool off and go to bed."

"Oh, no!" Rock protested. "I'll—"

"You," she said, "are going to bed. I'll wake you up when you got something to travel on."

Argument, he found, was useless and when his meal was finished he dropped on the bed and went out as if someone had slugged him. It was well after midnight when the snort of a horse brought him up. Swiftly he unlocked the kitchen door and stepped out, looking beyond Mrs. Nash to the dark outline of the Morgan. Then he looked back at the pale oval of the woman's face, loving her in that moment as he couldn't remember ever having loved his own mother.

"Any trouble?" he asked quickly.

"Not a bit. Like I figured, they rammed around, pawing the air until they decided you'd got hold of another horse and skedaddled. Then they all went home. I found your horse in Lackey's barn. Your guns were in his office and they'd locked it, but they hadn't boarded up that window you went through. That was the only hard part, climbing through that blasted window."

"You sure nobody saw you?"

"Plumb sure. Here's your hat and you better put it on quick. That white bandage shows up like a flag." She handed it to him and added, "And your guns."

Rock took them and slid them away, feeling the surge of confidence that came with being armed again. And just a few short hours ago he had thought he was licked! He put his hands once more on the woman's shoulders, at a loss for words.

"Most folks," Mrs. Nash said, matter-of-factly, "would figure I've done a terrible thing. But I can't help liking you, Rock, and I can't help believing you."

Impulsively, Rock leaned to kiss her on the forehead. "I'll tell you one thing," he said softly. "If I *was* the kind of man they think I am, I couldn't be again, after tonight."

"My boy," she whispered, and squeezed his arms. "Good luck!"

Rock rode out of town toward the east, sticking to the main-traveled road where his tracks would be inconspicuous. His impulse was to head straight back for the brakes to press for the proof he needed, but he knew that country wouldn't be safe. Every available man would be riding into it in the morning, and the brown horse was tired. He'd been fed and he seemed willing to travel, but Rock could feel the heavy fatigue dragging at his muscles.

"Been a hell of a day, hasn't it, old boy?" he said, resting his hand briefly on the stiff-dried neck.

Never had he felt more keenly the bond between himself and this brown Morgan. This was not the first time the horse had given everything he had in trying to get his rider out of a corner.

Rock pulled up in a secluded canyon at dawn, leaving the horse on good grass and water while he climbed back to the rim with his rifle. He was bone-tired himself, but their progress during the night had been slow and they were still dangerously close to town. However, he saw only three riders during the day, and they were far to the south of him, angling toward the mountains. They've all gone south, he thought grimly, and they won't give it up this time.

At sundown he moved on and rode out the night, circling wide before swinging toward the south and again bushing up during the daylight hours. A feeling of urgency pressed on him, but he knew that he would only be inviting destruction if he went back into the hornet's nest he had stirred up with either a tired horse or a tired body. He could only hope that Ash had no more messenger boys who would tear up the foundation he had laid with the Ballards.

Four times during the following days he spotted groups of riders but he deftly avoided them, making his way with slow care back to the rim and down into the sheltering brakes. It seemed like weeks since he had held the repentant Rita in his arms, and he wondered how she would receive him this time. No telling, he thought narrowly; but he found that any feeling of bitterness he had held toward her had vanished. She couldn't help her calloused nature and it was, in fact, no more hardened than his had been. The girl had never had a chance. Actually, he thought, she and Kathy Sinclair wanted the same thing—an end to these turbulent times—and maybe he had the means to that end in his hip pocket.

It was nearing sunset of a hot, windless day when Rock finally rode back into the Ballard clearing, his feeling of keen anticipation tempered by a cool wariness. However, the place had a calm, peaceful look about it, with a lazy smoke spiraling up from the chimney of the main cabin. Rock could see Tonto out at the corral, nailing a pole into place, and the measured clang of his hammer was somehow reassuring. Rock kept a sharp watch on the windows of the cabin as he rode up to the porch, but he saw nothing of Rita or her brothers.

The door to the men's cabin was wide open. The other door was closed, but the odor of cooking food was further reassuring to Rock. He dismounted and stepped up onto the porch, glancing through the open doorway and seeing no one. As he turned toward the main cabin, he noticed the two saddled horses grazing just beyond, reins dragging. He recognized the animals and wondered with a quick curiosity where Cherry and Tonto had been—or where they were going. The horses had not been hard-ridden. Maybe, he thought, he was just in time for something.

As he stepped up to the door and lifted his hand to knock, he heard the faint creak of a board behind him. He spun, instinctively reaching for his gun, and he saw Buck Ballard step from behind that open door with his gun already leveled.

# CHAPTER TWELVE

Rock threw himself, with the momentum of his spin, just as Ballard fired. The slug burned his arm but didn't hinder his lightning-quick draw. He fired before he hit the floor, twice, and saw both bullets take Ballard in the chest. The man dropped his gun and grabbed at the edge of the door, his eyes tight shut and his face twisted in a grimace of agony.

Rock tried to catch his weight on his left hand, but the force of his motion was too great and he crashed down on his side. The door slammed shut, and Rock heard Ballard fall against it, knocking the latch down into place. The man went on down with a heavy, muffled thud and Rock lunged to his feet, looking for Tonto. He couldn't find him and he whirled toward his horse just as a rifle cracked from out in the stump-dotted field. The horse shied violently, evidently nicked by the bullet, and with a wild snort he plunged away.

Then a second rifle cracked spitefully from the corral and Rock, caught in a deadly crossfire, threw himself at the door to the main cabin. He grabbed the knob and slammed his shoulder against the door, but it didn't budge. A slug splintered the wood right in front of his face and another drove into the casing behind him. With a desperate fury, Rock jumped for the far edge of the porch. A bullet clipped his boot heel, knocking his leg out from under him and sending him sprawling. He rolled off the edge of the porch, caught a glimpse of Tonto lying flat behind the bars of the corral and slammed three quick shots at him. He knew he missed, but the man ducked his head, cowering, and with that much of a respite Rock came to his feet and made a run for the two horses. One of them shied away from him but he caught the other, Tonto's dun, flung himself into the saddle and made a wild break for the timber.

He made it, shooting into the trees and catching one last glimpse of Tonto, rifle in hand, running toward the cabin. They were coming after him, then, and Rock swore as he realized there was no rifle on Tonto's saddle. He knew now, he thought savagely, where Tonto and Cherry had been—watching the trails for his approach. His delay in getting back to the brakes had given Ash time to get his message through, and Rock wondered with a quick-flaming wrath whether Rita was in on this plot. He wondered, too, whether there were other Bar Circle cowboys involved in this or whether Ash had come down himself. He would have had plenty of opportunity, helping the law as he was in its search for Rock Kendall.

The dun was a long-legged horse with a free stride and a willingness to run, and Rock kept him at it, dodging through the trees along the creek for a mile before turning up a low, timbered ridge. At the crest of it, he pulled up to scan his back trail, wondering how much of a start he had on them. His answer was the zing of a rifle bullet. He saw them, then, just at the foot of the ridge, Cherry in the lead and Tonto following on Rock's own brown horse. The sight filled him with a new rage, and he swore with vicious feeling as he spurred the dun off the far side of the ridge.

Timber here was thicker, and Rock dropped only halfway down the ridge before turning along it toward the east. He covered a fast two miles before climbing again to the top of the ridge, intending to pull up for a look back. Before he could do it, a bullet struck a rock directly ahead of him and screamed off into space; and Rock put the dun over the ridge without pause.

His anger now was tempered by the grim realization that Cherry Ballard was not going to be an easy man to shake off the trail. The man was more Indian than white and could apparently read sign without slackening his pace. Moreover, now he would be driven by more than his orders from Ash. He would be wanting revenge for his dead brother, and the thought of being knocked off his horse and caught alive by the black-eyed breed gave Rock a bad moment.

Briefly he considered laying for them, trying to fight it out; but he knew those two rifles would lick him and he kept going, crowding the dun down the slope. Just before he reached the thick brush along the creek, the rifle spoke again, flat and sharp. Then he was jumping the horse through the water to the flat ground beyond, turning up the valley and spurring into a hard run. He came into the road to Skeleton Creek, followed it almost to the town, then again crossed the creek and turned up the ridge.

He noted the buildings, looking drab and hungry in the small clearing. The sun was gone from there although it still shone, bright and colorful, on the upper walls of the rim. Rock saw nothing of the men trailing him and was thinking he had at least put himself out of rifle range when a bullet passed so close to his face that he instinctively ducked. Then he saw Tonto on top of the ridge less than a hundred yards away, his rifle leveled for another shot.

With a startled curse, Rock jumped the dun back down the slope. He hadn't seen Cherry, which meant that the breed was still on his trail and would undoubtedly stay on it while Tonto, better mounted, would see to it that he got no chance to cut back into rougher country. Fresh wrath flooded through Rock at the thought that they were using his own horse against him. As he reached the floor of the valley, he caught sight of Cherry coming fast and again he spurred the dun to his utmost. He was soon to find that he could not lose that Indian tracker, nor could he outdistance Tonto. Even with the dun on level ground and the brown fighting the brush and rocks of the slopes, the black-headed outlaw was constantly flanking him. Gradually, inexorably, their rifles were crowding him toward the rim. The men knew of the passes up there, and it was evident to Rock that they were determined either to get him or have him got.

Finally he had no other recourse. The last of the fading daylight found him climbing out somewhere beyond the spot where the stolen cattle had gone over the rim, in country that was strange to him but probably familiar to Cherry. Rock had a grim hunch that Cherry Ballard would stay on that trail if he had to follow it on his hands and knees.

"Damn Indian!" he gritted and wondered again where Rita stood in this.

He gained the top of the rim and turned back toward the west, keeping a sharp watch for fires that would mark the camps of possemen. He saw none and covered several miles before coming on a spring and stopping to give the dun a much-needed rest. The horse was game but he just didn't have it, nor was there any affection in him. Rock felt a keen sense of loneliness as he put a rope on this strange animal and put him out to graze. He missed the friendly nuzzling of the brown but he would not miss it for long. He'd get that horse back tomorrow.

He spent a dreary night, hungry, tired, not daring to light a fire, tormented by his thoughts. He had had the game in his hands, or so he had dared hope, but Ash had once more beaten him. Now not even the brakes were safe for him. This rim certainly wasn't safe and any movement here in daylight would be extremely dangerous; but with the relentless Cherry Ballard behind him and with the driving desire to retrieve his horse and outfit, Rock had to have a rifle and a fresh horse. He knew of only one place to get them.

If, indeed, he could get them there. Kathy Sinclair might know by now who it was who had stolen that kiss from her. Rock grew strangely empty at the thought that she might be waiting for him with a cocked gun.

Nevertheless, with the coming of morning, he oriented himself and set out for Kathy's ranch. As he had suspected, the dun had not responded like the brown Morgan to a few hours' rest and was still tired. Rock held him to a walk as he headed away from the rim, riding with every sense keenly alert. If he met a posse now, he would be in a bad way.

He was grimly aware, as he progressed, of the number of fresh horse tracks showing everywhere. Lackey evidently was keeping his men on the move and was undoubtedly being helped by cowboys from both Triple X and Bar Circle. However, Rock saw no one. He came in behind the Clear Springs ranch without incident and paused only long enough to note that there were only a few horses in the corral, which would indicate that the men were gone. Then he rode down.

As he swung to the ground, Kathy stepped out the back door and came quickly off the porch, a smile of eager welcome on her face. She was dressed as Rock had first seen her, in men's riding clothes, boots, a soft shirt; her head was bare, her hair shining gloriously in the sunlight.

"Howdy, stranger," she said gaily, extending her hand. " 'Bout decided you'd got lost."

There was a brightness about her this morning, a vibrant sparkle that was at complete variance with the stricken expression he had last seen on her face. Rock was suddenly confused. He felt the heat of blood in his face as he reached for his hat, then took her hand, struggling to return her greeting.

She had his hand in both of hers, gripping it warmly, but her smile vanished as she saw the fresh scar on his temple.

"You've been hurt!"

"No, it's just—"

He broke off, instantly wary as he saw the man step into the doorway. Kathy let go of his hand and turned.

"My brother, John," she said quickly, and Rock thought, with a queer hollow feeling, That's why she's so perky. "John, this is Jim Rocklin, that I was telling you about."

John Sinclair stepped forward at once. He was a tall, straight man, inclined to slimness, and he was dressed in the rough clothes of an ordinary working cowhand. Rock took sweeping note of the hang of his gun, his smooth brown face and the weathered wrinkles around his eyes. Then he got a good look into those eyes, the same direct blue gaze that characterized Kathy, and he met the man halfway, his hand extended.

"Glad to know you, Sinclair."

"And I'm glad to know you," John replied with significant emphasis.

His handshake was firm, his grin open and friendly. Rock, quick to form judgments, liked the man on the spot and he felt the other's approval, but he could not immediately free himself from the grip of tension. John Sinclair, he could see, was a man of keen perceptions, experienced on the range, and Rock couldn't help thinking that it wouldn't take him long to figure this out.

"We'd better go in the house," Kathy suggested, with a quick, nervous glance up the slope. "Had breakfast, Jim?"

"No," Rock said, "nor supper, nor lunch. I'm dang near starved."

Kathy laughed gaily, a sound that tingled through Rock and brought an involuntary grin to his face.

"Come on in the house," she ordered. "We can fix that right quick."

"Yeah, come on in, Rocklin," John said warmly, his hand on Rock's shoulder. "I was wishing you'd show up. Kathy near talked an arm off me last night, but I reckon I'd like to have your angle."

He ushered Rock into the kitchen ahead of him and there Rock paused, still tense and ill at ease. Kathy, however, seemed perfectly composed. She poured him a cup of coffee from the pot that was always on the stove and bade him sit down. John sat down opposite him, and Rock, reaching uncomfortably for tobacco, was aware that the man was studying him with a keen interest. He was also aware, vividly, of Kathy's quick, graceful movements as she hastened to prepare his breakfast.

John waited until he had his cigarette lit, then came to the point with a directness that Rock liked.

"I just got in last night, and Kathy sure filled me full of news. She told me how you had this rustling business doped out. Are you sure you're right about that, Rocklin?"

"Positive," Rock said.

"Have you got the proof?"

"No," Rock admitted with reluctance, "I haven't. Been doing a lot of riding. That's why I came in this morning. I need a fresh horse."

"I've got one," John said promptly. "A good one, and he isn't wearing a Triple X brand, either."

Rock nodded. "He'll fill the bill."

"I noticed you were riding a different horse," Kathy spoke up. "I hope nothing happened to that beautiful brown."

"Nothing permanent," Rock said and sincerely hoped she would say no more on that subject. He had a strong hunch that the brown Morgan was becoming almost as familiar a figure as he was himself.

"Nothing new, huh?" John prompted.

Rock shook his head. "Been having a little trouble."

John waited expectantly but Rock let it ride there, not caring to admit that from here on he'd be having more trouble. Getting proof of past raids seemed increasingly difficult, and the rustlers were now too busy chasing him to bother anyone's cattle.

"Well," John said finally, "reckon nobody figured it'd be easy. Dammit, Rocklin, I sure hate to believe that Jud and the Kid were in on that. I knew those men well. I'm not doubting your judgment, understand, but you can't blame Ed for not believing it. I'd sure have trouble believing it of any of my boys."

"Sure," Rock said, feeling his way cautiously. "But if you knew it was true, you'd fire 'em."

"I'd hang 'em," John said flatly, "the damn buzzards. You still watching the Ballards?"

"Trying to," Rock said and grinned ruefully. "They're not too cooperative."

"That's a slippery outfit," John conceded, nodding in quick understanding. "How many men you figure are in that gang?"

"That," said Rock, "has got me stumped. I know of six."

"Besides Jud and the Kid?"

"Including them."

"Not enough," John said bluntly, "to run off that herd the way they did."

"No," Rock admitted, "it isn't. But the way I figure, right now at least, is that Jud and the Kid helped get the herd started. Then the Ballards hired a few of their backwoods friends to help drive 'em to market. I may be figuring wrong, but I can't believe this gang could stay so secret and mysterious if they had very many men in it."

"Yeah," John agreed thoughtfully. "If there were too many, somebody would be sure to talk."

"You going ahead with this next herd?"

"It's on its way," John said, nodding emphatically. "That's the way to build this country, with cattle, and I'll be damned if I'm going to back up. I won't go after any more, though, until things settle down around here."

There was a hard, grim light in his eyes, and Rock suspected that it wasn't the cattle he was thinking of. It was Kathy, alone here at the ranch too much of the time. John's next words bore him out.

"That damn Rock Kendall! Every time I think of Kathy being out here with that wolf running loose, I get the cold shakes."

"Yeah, I can see how you'd feel," Rock said dryly, "but I kinda hope the jigger sticks around awhile. He's the one who tipped me off to Jud and the Kid."

"Yeah, and I can agree with you that he was probably right about Jud, but that's as far as I can go with that skunk. Damn him! He's just trying to ruin Ed, to torture him before he kills him. This country's got enough troubles without having a killer like him running loose in it."

Rock looked down at his hands, feeling a dull familiar ache somewhere inside him.

"Kathy tells me," John went on, "that you think somebody killed Jud to keep him from talking. Got any idea who did it?"

"Yeah," Rock said, his voice suddenly hard. "I know who did it, but I can't prove it."

"Who?" John queried sharply.

"The boss of the outfit."

John was leaning forward with a strained eagerness. "You know who he is?"

"Yes."

"Well, who, for hell's sake?"

Rock glanced at Kathy, who had whirled from the stove and was standing rooted, her lips parted and her eyes filled with apprehension. Rock knew that if he said it she'd believe it now, but he found that he couldn't say it. He looked down at his cigarette and spoke slowly.

"Maybe," he said, "I better wait until I *can* prove it."

John obviously hated to leave it there, but he did not press the point. Kathy brought Rock's breakfast, giving him a queer little smile as she set it before him. Then she took a place at the table, her chin in her hands. Rock was acutely aware of the fact that she was watching him as he started to eat. John smoked in thoughtful silence, respecting his hunger, and Rock made short work of the ham, eggs and potatoes Kathy had cooked.

"You *were* hungry," she commented when he had finished. "Sure you've had enough?"

"Plenty," Rock said with a grin of thanks. "I can go for another week now."

Her eyes sparkled with a high humor as she started to answer him, but John interrupted.

"Kathy tells me," he said grimly, "that Ed caught Kendall the other day."

"Oh?" Rock said in surprise. "They finally got him, huh?"

"Yeah, they got him, but that damn Lackey let him get away!" John shook his head in fierce disgust. "They'll get Kendall, sure, but I hope to God they do it before he kills Ed. He sure is a nice fella."

Rock glanced at Kathy to see that she was struggling with a sudden confusing emotion. Her cheeks were hot, and abruptly she reached out a hand and started worrying the salt shaker around a pattern in the oilcloth. Rock knew she was thinking of his last disturbing visit, and irresistibly he looked at her lips. They were set in a grave line, almost sad. The sight startled Rock, and suddenly he knew that Kathy Sinclair had not voiced the speculations that had upset her that night. Ash Carlton was a friend of hers, and she'd make no condemnation until proof of his guilt was offered.

Rock felt a stab of jealousy, but it wouldn't hold under his awareness that she was just showing the very loyalty that he admired in her. And he was infinitely glad that he had kept his unverifiable information to himself. She'd find out eventually, and it would be better that way.

Abruptly he picked his hat off the floor and stood up. "Reckon I better be going. You got a rifle I can borrow?"

John nodded. "An extra one in the saddle shop. I'll get it for you."

He stood up and Kathy, too, came to her feet. Rock waited, held by an intent light in John's eyes. The man seemed to be debating something but abruptly made up his mind, smiling as he stepped around the table to face Rock.

"Rocklin," he said frankly, "I don't mind saying that if I'd been here I wouldn't have been so quick to take you up on this job. It sounded like a wild idea to me, but I reckon I can see now why Kathy fell for it. I like your looks. The job sure needs doing, and I hope to God you can get it done without getting yourself killed. I'll back you any way I can, and here's my hand on it."

Surprised and pleased beyond expression, Rock took his proffered hand. He flicked a glance at Kathy, saw the proud, happy light in her eyes; he thought that that, if nothing else, would drive him on to win this fight. Confidence was surging up strong in him when he heard the door behind him flung open with jarring suddenness.

Rock broke away from John's grip and turned sharply to see a young, lean-faced cowboy whose brown eyes were snapping with excitement. Rock heard them then, horses moving along the side of the house toward the back, and he felt a quick, cold fury at his own carelessness. Silently he cursed the thoughts and emotions that had held his attention. He couldn't leave now, and if anyone in that group recognized him, he certainly wouldn't stay long.

Then the cowboy caught his breath and blurted, "We've caught Rock Kendall!"

It hit Rock like a sledgehammer and for a moment he could only stare, unbreathing. The shock of it held John and Kathy, too, until John came out of it to slam a fist into his palm.

"You got him!"

"We sure got him," the cowboy said flatly. "Jumped him over here not a mile from the ranch. He claims he ain't Kendall, but he fits the description. Big and black-headed and gray-eyed. And we shot that brown Morgan out from under him."

A pang, as biting as a north wind, cut into Rock and then was gone, leaving him sick.

"The feller that was with him got away," the cowboy added. "Don't know who it was but we let him go, figurin' Kendall was the one that counted. What should we do with him?"

Rock flashed a swift glance at John. The rancher's jaw was corded, his eyes glittering with a hard light, and Rock read the answer before it was voiced.

"I'll show you," John said through his teeth, heading for the back door. "By God, I know what to do with a woman killer!"

Rock stood rooted, suddenly cold all over. He stared blankly at the open doorway as John stalked through it and turned along the porch, the cowboy right behind him. Then, impelled, he moved slowly to the door and stopped, aware that Kathy was edging in beside him.

The group of cowboys had stopped just past the end of the porch, and they split as John strode toward them. Rock saw Tonto sitting on a strange horse, his face ashen, his hands tied behind his back. Evidently he was too stunned by what was happening to notice his own dun horse standing there in the yard or to notice Rock in the doorway.

"What will they do to him?" Kathy whispered.

Rock's answer was as barren as death itself. "Hang him, probably."

He felt the shudder that went through her but he kept his hard gaze on Tonto, fighting the icy passion that gripped him. The man was a rustler and a killer, a sneaking bushwhacker who deserved to meet his death at the end of a cowboy's rope. If he hadn't tried to commit a cowardly murder, he wouldn't have been riding the horse that damned him. Now the big Morgan was dead, and Rock felt a driving, personal hatred toward this man who had ridden him into a bullet trap.

He saw John come to a stop before the prisoner, his hands on his hips as he looked the man over. He heard the urgent run of Tonto's voice, but the words couldn't penetrate the continued hard line of his thought. If word went out that Rock Kendall was dead, it would ease the pressure on him, give him the time he needed to get the proof against Ash. This was a break for him, the best break he'd had. and Rock knew it.

But he knew something else, too, something that he couldn't push out of his mind. Someday, inevitably, the girl quivering beside him would find out who he was, and she would know that he had let an innocent man die in his place. Irresistibly Rock looked down at her. Her face was as white as the prisoner's, her fingers pressed tightly against her lips as she watched in silence. She felt his glance and looked up at him, her eyes wide with a terrible dread; and Rock knew then that he couldn't do it.

He heard John's voice, flat and deadly. "We'll take him down back of the corral."

For one fleeting instant, Rock thought of the tired dun horse and he thought remotely, I'll never get away. Then, as the men stirred to motion, too intent on their prisoner to notice him, he reached out his left arm and swept Kathy back into the kitchen. With the same continuous movement, he pulled both guns and took a long stride away from the door.

"Hold it!"

The men jerked their horses to a halt, and John whirled in startled wonder. He stopped short at sight of the guns in Rock's hands, staring blankly.

"Turn that fella loose," Rock ordered evenly.

A moment longer John stared. Then anger leaped into his eyes and he took a short step forward, his fists clenched. "What's the idea?" he demanded.

"You've got the wrong gent."

"Wrong gent, hell! It's Rock Kendall!"

"Your mistake, Sinclair," Rock said coolly. "I'm Rock Kendall."

"You!"

"Yeah." Rock was bitterly aware of Kathy's presence just inside the doorway and he added in an acrid drawl, "Mr. Rocklin James Kendall, callin' the dance."

Incredulity held John in his tracks, but a cowboy sitting his horse beyond him made an impulsive grab for his gun. Without hesitation Rock shot him, aiming high. The man made a grab for his right shoulder as, his face contorted, he tumbled out of his saddle. With Kathy's gasp knifing into him, Rock swept a challenging gaze over the other men.

"Turn him loose," he repeated in icy tones.

One grizzled rider, less stunned than his companions, moved carefully to obey, reining up beside Tonto and reaching out with deliberate caution to untie his hands. The sudden, deadly efficiency of Rock's action held the others frozen, staring down at their writhing bunkmate but making no move to help him. Rock stood stone still, grimly watchful, but his circumspection did not keep him from noting the look of awed disbelief stamped on Tonto's face.

That wonder, however, did not keep Tonto from bolting the second his hands came free. With desperate haste he leaned to jerk the reins away from the man holding them. Then, without even a glance at Rock, he hauled the horse around and spurred him into a lunging run around the corner of the house.

Moving sideways, Rock stepped guardedly off the porch and backed to the dun, but there he paused. He could sense a change coming over the Triple X men. Their shock was wearing off, giving way to a deadly resolve that this was not finished; and the hunched shoulders and glittering eyes of John Sinclair told Rock that he had to give the tired dun as much head start as possible. It still might not be enough.

"Sinclair," he ordered abruptly, "unbuckle your gunbelt and let it drop." The order was obeyed in grim silence. "Now the rest of you, one at a time, starting on the right."

One by one the gunbelts dropped, and with each one Rock's tension mounted. He could feel the sweat standing on his upper lip, could feel it cold and slippery on the butts of his guns. Out of the corner of his eye he could see Kathy still standing just inside the door, could feel her gaze on him; and he thought, She'll be riding with them when they come after me.

When the last belt had dropped, he ordered the men to dismount and move away from the horses. He sheathed his right gun, wiping his hand on his pants before reaching behind him to get a good grip on the reins.

"You," he ordered then, to the grizzled man who had freed Tonto, "spook those horses out of here."

The cowboy gave him a long, hate-filled stare before sweeping the hat off his head and throwing it at the animals. He accompanied the action with a shrill whoop, then ran at the bunch, waving his arms. With startled snorts, the horses shied away and stampeded, but Rock knew they would only go as far as the corral.

He backed against the dun, holding the one gun still leveled as he slipped the reins over the horse's neck. He felt for the horn and stepped into the saddle without losing the drop. Then, step by step, he backed the horse toward the corner of the house, noticing that the cowboys were flicking calculating glances at their guns, looking beyond to see where their horses had stopped. He was aware that John stood rooted, his fists doubled; but not until he reached the corner did Rock pause to give the young rancher his full attention.

John's eyes were fastened on him in an unswerving glare, and for the first time it really hit Rock that he had probably just sacrificed his last chance. This man who had just shaken his hand and offered to back him in the fight he was making knew now that a man he considered to be pure poison had been hanging around his sister, perhaps making love to her. Rock realized with a strange sick feeling that John Sinclair was now his greatest enemy, and this outfit would take his trail with the full knowledge that he was riding a tired horse and that he had no rifle.

Rock grinned without humor. "I'll no doubt be seeing you gentlemen," he drawled.

Then, with a quick, hard rein, he wheeled the dun and spurred away.

# CHAPTER THIRTEEN

THE DUN horse was still game. He jumped into a run, flashing down the length of the house and sailing over the creek beyond it. Then Rock was swerving him through the scattered pines, dodging and weaving as the first quick shots boomed out behind him. There weren't many guns in on the firing and those few ceased abruptly, which indicated to Rock that their owners were legging it for their horses along with the other men.

He hit the brushy slope beyond the ranch with the dun running hard, and he did not look back until he had gained the top of the ridge. Brush and timber cut off his view and he turned up country, seeing the tracks of Tonto's horse in the ground ahead of him. He lost them in the thick brush and rocks that dotted the ridge and he put his horse off the far side, thinking grimly that if there were no Cherry Ballards in that outfit he might make it.

He cut diagonally across a rough canyon and gained the far ridge with neither a shot nor a yell ringing out behind him. A glance back showed him nothing but a screen of foliage and again Rock turned straight up country, a fierce hope rising in him. If he couldn't see them, they couldn't see him, either; apparently there *weren't* any Cherry Ballards riding for Triple X.

Rock gained the rim without once having glimpsed his pursuers. He turned along it, heading for the nearest trail down, and again he saw Tonto's track. The black-headed outlaw had still been running, nor had he pulled out of his run until he turned down the trail, dipping into a canyon that opened out a little above the Ballard ranch. Rock turned for one last look behind him, seeing nothing except the majestic pines that towered over the rim. As he swung back and reined the dun onto the trail leading down, he wondered with a sudden, sharp loneliness whether he would ever again see that beautiful wild country or the girl who loved it.

Rock hadn't really hoped to elude Triple X this long, but now he turned his thoughts to Tonto and he crowded the dun going down, hoping to overtake the man before he reached the Ballard place. Tonto's gratitude might make him willing to talk, and Rock had the urgent certainty that his time was growing short. They'd been crowding him too hard, from too many sides. And now he had lost his last sanctuary.

He caught no sight of Tonto as he emerged from the canyon, but he stayed on the man's tracks, riding at a stiff trot. He was surprised, on coming to the Skeleton Creek road, to find that Tonto had crossed it, going straight on toward the opposite ridge. Rock hesitated only briefly, wondering; then he kept on, following the tracks over the ridge and into the valley beyond. Tonto had turned along this winding valley, apparently making no effort to kill his tracks but keeping his horse in a hard trot that would put the miles behind him.

With a hard suspicion growing in him, Rock lifted the dun into a lope, keeping a sharp watch both for the tracks and the horse that was making them. He saw nothing of the horse, but he followed the tracks for perhaps two miles along the valley floor, then up a steep, high ridge to the west. At the top he pulled up, seeing where the tracks went on down into the brush and timber of the rough canyon beyond and knowing it was useless to follow them farther on a tired horse.

For several minutes Rock sat motionless, gazing down into that tangled wilderness and fighting a bitter discouragement. He knew now that one brush with the rope had been enough for Tonto. The man was leaving the country, and one more possible witness had passed out of Rock's reach just as surely as if Ash had shot this one in the back, too. That left Cherry—and Rita. At least one of them, and perhaps both, would now kill him quicker than anyone else because of the death of Buck.

With a disheartened sigh, Rock turned and started slowly back toward Skeleton Creek, trying to pick up any significant pieces there might be in this frustrating day. He thought of that business at Clear Springs and knew that it would leak out, however much John might try to cover it up. The range, including Ash Carlton, would very soon find out that Rock Kendall had been working for Kathy Sinclair. Ash at least would guess that Rock had been with her—alone, and he would know that Rock had approached her merely because she was his woman. That would be more than enough to stir his jealousy to an insane pitch and possibly to goad him into the rash action Rock had hoped for. But Rock found that the thought of it now brought him nothing but shame.

It was late afternoon when he emerged from the timber into the drab clearing at Skeleton Creek. The only person in sight was the proprietor of the saloon, leaning in bored idleness in the doorway of his establishment. Rock nodded to him and rode on back to the stable, looking for Jimmy. The boy was not in sight, and Rock swung off to care for the horse himself, wondering which of those cabins back in the brush the kid occupied. He wanted to see Jimmy, and he wanted to ask a favor of him.

Rock was stiff from too many hours in the saddle, and he moved with a cramped awkwardness as he led the dun into the dim interior of the stable. He had just cleared the doorway when he felt rather than saw a movement in the shadows on his left. Rock spun toward it, caught a flashing glimpse of a knife held low and driving in toward his body. Instinctively he flung out his left arm to ward the blow, knocking the knife aside but failing to get a grip on the hand holding it. Then Cherry Ballard smashed into him, staggering him; and he saw the knife, quick and deadly as a striking rattler, come in at him again.

Rock twisted and threw himself against Cherry, grabbing again for that slashing right arm. His fingers closed briefly around muscles as smooth and hard as rubber, but he couldn't hang on. The next instant, while he was still off balance, Cherry grabbed him around the neck and twisted to throw him hard, face down. Cherry kept his grip and fell on top of him; but before he could drive the knife home, Rock lunged up and flung himself over onto his back, pinning the man's arm for one brief moment against the ground. Rock slammed his head back into Cherry's face, hearing the crunch of bone and cartilage, feeling the man's nose flatten out under his skull. Cherry's grip loosened and Rock, wrenching free, rolled away and scrambled to his feet. He'd barely made it when Cherry bounded up and plunged in again, snarling, the eyes in his bloody face glittering with a hellish hatred.

Rock closed with him, grabbing again for that knife arm. He got a good grip on it this time and threw his right arm around the man, wrestling to throw him. He couldn't do it. Tired and stiff as he was, he was no match for the supple Indian. Again he was thrown off his feet, going down solidly on his back; but he kept his grip on Cherry's arm and shoved the knife away from his body as the breed fell on him.

The fall jarred him badly, knocking most of the wind out of him. For a second his sight blurred but he could feel his grip loosening, feel his arm bending as Cherry strained to drive the knife into him. Cold desperation came over Rock. He knew that if that knife ever reached him, weakened him, Cherry would carve him up like a butchered beef. With a sudden, furious lurch, Rock threw the man off him, but he couldn't hold him down and they rolled, kicking and thrashing, across the hard-packed dirt floor.

Rock's head was hammering, his chest bursting; but he was on top when they hit the wall, Cherry's arm twisted above his head. For a fleeting, triumphant moment Rock thought he had him. He'd never heard Cherry speak, but if he could hold out for a few more minutes he'd damn well find out what the man's voice sounded like. Then he felt Cherry double up under him, curling up like a snake before lashing out with both heavy boots. He had the wall at his back for leverage, and Rock was thrown off violently.

He tried to get to his feet, reeling backward, but his shoulder struck the end of a stall and he caromed off. As he was falling, he saw Cherry leap up with a wild, certain rush, the blade of the knife winking wickedly in his hand. Then Rock lit sprawling, his back to Cherry, and knew he could never get up. With a silent curse, he threw himself over and reached for his gun. He saw Cherry looming over him, starting to spring, and lying flat on his back he fired three times as fast as he could pull the trigger. The heavy slugs stopped Cherry as if he'd run into an invisible wall. For a moment he swayed drunkenly, his eyes widening into a blank stare. Then, as a bloody froth appeared on his lips, he crumpled into a loose heap.

Rock rolled over and struggled to a sitting position against the stall, gasping for breath. Cherry hadn't moved and wouldn't again under his own power; but Rock saw that he still clutched the knife, his fingers just now relaxing their convulsive grip. Rock tipped his head back against the stall and closed his eyes, his fury draining out into a queer sense of defeat. He had saved his life, but in doing it he had put still another possible witness against Ash forever out of his reach. And it was entirely probable that Cherry was the last one who had ever taken a rustling order from the man.

Exhausted and sick, Rock was climbing to his feet when he heard a faint movement at the door. He grew rigid, waiting. Then the gray, hard face of the proprietor appeared stealthily around the door casing.

"Cherry?" he called uncertainly.

Rock stepped out of the stall, his gun leveled. The man jerked and then froze, his eyes flicking in panic from Rock to Cherry's limp form and back again.

"Yeah," Rock said harshly. "He had a wreck. Where's the kid?"

"In—in his cabin."

"Which one?"

The man jerked his head toward the brush. "Under the big pine."

"Get out of here," Rock said. "If I see your mug again today, I'll slam a shot at it."

The man disappeared at once and was not in sight when Rock limped out of the building. He caught the dun horse, which had spooked out during the fight, and led him toward the small cabin partially concealed back in the brush. Fatigue put a drag in his steps, and depression weighed on him heavily. Try as he would, he couldn't throw off the feeling that he was about half licked, and he wondered how much longer he could last.

The door to the cabin was closed, and Rock hit it once with his knuckles before opening it and stepping over the threshold. He noted the neatly made bed in the left end of the one room. Then, as he stepped on inside, he saw the boy sitting near the rough board table in the center of the room, and he stopped short. Jimmy was tied to the chair, a red bandanna bound over his mouth, a sick light in his blue eyes. As Rock hesitated, he saw that sick light vanish before an incredulous relief.

Rock swore as he grasped the significance of this. Then he slammed the door and in two long strides reached the boy and pulled the bandanna from his face. Jimmy's lips were white from the pressure, but he tried to grin, looking up at Rock with glad eyes.

"Gee," he whispered, his lips so stiff he could hardly be understood. "I heard those shots and I thought—did you get him?"

"I got him," Rock said grimly. He dug out his knife, thinking with cold anger of the face that he already wanted to slam a bullet into. "Who tied you up like this?"

"Cherry. He saw you come over the ridge awhile ago. I heard 'em talkin'. Thought it was you he was layin' for and I tried to sneak off, but he caught me."

Rock cut the rope, then helped the boy to his feet, holding him; but Jimmy evidently had not been tied long and seemed to be all right. Rock pocketed his knife, looking down at the kid with a growing warmth.

"Would you really have tipped me off?"

"Sure," Jimmy said quickly. Then he hesitated, a frown of uncertainty clouding his eyes. "You're not Rock Kendall, are you?"

The question hit Rock like a hard fist in the stomach, and all at once he felt so tired that nothing seemed to matter. He pulled in a heavy breath and looked down at the floor. "Yeah," he said wearily, "I am, Jimmy."

There was a long moment of silence. With an effort Rock looked up again, expecting to see the hatred his name always aroused, but Jimmy was only staring at him, wide-eyed. And suddenly the boy was fierce.

"I don't care who you are!" he burst out. "I like you, and I still woulda tipped you off!"

An unfamiliar emotion tightened Rock's throat and, unable to speak, he laid a hand on the boy's head. Then impulsively he pulled the kid up against him. For a brief moment he felt those slender arms around his waist, hugging tight, and a loneliness such as he had never known swept over him.

"A couple of mavericks," he murmured and knew then what was the matter with him. Unconsciously during these past days he had been dreaming of a home, of someone to love and to love him, and he realized with a lost, hopeless feeling who that some-one was. It had caught up with him.

Abruptly he swung away, reaching for tobacco. "Do me a favor, Jimmy?"

"Sure," the kid said promptly.

"Know where Clear Springs is?"

"Yeah. I was up there one time with my dad."

Rock turned back slowly, almost reluctantly. "If I was to write a letter to Miss Sinclair, would you take it up there this evening?"

"You betcha," Jimmy said, bobbing his head eagerly. "Cherry left his horse out here in the shed. You want somethin' to write on?"

"Yeah," Rock said and sighed miserably. "Dammit!"

He knew it was not going to be easy, but he hadn't expected it to be so utterly impossible. Long after Jimmy had gone out to take care of his horse and buy some food, Rock sat immobile, his elbows on the table and his eyes on the far wall. He had to do now what he hadn't been able to do the night he kissed Kathy—make a clean breast of the whole thing. And he didn't know how to begin.

He wanted to tell her the truth about Ash, too. He had no hope that she would believe him now that she knew who he was, but he had to tell her before it was too late. Rock felt a gloomy certainty that he had about reached the end of his rope—or somebody else's rope.

With that urgent thought, he suddenly quit trying to find ways of saying things. He just started at the beginning and told her the truth of the whole business as if he were talking to her. He was unaware that Jimmy came back and quietly started preparing a meal, but still he kept on, writing with a hand that was swift and sure now. He told her exactly what had happened there in Texas, of the jealousy that he had hoped to arouse in Ash here. He told her of the suspicion that had prompted him to go after the rustlers and said he knew now that his suspicion had been justified.

"I don't expect you to believe all this," he finished, "but if I live long enough I'll prove it to you. If I don't live that long—well, it couldn't matter then, but I want you to know. I love you, Kathy, and for that reason I want to clear my name so bad it hurts. If I don't make it, keep a place in your heart for an outlaw who fell in love with you and was a better man for it."

He signed his name hurriedly and folded the letter without reading it over. Then for a long moment he sat staring at the wall, his heart thudding dully against his ribs.

"Get her done?" Jimmy asked cheerfully.

Rock pulled in a deep breath and abruptly stood up. "Yeah, I got her done. As soon as you've eaten—"

"I'm all done," Jimmy interrupted. "I've been eatin' while you were writin'. And I got Cherry's horse all ready to go."

"All right." Rock hesitated, wondering whether the boy would be running any risk. He thought of John Sinclair, a forceful man but not a hard one, and he said slowly, "They may hang onto you, Jimmy, when they find out you know where I am."

"I don't know where you are," Jimmy retorted, looking him right square in the eye. "Shucks, I don't even know *who* you are. I met you down here on the creek way below the Ballard place while I was fishin'. You give me that letter and then took off. Last I saw of you, you was ridin' like hell for somewhere else."

Rock could not help grinning. "Got it all figured out, have you?"

"I been thinkin'," Jimmy said. "What you said about folks talkin'—you meant that, didn't you?"

"Jimmy, I *sure* meant it," Rock said earnestly.

"Ahuh." Jimmy nodded solemnly. "You look to me like they been givin' you hell."

"Jimmy," Rock said, suddenly compelled to justify the boy's trust. "Son, I've never killed a woman."

"Figured that," Jimmy said, surprisingly. "Folks talk, and we're just a couple of mavericks. But don't you worry about tonight, Rock. I won't let nobody have this letter but your girl, and I'll find out what they're cookin' up. There won't be nobody followin' me when I come back, neither."

For a long moment after the boy had gone Rock stood rooted, mired in his painful thoughts. He understood now, fully and hopelessly, the change that had come over him. Jimmy had summed it up in two words: your girl. Kathy Sinclair had taken possession of him, filling him with dreams and desires that made his lot only the more agonizing, and Rock unconsciously clenched his fists as he realized that if he were caught now he would be losing infinitely more than just his life.

He forced himself to eat the meal Jimmy had prepared, then checked the shed to be sure the dun horse had been well cared for. On his way back to the cabin, he favored the saloon with a bleak survey. He had no illusions about the proprietor's actions if a posse or a bunch of cowboys came along, but it was a risk that had to be taken. Both he and his horse were worn out. Propping a chair against the door, Rock stretched out on Jimmy's bed and was almost instantly asleep.

Nor was his sleep broken until Jimmy got back, late that night. As soon as the flickering candle revealed the boy's strained face and clouded eyes, Rock knew that the news he carried wasn't good and he felt a hollow spot open up in the pit of his stomach.

"Trouble?" he asked sharply.

"Not for me," Jimmy said, "but you sure got some. Gosh, Rock, there was a lot of men there. Bunch of cowboys from Bar Circle and the feller that owns that outfit—gee, he was mad. Rantin' and ravin' all over the place."

"Oh, yeah? What'd he say?"

"He said that nothin' or nobody would be safe as long as you were alive. Gee, he hates you, Rock. He said he'd been figurin' on the law to get you, but if Lackey couldn't hang onto you, then it was up to the ranchers and other folks. They're gonna get you, Rock."

"Maybe," Rock said grimly, studying the boy and sensing that the real cause of Jimmy's worry hadn't yet been divulged. "What's Ash got in mind?"

"That," said Jimmy, "is what's got me so scared. He said you had to be got, and he was, personal, gonna dig up another nine thousand dollars to add to the reward that's on you."

Rock felt the breath go slowly out of him, leaving him with a numb, blank feeling. He groped for a chair and sank into it, still staring at Jimmy but hardly seeing him.

"Ten thousand dollars!" he breathed.

"Yeah." Jimmy hesitated, fidgeting. "That—kinda puts you up a tree, don't it, Rock?"

Rock nodded, then looked directly at Jimmy as a demanding question crossed his mind. "What'd Kathy have to say about that?"

"Nothin'. She didn't have nothin' much to say at all. I gave her the letter and she looked to see who it was from and then asked me where you were." Jimmy shrugged, then frowned again. "Rock, what's the matter with that feller, anyway?"

"Jealousy," Rock said and his voice turned hard. "I started out to make him jealous, and I sure as hell got the job done!"

"What'll they do?" Jimmy asked anxiously. "They were talkin' about the sheriff and a posse bein' right there close, too. They'll be comin' after you, won't they?"

"All of 'em," Rock said grimly. "With that kind of a reward, every man in the country will drop whatever he's doing and hit my trail. And they won't be chasing this time, either. They'll be shootin'!"

Jimmy shivered. "Gee, Rock, you better get out of the country."

"No point in it, Jimmy." Rock dropped his head into his hands, and he knew then just how hard this had hit him. "If I can't clear myself, I reckon I'd be better off dead."

"But what'll you do?"

"There's only one thing I can do."

Rock stared blindly at the floor, knowing there was only one chance left for him. He would have to try once more to get Rita to tell what she knew—and hope that she knew enough. If he could prove that Ash was a rustler, the ranchers would stop him. If Rita wouldn't or couldn't supply the proof, then Rock Kendall was a dead duck.

The sun had barely risen the next morning when Rock pulled up on the ridge behind the Ballard place, studying it with minute care. He had circled the clearing, made cautious by the fact that too many people knew he'd been hanging around here, but had seen no evidence of recent riders. Nor did he see anything out of the way as he looked down now. There were no horses in the corral, nothing moving about the yard. Except for the smoke issuing lazily from the main cabin, the place appeared deserted.

With a tight-drawn breath, Rock turned his horse down the ridge, riding slowly and warily. Rita had shown no love for her brothers, had even stated that she wouldn't care if they never came back, but that was before they had both been killed by the same man. And Rock still wondered whether she had been a willing accomplice to that ambush.

As he emerged from the trees at the foot of the ridge, he watched the windows and the open door of the cabin with increasing tension. With the money he had in his pocket, he could offer the girl a chance to get out of this country that she hated, away from the sordid life she'd been living. Rock dared to hope that such an offer would induce her to talk—if she didn't put a slug in him before he could make it.

He saw nothing of her as he rode up to the porch and dismounted. Quickly he stepped to the doorway and was just entering when he saw Rita appear from behind the partition. Remembering the first time he had come here, he took two long strides into the room before stopping, tense and ready to jump at her. But Rita had no gun in her hand and nothing but a bright, almost eager, light in her eyes.

"Rock," she said breathlessly, and came straight up to him. "I've been hoping you'd come back. I was afraid they'd—get you."

Rock let his breath out carefully and reached for his hat, noting the tentative smile that was playing around her lips. She lifted her hands to his arms, looking up at him expectantly, and Rock felt his face grow suddenly hot. She was obviously waiting for his kiss, and he couldn't give it to her. Not now.

"Rock," she said, drawing back, "what's wrong? Do you— think I had anything to do with that?"

"I've been wondering," he said, with an effort.

"No, Rock. I swear it. Buck said he'd kill me if I didn't stay in my room and keep still. I was afraid of him, terribly afraid."

Rock felt a slight easing of the tension inside of him, and he said slowly, "Then you don't hold it against me for killing him?"

"I'm glad you killed him," she said, her voice flat and hard. "I've been hoping you'd kill Cherry, too."

"I did, Rita. He was laying for me again yesterday. I hated to tell you."

"You didn't need to. I didn't give a hang about either one of them. Did you get Tonto, too?"

"He left the country."

Rock looked down at his hat, aware of a painful embarrassment that was not all due to his inability to respond to her. He had despised Buck and Cherry Ballard himself, but seeing the same utter disregard for them in their own sister jarred him.

"You're tired," Rita said, with sudden solicitude. "Sit down, Rock. I'll get you some coffee."

She stepped away from him and Rock turned slowly, watching her as she got a cup from the cupboard and went on to the stove. He was thinking of the warmth of feeling she had shown him the last night he had seen her, remembering his skepticism concerning it. She was showing him the same warmth now, and Rock couldn't help wondering whether perhaps her feeling ran deeper than he had believed. If it did, she might not accept him as a friend with a straight offer of help in exchange for help.

Then she smiled again, over her shoulder. "Everything's all right now," she said clearly.

Rock grinned and relaxed. Confidence surged in him and he pulled in a slow breath, seeking the right words with which to broach his proposition. Before he could speak, he felt a stir of movement behind him at the end of the partition. Then Red Mayberry's voice bit out a cold, deadly command.

"Turn around and take it, Kendall!"

Shock knifed through Rock, stiffening him. He saw Rita's smile turn venomous, and he knew then that she'd been speaking to Red rather than to him when she said everything was all right. She had put his back to the door! The thought that they had him flashed through his mind and was lost in an icy murderous wrath.

He lifted his hands away from his sides, the right one tightly gripped around the brim of his hat, and started to turn slowly. He looked back over his shoulder as he came around, seeing Red standing clear of the partition not over six feet away. He saw the grim determination stamped on the cowboy's face, saw the cocked gun in his hand. Then he spun and made a desperate, swerving lunge at the redhead.

The shot crashed out and Rock felt the bullet, white hot, cut along his left side. Then he was on Red, slamming his hat into the cowboy's face. Red staggered back, blinded and off balance, and Rock drove into him, grabbing his gun arm as they hit the wall. He jerked the arm up and in one movement smashed it viciously down against the window sill. Red grunted in pain as the gun flew out of his hand, and Rock stepped back, grabbing at the cowboy's shirt and intending to slug him. Before he could swing, Red shoved violently away from the wall, ducked in and grabbed him around the body.

Rock could feel the cowboy's hand groping at his holster, and a fresh anger rose in him, turning him hard. He didn't want to kill Red. He couldn't blame the boy for the way he felt and it was important to Rock that this brother of Dorene Mayberry learn the truth, but he knew he had to end this at once.

He twisted, throwing his left arm up against Red's chin as he wrenched the boy's hand away from his holster and drew the gun himself. He shoved Red back and in one long sweep of his arm brought the gun down on the cowboy's head. Red caught his breath as his eyes shut tight in pain. Then, his face going slack, he dropped.

With the fury still in him, Rock whirled and saw Rita on her knees beside the wood box, in the act of snatching up a hidden gun. He started for her but took only one stride and stopped, knowing he couldn't reach her in time. With frantic haste, she was dropping back on her heels against the wall, striving to catch her balance as she brought the gun up with both hands.

Rock snapped his own gun to a level, his thumb on the hammer, his eyes on the target—her heart. But he couldn't fire. He could see the line of her breast, firm and full under the worn buckskin, could see it heave with her ragged breathing. He strained forward, snarling, gripping the gun so hard his hand shook. But he couldn't do it. Even hating her from the bottom of his heart, he couldn't bring himself to drive a bullet into that breast.

For a fleeting instant, he looked into her eyes, wild and black with intent. Then he looked at the gun, steadying now, centering on his chest, and sickness washed through him. With the last of purpose draining suddenly out of him, he let his gun sag and straightened, waiting.

# CHAPTER FOURTEEN

THE GUN in Rita's hands wavered. She seemed to sink back lower, cowering, her eyes fastened on him with an hypnotic stare.

"Go ahead and shoot," he said bitterly. "You've killed me, anyway."

"No," she whispered. Slowly she lowered the gun into her lap, still staring at him, obviously shaken by something in his expression. "Rock, he—trailed you here night before last."

"And you threw in with him again, for the money!"

"No, not—altogether," she faltered. "He promised to see that I got a chance to get out of the brakes."

"That's what I came to offer you," Rock said, his lip curling. "I got to feeling sorry for you, thinking you'd never had a chance. You black-hearted little—" Rock bit down on his words, then turned harsh. "You don't deserve a chance, Rita. You're rotten, rottener than Buck and Cherry ever thought of being. At least they were true to each other, but you're not true to anybody. You're on the side of the last man who kisses you, regardless of who he is, and you'd throw any of them over for four bits, Mex. There isn't a spark of truth or loyalty or decency in you anywhere, and I hope to God Red finds that out before you stick a knife in *his* back!"

The girl had dropped her head. Rock could see that her face was flaming, but it had no effect on him. He had seen her once before when she appeared repentant.

"If you're not going to use that gun," he said coldly, "put it down and get up."

Without a word, she laid the gun across the corner of the wood box and shoved to her feet, still not looking at him. Rock sheathed his own gun as he strode over to her. He grabbed her arm and pulled her away from the stove, then ran his hands down over her body, feeling swiftly and roughly for a knife. He found none and straightened to look down at her with open contempt. For only a fleeting instant did Rita meet his gaze, then looked down at the floor again, her lips quivering.

Rock glanced down at his burning side. Blood had saturated the lower part of his shirt and he could feel it oozing, warm and slick, down under his belt. He knew the slug had cut only a groove through the muscles, but apparently it was a deep one and was still bleeding.

"Rig up a bandage," he ordered abruptly. "Then you're going to do some talking, Miss Ballard!"

Rock had no chance, however, to question her. As he reached for his shirt to unbutton it, he heard the whinny of a horse somewhere above the cabin in the direction of Skeleton Creek. He jerked his head up, then shoved Rita out of his way and stepped swiftly to the window. He saw movement in the trees just beyond the edge of the clearing, saw the shoulder of a bay horse flashing in a spot of sunlight. Then a rider emerged, tall and square in the saddle. With a sudden blank feeling, Rock recognized Ash Carlton, a rifle across the saddle in front of him, a group of cowboys riding out of the trees behind him.

At that moment Red stirred on the floor and groaned. Rock spun away from the window, flashed one swift glance at the rousing cowboy and knew he'd have to run for it. If he tried to fort up, he would have two enemies inside with him and he'd go down before he could get the information that might save him. With a bitter curse, he turned and bolted out the door.

The cabin kept them from seeing him and Rock vaulted into his saddle, hoping to make it to the brush before they spotted him. He had no more than wheeled the dun when a wild shout went up from the ridge above him. Rock saw them then, four or five riders plunging down toward him, yelling and pointing, and he turned the dun toward the stump-dotted field and spurred him into a run. Almost immediately a rifle opened up behind him, then a second from the direction of the cabin. Rock knew that Ash had rounded into sight, but he didn't look back until he was nearing the edge of the clearing. Then he turned for a grim survey.

There were at least fifteen men besides Ash, spread out across the field and coming hard. Rock could see the horses running with a fresh, eager stride. He could see the rifles glinting in the sunlight, and he faced ahead again with a barren feeling inside him. They were going to get him and he knew it, but he put the dun into the sheltering trees and stretched him out, heading as straight down the valley as brush and timber would permit.

His hat was still at the Ballard place, leaving his head unprotected, but Rock was oblivious to the limbs that slapped at his face as he scanned the trees ahead of him. Ash and his men had come from the direction of Skeleton Creek, which would indicate that they had spent the night at Triple X, and they certainly hadn't ridden out alone. Where, Rock wondered tightly, was that other outfit? Down here in the brakes somewhere? Or up on the rim, waiting for Ash to run him out?

Rock passed the trail to Bar Circle but dared not turn up, and he plunged on into country that was strange to him. The dun was still running smoothly, but Rock knew that one night on good feed hadn't rested him and he wondered how long he could last. He hadn't glimpsed his pursuers since he entered the timber, but he knew they would be spread out behind him, riding fast and watching close. They had caught him once, and Rock knew they would be savagely determined to do it again.

The valley widened, swung to the south. A long green meadow opened before Rock and he swerved away from it, hugging the timber as he started to circle it. He intended to swing back, to hold to the comparatively level ground, but a couple of riders burst out of the trees abreast of him, dangerously close, and Rock turned his tiring horse up the steep ridge to the west. A wild yell went up as the men spotted him, and the sound sent a chill up Rock's back. They were gaining on him, steadily and surely.

His horse was laboring by the time he gained the crest of the ridge, and Rock looked down briefly into a tangle of brush and rocks and broken ridges. The yellow wall of the rim loomed on his right and ahead were other jagged walls, shadowing timbered canyons. Then the horse was plunging down the steep incline and Rock was clinging to the fork of his saddle, trying to brace himself against the rending pain in his side. By the time he reached the bottom, he was wringing wet, breathless, fighting against the certainty that he couldn't get away from them. He could hear them crashing down the slope behind him, closing in. A passionate urge seized him, to stop and fight it out now, to take it from their guns rather than from their ropes when *this* horse went down. But he didn't pull up. A stubborn pride wouldn't let him admit defeat even when he was facing it.

The dun was lathered and stumbling by the time Rock came to the jutting edge of what appeared to be a butte. He turned along it, still in heavy timber; but he had gone no more than half a mile when he rounded a corner and saw, through thinning timber, the sheer walls of a box canyon. Rock jerked to a stop, instantly wheeling the dun; but a fierce yell sounded from the trees, echoed by the crack of a rifle. A bullet thudded into a tree right beside him, and Rock swung the dun back up the canyon, spurring him through the brush and looking desperately for a jumble of rocks. They had him cold, but if he could find good cover maybe they wouldn't get him for nothing.

The canyon narrowed, and the brush, while still thick along the sides, thinned in the middle. Rock saw the old cabin squatting against the back wall two hundred yards away, and with a burst of hope he spurred the faltering horse toward it. He had covered but a part of the distance when a rash of firing broke out behind him and he knew the men had pulled up, trying to nail him before he could reach cover. He could hear bullets whining and screaming off the cliffs all around him. Then, fifteen yards from the yawning doorway of the cabin, the dun gave a convulsive leap and went down, somersaulting as he hit the ground.

Rock threw himself clear, rolling away from the flailing hoofs and coming up on the run. He didn't have any wind in him and there was a haze swimming before his eyes, seeming to dim out everything except the dark opening before him. He couldn't even hear the guns now. He stumbled as he reached the door and fell into the casing, but he grabbed it and swung himself through into the dim interior. As he was dodging away from the doorway, he tripped over a box and pitched headlong to the littered dirt floor.

For what seemed like a long time he lay where he had fallen, fighting to get his breath, hearing nothing except the roaring in his head. Gradually his senses cleared and he became aware of the bullets that were peppering the old cabin, some of them feeling out the chinks and buzzing in to whine off the back wall. Rock wondered about that and with an effort he rolled over to inspect his shelter.

It was more of a lean-to than a cabin, evidently built by some prospector who was content to use the cliff itself as a back wall. There were no windows. The only opening was that doorway; and Rock, realizing that he had his back literally against the wall, could not restrain the dreary thought that, deep down inside of him, he had known the moment he saw Ash in the garden there behind the dance hall that he couldn't whip him. Now it would end here.

The firing ceased abruptly and a deadly silence fell over the canyon. For a moment Rock lay quiet, listening. Then he crawled to the front wall and flattened himself behind the bottom log, peering through a wide crack. He could see them bunched out there in the center of the canyon, still sitting their horses. Then he spotted Ash, standing in his stirrups and giving directions with wide gestures. He was obviously fanning them out to hit the cabin with a crossfire, and Rock swore at him with vicious fervency. He knew they were beyond effective revolver range but he drew his gun anyway, slipping the barrel through the crack and holding high as he fired.

He didn't see where the bullet carried, but the sound of the shot was enough to scatter the men like startled deer. Rock watched coldly as they jumped their horses into thicker brush and flung themselves from the saddles. Then one by one they took up positions across the canyon floor, dropping down behind rocks or brush and starting a steady, methodical firing. Several of them were in plain view, sighting coolly and leisurely along their rifle barrels, safe beyond the range of his sixgun. Again Rock swore in helpless rage. It was only a question of time until one of those slugs tagged him, and he looked for Ash, once more feeling the savage desire to take his enemy with him. He couldn't immediately locate him and thought with contempt, He's playing it safe.

A feeling of weary futility crept over Rock and he dropped his head onto his arm. He was aware that the left side of his shirt and pants were soggy and that the wound was still bleeding, but it couldn't make any difference. That would be just the first one. He listened to the bullets, thudding into the logs with the irregular beat of the first drops of rain, sometimes hitting the chinking and sending it down in little showers of dust. Then, all at once, it occurred to him that all of those slugs were hitting high.

He jerked his head up, wondering, and he saw Ash on the left side of the canyon darting furtively through the brush. He was close, no more than fifty yards, and Rock brought his gun up with a driving impulse. But he didn't fire. He watched, suddenly tense, as Ash dropped down behind a rock for a moment, then came on, bent over and hugging the wall of the canyon as he ran for the next bit of cover.

Rock flashed a glance over the canyon, but he could see no one else moving. He looked up at the wall above him, noting that every bullet that struck was at least three feet high. Apparently those cowboys were only supposed to keep him pinned down and were taking no chance of killing him. That was a job that Ash Carlton evidently wanted to do himself. Rock looked back to the left in time to see Ash advance another ten yards, exposing himself recklessly. He was obviously intending to come in at the side of the cabin, and he was, also obviously, very sure that Rock wouldn't kill him except as a last resort.

Rock grew rigidly still, his hand tight on his gun. The desire to kill Ash was still burning in him, and the thought that there might be a way out of this was slow in coming to him. He twisted for a look at the left wall of the cabin. The chinking was in good repair, which meant that Ash would have to come to the doorway and jump him at close range. Again Rock looked down at his bloody side, knowing that he wouldn't last long in a fight, knowing too that if he lost the fight he would leave Ash, alive and free, behind him. But the desire to try it put a pound in his blood. If he *could* whip the man, he could use him as a hostage in getting out of here—and he'd have Ash in his hands at last.

Rock took one last look through the crack, watching with a sudden, tight eagerness as Ash arose from behind a rock, then ran to disappear from his view at the end of the cabin. Rock thought grimly, Let him come! Swiftly he crawled over next to the doorway and waited, marking Ash's progress by sound. For the space of several minutes he heard nothing. Then came the crack of a twig, close, and Rock came up on one knee beside the doorway, crouched, ready to spring. He had laid the spare gun aside but the other he held gripped tightly in his right hand, his arm half lifted to strike.

It would have to be done fast or he knew he'd go down. He waited breathlessly, hearing the faint brush of movement just beside the door. Then the light was momentarily blotted out as Ash sprang through the doorway, gun in hand.

Rock lunged up like a panther, throwing himself against Ash and grabbing the man's right arm. He shoved it aside, brought his own gun up to strike; but Ash moved as quickly. His hand closed like a steel vise around Rock's wrist and for a second Rock stood rigid, meeting those cold blue eyes and hating everything he saw in them. Then he lurched ahead, knocking Ash off balance and slamming him back against the wall. Rock heard the man's elbow strike solidly, felt the gun drop out of his hand. With a fierce confidence, he let go of Ash's arm and twisted to drive his shoulder into him. He heard Ash's back grind against the logs and he threw his arm back, trying to break the man's grip; but again Ash was as quick. His right arm flashed around Rock's neck, jerking his head back. The next instant the man had shoved away from the wall with a violence that staggered Rock.

He grabbed at Ash with his free hand, getting a grip on the back of the man's vest as they wrestled. Then their legs tangled and they went down hard, crashing into the box that had tripped Rock before. He felt the wood splintering under his shoulder, heard the grunt from Ash as a corner of the box caught him in the chest. Then his arm hit the dirt floor with jarring force, and Rock felt the gun fly out of his hand. He brought his left arm in against Ash, shoving at his shoulder at the same time that he brought up a leg to kick the man away from him. Ash let go of him and rolled clear, coming up in one continuous motion, and Rock bounded to his feet.

He didn't even look to see where his gun had gone. With three years of enmity driving him, he forgot his wound and tore into Ash with a furious onslaught that drove the man slowly backward. Rock was oblivious to the blows that struck his own body as he smashed time after time at that snarling face. He felt his knuckles grind on bone, saw blood spurt from Ash's cheek, and he drove his other fist into those gleaming white teeth. Ash staggered back, swearing thickly. He brought up his left arm to shield his face, and Rock stepped in to slam a fist into the pit of his stomach. He was swinging again at the man's face when Ash suddenly bowed his neck and surged ahead to grab him around the body.

Rock twisted sharply, bringing his fist down like a sledge-hammer on Ash's neck. As he did so, the arm around his wounded side dug in like a rasping cable, and Rock felt a shudder go through him. For a second pain took his breath and he grabbed at Ash's shoulders, trying to flinch away from that encircling band. Ash's arm clutched tighter, and nausea hit Rock like a physical blow. He could feel weakness creeping over him, and in sudden desperation he threw himself backward.

Ash let go of him as they went down and Rock grabbed his arms, using them as leverage to swing his legs up the moment he hit the floor. Ash was catapulted over the top of him, and Rock heard the grunt that was jarred out of him as he landed solidly on his back. Rock rolled over and struggled to his feet, but the fall had taken a lot out of him. His wind was gone, his head spinning. Through a haze, he saw Ash roll to his knees in the doorway, his eyes darting over the floor in search of the gun he had dropped. Rock saw it, closer to Ash than to him, and as the man started up, Rock dove at him.

He caught him around the upper body, hitting him with a force that knocked him backward out the door. Rock fell on top of him and for a moment he tried only to hold him down, fighting back the nausea that was turning him weak. He knew it was the loss of blood that was getting him and he lay heavy on Ash, pinning his arms, struggling for breath. For a moment Ash lay quiet too, his chest heaving. Then with a sudden, twisting lurch he threw Rock off him.

Rock rolled away and came up, staggering back against the cabin as he gained his feet. He was aware of movement out in the brush, figured the cowboys were coming in to help with the kill. He knew he was licked but he shoved away from the wall and met Ash head on, swinging savagely at the bloody face in front of him. His strength was going fast and this time he was the one who was forced to give ground, moving back inch by hard-fought inch until he felt the cabin directly behind him. Then a blow came out of nowhere to land against his jaw, and he slammed into the wall with stunning force.

His head rang against the wood and his knees started to buckle, but he caught himself and lashed out doggedly as Ash closed in on him. He got in two more blows at that bleary, hated face. Then he felt his arms flung wide as Ash lunged in against him and grabbed his throat. Rock had a fleeting glimpse of the triumph glittering in Ash's eyes before those fingers closed around his neck in a throttling, blinding grip.

Rock got his hands up and found Ash's arms, but his muscles had gone rubbery and his shoving and straining availed him nothing. There was no power in him to stop Ash as the man jerked him away from the building, then smashed his head back against it. Pain exploded in Rock. Again Ash slammed him against the logs, and Rock felt his hands fall away. He knew he was sagging when he was jerked away from the wall again and thrown down on his back. For one brief instant the hands on his throat loosened, and Rock dragged in a painful breath, his sight clearing enough to show him Ash straddling his chest. Then those fingers closed again, and Rock writhed futilely as the world seemed to go up in flame.

The flames were dancing, dimming out, when that grip was violently torn loose and Rock could once more drag in air. He filled his lungs twice, three times. The pain was easing and his head was starting to clear when he felt hands on him, pulling him over on his stomach. The next instant his arms were jerked behind him and he felt the cold grip of steel around his wrists. The sheriff, he thought dully, and wondered what difference it could make now.

He was still groggy, breathless, when he was hauled to his feet and shoved back against the wall. Rock leaned into it, aware of the clamor of heated voices but paying no attention to them as he struggled to steady his vision. Gradually his sight cleared, and he saw Lackey directly in front of him, gesturing angrily. Everyone seemed to be shouting at once, the sound beating against Rock's ears and adding to the throb in his head.

With the thought that the sheriff was wasting his breath, Rock pushed himself away from the wall and straightened, glancing over a crowd that was surprisingly large. He saw Red, his face pale and tight, and Rita, who was staring at him with a queer intentness that roused his resentment. Clamping his teeth, he swung his gaze on around the circle of yelling cowboys, bringing it up with a cold shock against the wide blue eyes of Kathy Sinclair.

For a moment Rock stared at her in blank incredulity, not wanting to believe she was there. He swept his glance past her, to John, her cowboys, then back again; and he knew she *was* there. With a slow breath swelling and jamming in his chest, Rock looked away, lifting his head to stare blindly over the heads of the crowd. They'd hang him this time, and the woman to whom he had admitted his love would watch him die.

A feeling of utter desolation settled over Rock. The hot words of the argument finally penetrated his consciousness but were as powerless to affect him now as if they'd been spoken about a stranger.

"The hell with you, Lackey," Ash was saying harshly. "You tried to jail him once, and he got away from you."

"He won't get away this time."

"You're damn right he won't! By the time we turn him over to you, he'll be too damned dead to do anything!"

"Now, wait—"

"Wait, hell!" someone yelled, and a dozen voices joined him. "Get a rope!"

Ash's voice was flat. "We're going to hang him, Lackey, right now. And if you don't want to watch it you can go on back to town. We'll bring his carcass in, to show folks how a woman killer ought to look!"

A concerted shout of approval greeted his words, but still Rock kept his gaze on the far line of a cliff, wishing only that it were over. He could feel Kathy's eyes on him, and that added the final, unbearable weight to the disgrace that would be his.

Then Rita's voice broke through the clamor with startling effect.

"You're hanging the wrong man!"

Rock jerked his head around to stare at her in blank amazement. The girl had brushed past Red and was facing Lackey resolutely, her chin thrust up at a defiant angle. In the abrupt silence, her voice rang out with an even, swift conviction.

"Mr. Lackey, I don't believe he killed that woman. There's been twice when he should have killed me, and he didn't do it. The first time I tried to kill him, he jumped me, took the gun away from me, but this morning he was too far away to do that. He had a gun in his hand, but then, even with me pointing a gun right straight at him, he just—dropped his hand and stood there."

"And let you plug him?" Lackey asked incredulously.

"I didn't. There was something about the way he looked—" She shook her head, shame turning her face hot. "But he wouldn't shoot me even to save his life, and I don't think he ever killed any woman."

For a taut second her words held the crowd spellbound, open-mouthed, and Rock felt a glimmer of warmth at this unexpected defense. Then Ash took a long stride forward, flipping his hand in a furious gesture.

"The hell he didn't," he bit out. "Lackey, it's obvious the girl is just making this up in an effort to save Kendall's life. He's undoubtedly had an affair with her, as he has with so many women."

Rock flashed a blazing glance at him, then swung toward Kathy, a protest welling out of him before he could stop it.

"I've never had but one affair that counted," he said harshly. "I meant what I said in that letter, Kathy."

"Yes," she said with surprising readiness, "I expect you did. And you said plenty." She glanced at Ash, one brief, hardening survey, before bringing her gaze back to Rock; and he saw then the turbulent emotion that was rushing through her. "Apparently," she said, "I haven't done too good a job of controlling my heart. Started to give it to a man who will probably hang for rustling, and ended up giving it to a man who will undoubtedly hang for murder. Foolish of me, wasn't it?"

Rock's breath stuck in his throat as he stared at her, hardly aware of the ripple of wonder that swept through the crowd. He doubted that he had heard her right, that he had grasped the real meaning of her words, but the intense light in her eyes convinced him that he had.

Ash saw it, too, and he lifted a hand in shocked protest. "Kathy!" he burst out. "You can't be in love with him! Not when you know who he is!"

"I've known who he was right along," Kathy retorted. "Found it out the day after he came to the ranch the first time. That didn't make any difference."

Rock was stunned. He breathed incredulously, "You knew—when you kissed me?"

"Of course, I knew. That's why I asked you to stay for dinner that night. I wanted to find out what you were really like." Her eyes seemed to burn a hole clear through him. "I found out, all right. I was falling in love with you then, and yesterday when you made them turn that man loose—that finished me. You didn't even expect to get away, did you?"

Rock shook his head, his throat suddenly too tight for speech. Kathy started to speak again, but John beat her to it.

"Well, I can tell you why you made it," he said bluntly. "She threw a double-barreled shotgun on the outfit! Told us you were her man and she'd plug the first jigger that started after you. By God, I believed her!"

*"Her man!"* Ash sounded as if he were strangling. "Kathy, you invited him to dinner? You let him *kiss* you?"

"Why not?" she flashed, her voice suddenly hot. "I let you kiss me—and all the time you were stealing my cattle!"

"That's a—" Ash caught himself, but rage had turned his face gray and his whole body rigid. His voice was deadly. "Who says I was?"

"Rock Kendall!" Kathy shot at him. "That's what he was doing for me—trying to find the leader of these rustlers. And he found him. You!"

Lackey snapped, "How about that, Kendall?"

"It's a lie!" Ash spun toward Rock, his eyes glittering, his right hand quivering. "I haven't had anything to do with this rustling, and I dare you to prove different!"

Rock knew then that Cherry *had* been the last of the gang. He could feel the cowboys straining forward, waiting for the proof he couldn't give, and frustration tortured him as he turned his gaze back to Kathy.

"I didn't live long enough," he said roughly.

Kathy sucked in her breath, and her eyes turned desperate. "Oh, Rock!" she whispered.

Ash swore a savage, snarling sound that was barely coherent. Rock knew the man's inflammable jealousy was racking him, threatening to destroy his judgment, but he could see no way now to use it. Rather, it would only hasten his death. As if in echo to his bitter thought, Ash spoke thickly.

"Let's get this over with. Come on, Kendall. Or do you want us to drag you down to the nearest tree?"

"Just a minute!"

It was Rita's voice, harsh and imperative. Rock saw that she had squared off toward Ash, and a thrill of hope shot through him.

"You're not fooling me any," she said flatly. "I know why you're so anxious to kill him. You're afraid of him and I know why, and I'm going to spill it!"

Ash took a threatening step forward, his fists doubled ominously, but Rita was not to be stopped now. She turned flashing black eyes to the sheriff and pointed a rigid finger at Ash, her voice rising shrilly.

"Lackey, he *is* the boss of the rustlers! He organized that new gang and planned those raids on Triple X. I heard him tell the boys and Tonto to get Rock before he got the goods on them. I heard him say he shot Jud Moore to keep his mouth shut, and I *saw* him kill that lawman right there in our—"

The blast of the gun drowned out her voice—and silenced it forever. Rock saw the bullet strike, full in her breast, and for a fraction of a second shock held him paralyzed. Then he spun toward Ash. He barely had time to glimpse the small hideout gun before it exploded a second time, and a sickening, numbing blow struck the side of his head. He staggered, trying to keep his feet, but his legs dissolved under him. As he was going down, he saw the gun spout flame again but he didn't know whether or not the slug hit him.

He lit hard on his stomach, his face slamming into the ground, and for a moment dizziness possessed him. He felt dirt splatter his cheek as Ash fired again, and he tried to get up, fighting the steel bonds that held his arms behind him. He couldn't turn himself, but he got his head off the ground and saw, as through a thick haze, the same hideous mask of insane hatred he had seen on Ash's face once before. And he saw the muzzle of the gun centering between his eyes.

Then Ash staggered, and Rock saw the blood that popped out on the man's shirt. He twisted his head, seeing the blurred figures of John Sinclair and several cowboys leveling their guns at Ash to stop him, and panic seized Rock. Again he tried to get up, jerking his hands furiously against the cuffs holding them, trying to yell.

"Don't kill him! For God's sake! *Don't kill him!*"

The words ran through his reeling mind, but he couldn't hear the sound of his own voice. Then his strength ran out and his head dropped, but he had a last dimming sight of Ash, sagging, going down. Rock knew they were killing him, and a pang, terrible and devastating, hit him as the darkness closed in. He'd lost his chance ....

He awoke to the feel of water on his chest and face, fresh and cooling, and he looked up dully at the circle of faces above him. He saw Kathy kneeling at his right, John beside her. He saw Red hunkered down, but his glance swept on until he found Lackey on his left and it was to him that he spoke, his voice husky and coming with an effort.

"Is he dead?"

"Too damned dead to skin," Lackey said grimly.

Rock closed his eyes. "I tried to yell," he mumbled.

"You did yell, Rock," Kathy said quickly.

He felt her hand closing around his, lifting it into her lap, and he realized then that the handcuffs had been taken off of him. He looked up, wondering, and saw the clear, glad light shining in Kathy's eyes.

"You were yellin' like a Comanche," John said gruffly. "I heard you, but that just made me all the more certain that I wanted to kill that skunk."

Rock stared at him incredulously for a moment, then looked to Lackey with a question he couldn't voice. The old lawman grinned.

"Cowboy," he drawled, "any time a man is yellin' for the other feller at a time like that, it's a pretty good bet he needs him *alive*. Red told us your version of that shootin' in Texas, and after seein' the way Ash acted here today, we can sure believe it. If you'll stand trial, Rock, I'll guarantee that with our testimony, any jury in the country will acquit you without ever leavin' the box. I might even be able to get those charges dropped so you wouldn't have to go back."

Rock's brain was spinning. Dazedly he looked at Red and saw the young cowboy nod, his face grave.

"Rita told me about Ash on the way out here, Rock. I was sure findin' it hard to believe, and if Ash hadn't blown up—but, well—now we all know the truth." He hesitated, flushing. "I don't reckon you'd want to shake hands with me after the trick I pulled."

A riot of feeling welled up in Rock and choked him. Mutely he extended his hand and, as Red gripped it, he saw a light in the cowboy's green eyes that dispelled once and for all the memory that had haunted him.

"Course," Lackey said dryly, "there's a little matter of you shootin' my town up the other evenin', but only one of those fellers kicked the bucket."

"Self-defense," Kathy said and helped herself to Rock's hand again.

He looked up at her, feeling dizzy and weak and wondering whether this was really happening. "You knew," he murmured, "all the time."

Kathy nodded, smiling. "Lackey came by the day after you were there and described you and your horse, said you'd called yourself Rocklin. But you had told me as plain as you could that you'd been framed, Rock, and you struck me right. So I decided to keep out of it and watch you and Ash fight it out. And I knew you told me the truth in that letter."

"You believed me—even before today?"

"Hell," John snorted. "What did you think we were doin' down here? After she threw that gun on us yesterday, she told me how she had it doped out. I sure wasn't convinced, but I was willing to back off till I found out. And after she got your letter—! She rounded up the sheriff and whipped us all out on Ash's trail. Said if she could get the two of you together, she'd make him jealous and help you force the truth out of him. She sure did it, although I thought for a minute she was gonna be wastin' her love on a dead man."

Rock was suddenly in a tumult that made him oblivious to the ring of watching cowboys, oblivious to everything except the woman beside him. The dreams he hadn't dared admit during the years of loneliness crowded in on him, and he struggled to get up on his elbow. Kathy grabbed his left hand and helped him, then held him steady until the dizziness passed. Her face was close, her lips parted.

"Kathy," he said, feeling for words, "there's a kid up at Skeleton Creek—"

"The one who brought your letter?"

"Yeah. He's a maverick, like me. If I can get my name cleaned up a little—"

"No ifs, cowboy," Kathy warned soberly. "You might be fast enough to dodge posses, but you'll never get away from me."

Weakness was stealing through him, making him waver; but he looked at her lips, rich and full and for him, and he whispered, "I'm tired of runnin'."

Then, as his neck turned limber, Kathy caught him and pulled his head into her lap. Rock could feel her arms around him, strong and warm and possessive, and with the past dimming, fading out, he let himself sink into the deep comfort she offered.

www.ingramcontent.com/pod-product-compliance
Lightning Source LLC
Chambersburg PA
CBHW031230260626
47169CB00007B/2226